How Sweet It Is!

Also by Thane Rosenbaum

Novels

The Stranger Within Sarah Stein
The Golems of Gotham
Second Hand Smoke
Elijah Visible

Nonfiction

Payback: The Case for Revenge
The Myth of Moral Justice: How Our Legal System Fails to Do What's Right

Anthologies

Law Lit: From Atticus Finch to The Practice, *A Collection of Great Writing About the Law*

How Sweet It Is!

Thane Rosenbaum

Mandel Vilar Press

1915 • 2015
MIAMIBEACH

Copyright © 2015 by Thane Rosenbaum

This book is typeset in Adobe Garamond Pro. The paper used in this book meets the minimum requirements of ANSI/NISO Z39.48-1992 (R1997). ∞

Publisher's Cataloging-In-Publication Data

Rosenbaum, Thane.

How sweet it is! / Thane Rosenbaum.

pages ; cm

Includes bibliographical references.
ISBN: 978-1-942134-00-8
978-1-942134-02-2   Kindle
978-1-942134-16-9   E-Pub

1. Holocaust survivors—Florida—Miami—History—20th century—Fiction. 2. Jews—Florida—Miami—History—20th century—Fiction. 3. Miami (Fla.)—Social life and customs—20th century—Fiction. 4. Miami (Fla.)—History—20th century—Fiction. 5. Historical fiction. I. Title.

PS3568.O782 H69 2015
813/.54

Printed in the United States of America
15 16 17 18 19 20 21 22 23 / 9 8 7 6 5 4 3 2 1

Mandel Vilar Press
19 Oxford Court, Simsbury, Connecticut 06070
www.americasforconservation.org | www.mvpress.org

Acknowledgments

I am deeply grateful to many loyal and loving friends who sweeten my life and make it possible to write a novel with such a nostalgically sugary title. They are Hugo Barreca, Paul and Judy Berkman, Sandee Brawarsky, Sam Dubbin, Erin Bundra, Eva Fogelman, Danny and Sarah Goldhagen, Robert Goldblum, Sol Haber, Tom Hameline, Angela Himsel, Robert Hollweg, Annette Insdorf, Carolyn Jackson, Gary Klein, Andy Kovler, Jim Leitner, Alex Mauskop, Brett Paul, Paula and Maya Rackoff, Danny Retter, John Thomas, Henry Timms, and Robert Wertheimer.

My agent, Ellen Levine, and I have been at this for over twenty years now and I am thankful for her efforts and friendship along the way. My editor and publisher, Robert Mandel, a truly distinguished man of letters, has been a friend and mentor for many years and I am proud to be a part of his latest venture.

This novel is a valentine to a small beachfront city where I spent my childhood. Long before South Beach and the Art Deco District, there was just Miami Beach—quiet, unadorned, and yet enchantingly magical. I extend thanks to Jimmy Pomerance, whose father, Rocky, is a character in this book, for indulging me with his own evocative memories of his childhood tagging along with the city's police chief. I also wish to acknowledge the late Seymour Gelber, a former Miami Beach mayor, for his book, *The Summer That Changed Miami Beach: A Diary of the 1972 Democratic and Republican Nominating Conventions* (2004), which I availed myself of in recalling that summer when Miami Beach was, for a brief moment, the center of the world.

Lastly, I wish to express my love and gratitude to my children, Basia Tess, Zofii, Elska, and Solènne Rose, and to my partner, Roz, for the life we all share.

Contents

How Sweet It Is!

Prologue: *The Fat Man*

veryone loves the fat man, the cellulite clown, the obese freak. Show me a fat man and I'll show you a laugh that is worth its weight in comedic gold. Add bulging eyes and dangling chins to undulating flesh and, honestly, you have a show right there.

As I always say, whenever there is the premise of a joke or the presumption of laughter, don't waste it. Funny doesn't come easy. With some audiences you can't even buy a laugh. So if it's funny, hurry up and get what you came for. Nobody cares if the sad clown is actually melancholy or whether the overweight man is crying a river of fat cells though his bloodstream. Comedy is all about timing. We respond to the tittering moment, the gut-busting sight gag. Throw in some farting and you can charge extra.

Here's the trick, the dirty little secret that makes an underactive thyroid so hilarious: the fat man can't be taken seriously because he doesn't take himself seriously. Excess weight is his calling card, his message to the outside world. What he is saying is: I have lost my self-discipline, so go ahead and subject me to public ridicule. I deserve it. My weight is a badge of dishonor and it's not easily removed. It is a scarlet letter F without having to sew anything on.

It's already on.

But it's a self-inflicted wound; the brand is stamped in uncounted calories and jiggling flab. It's no comfort to the fat man that our giggles might start out as nervous before ascending to hilarious. Either way we're given little choice but to laugh. Every fat joke is a cautionary tale. There but for the grace of God, and pride in my appearance, go I. The fat man is what you can become if you lose all self-control, if you let everything go to pot . . . belly. And if you do, beware: you're a pratfall waiting to happen. The public can't be faulted for mocking. The fat guy, after all, is a glutton—for everything, including his own punishment. He's without moderation or the common decency to eat only his fair share. And no one forgives the fat man for not being entirely aware of how much space his body actually consumes.

"Oops, sorry about that vase."

"I have managed to get myself stuck in this revolving door."

"Pardon me, I see that I have taken up two seats."

W. C. Fields, Fatty Arbuckle, Lou Costello, and John Candy, all made a sloppy but substantial living from eating too much. Is that a respectable career? What next: professional eating? Hey, I guess it beats driving a bus. Shouldn't everyone market his or her best attribute? Some people have a head for business, others exploit their legs for dancing or running, and still others have a body for sex. Some people just have too much of a body. Shouldn't those with low self-esteem and a penchant for flab be able to cash in on the one asset that is primarily located on their asses?

A friend of mine who is a writer once told me about this other writer, some Jew from Czechoslovakia who wrote a story about a hunger artist—a guy in a freak show who lived in a cage and starved himself for over a month at a time. People would pay to see the man sitting in his cage, surrounded by straw and starving to death, day after day. After a while the villagers had gotten so used to the hunger artist's act, they forgot about him. He became part of the scenery, like a lamppost or a trashcan. They would pass his cage each day no longer taking any notice of him—even though he was breaking all sorts of records for not eating.

One day, when the hunger artist was nearly dead, a man discovered him still lying there in his cage. He prodded him back to life, and the hunger artist said, "I always wanted you to admire my fasting."

The man replied, "But we do admire it."

The hunger artist then said, "But you shouldn't admire it."

When it gets right down to it, I never could understand why the absence of will power, or having a glacial metabolism, is so fucking funny. But I don't have to understand it. Laughing at the fat man is a universal occurrence—

every culture responds in unison to the same laugh track. Even Buddha had to develop a thick skin over his big belly. In the vast unspoken anatomy lesson of how our funny bones have evolved over time, somehow the guy who ate too much was bound to get the last laugh.

Why am I telling you all this? Well, I *am* the fat man. But I'm not just some ordinary schlub, some mute poor soul, a fat guy from Minnesota with a pool cue in his hand. I'm *THE* Fat Man, the most famous overweight person in the world. All other fat people would bow down to me if, of course, they could bend.

I am called the Great One. And this greatness is not tied solely to my girth. I'm America's most beloved entertainer. I pioneered early TV situation and sketch comedies in the 1950s, and my variety shows owned Saturday nights for thirteen years. And even though I have been off the air for a year now, all three networks are throwing money at me to come back. Well, I wouldn't exactly say throwing money—but there is interest; my agent has had some meetings.

I don't think I will be on the air anytime soon though. I've got this health problem, you see. Apparently smoking four packs of cigarettes a day isn't a recipe for a long life. Turns out, those Surgeon General warnings aren't a scam. How do you like that? Filtered sticks made me look suave, especially when I was in character as Reginald Van Gleason III. But they were killing me! And I drank too much. Hell, without the booze, without the sauce, I would never have had the courage to get up on stage to do my act. I was able to outdrink everyone. And all this extra weight hasn't helped either.

Now they got me holed up in my own private suite here at Mount Sinai Medical Center on Miami Beach, Florida, the same city where I brought my variety show in 1964. You remember how we used to do it: I began each show with a long shot of the Atlantic Ocean as if the camera starts out in New York City, and then it jets south like a high-speed racing boat along the Atlantic coastline, finally zooming in on the seawall of Ocean Drive on Miami Beach. Then you hear my voice-over, "Come on down!"

Those were the days. Man, it was something, really something. It was a riot, I tell you, a regular riot! It was filmed at the Miami Beach Auditorium in front of a live audience, and for an hour you were transported to a small island where palm trees were abundant and faux stuffed alligators were the souvenirs of choice. In the audience, on the streets, lying on the sand were retirees, northeastern transplants, Miami natives fishing for marlin, Jews, Cubans, and some who were both Cuban and Jewish. An odd mix, really, with deep divisions that could have sunk a less buoyant strip of land. Many of them were forced upon one another by tragic political events. But they somehow all managed to get along, to share the island like castaways, which many of them were. Of course the tantalizing weather helped. In the end, all made for quite a Florida family, like one of those family portraits where you can't figure out how all of these strangers ever got in the picture.

On my stage there was laughter, with some of the biggest names in show business who "came on down" to entertain my audience—Milton Berle, Jack Benny, Bing Crosby, Groucho Marx, Tony Bennett, George Burns, George Carlin, Dean Martin, Gene Kelly, and Bob Hope. They walked out in their tuxedos and gowns (Carlin never wore a tux; being a whacked-out hippie was part of his act), their faces ghostly white from pancake makeup, while my audience sat there, their faces flushed from their golden tans. You didn't even need a color TV to see that my audience was the picture of perfect health and vitality. Meanwhile, back up on Broadway in New York City, Ed Sullivan's audience, like Sullivan's morgue of a mug, looked like they were all about to drop dead.

Now what we had was a real variety show. From the stage I used to say, "As always, the Miami Beach audience is the greatest audience in the world!" What a life I made for myself down here. How sweet it was. How sweet it is!

The Miami Beach Chamber of Commerce still tells me that I did more for building up this city and promoting it to the world than anyone else. The rest of the state needed oranges to make money, or they launched rockets into outer space to leave their mark, but Miami Beach had the Great One. I made everybody rich. And I'm not made from concentrate, and I never had to leave the ground.

And so this became my city, my adopted home, my private playground— my own personal peninsula? I'm the biggest celebrity on this man-made island, and I am very much a self-made man. I grew up fatherless in Brooklyn and ended up the King of Miami Beach.

This Miami Beach, this paradise, stretches seven miles across the Atlantic seaboard like a sun-drenched Band-Aid. You've heard the story before, heard the Miami Beach carnival barkers, bought the tourism pitches: warm weather all year round, golf courses galore, great hotels like the Fontainebleau, the Eden Roc, the Doral and the Deauville—each with their big-name stars appearing nightly. The guys who did my show would stay on for the week to headline at one of those places along the strip. And the food, which for a guy like me is as second nature as putting on stage makeup, those ribs at Embers, sirloins at the Forge, stone crabs at Joe's, veal cutlet parmesan at Piccolos, and the stuffed cabbage at the Famous were well worth the risk of having to one day spend some time in a hospital. And Cuban food—the yucca in garlic sauce, the black beans dripping in pork fat. All of this on such a small patch of a peninsula. Name me another city like that in America, or anywhere, for that matter.

And get this: no state income tax and a generous homestead exemption. Why do you think all the crooks and thieves end up living down here? It's not *just* the weather, believe me. There's also the immunity to civil damages. With all their assets socked away in those waterfront properties, Florida gives goniffs a license to steal. Yes, of course I picked up some Yiddish while living here. What do you expect? I'm not deaf. And I'm from Brooklyn. Anyway, the way I see it: Florida is a safe haven for those who owe money elsewhere. It's genius, a far bigger draw than the suntans. Devils are lounging on the beach, soaking up the rays and firing up their pitchforks. Florida is a furnace for reasons apart from its proximity to the equator.

Miami Beach is magical, but it is the magic of the dark arts. Black magic masquerading as enchantment. A fatal attraction draws you in with Bermuda Triangle efficiency, and with similar consequences. Miami Beach is a magnet for the lost. A short stay on the island acquaints all visitors with the ruination that is the one true residency requirement of this city. Failure pervades Miami Beach like a rite of passage. Our tourism brochures have the good sense not to reveal such information. It's caveat emptor all the way, and buyer's remorse after that.

Perhaps that explains all the retirees, refugees, and escapees. For years I sold everyone on an illusion: Come on down and live out your dreams. But Miami Beach is not where people arrive by choice. It is a default destination, Devil's Island in drag. People arrive here having left elsewhere in a hurry. And they have no plans of returning. And it is not because they have been placed in witness protection. Most come here either to avoid something or to die. Burial plots are purchased well in advance, the head-stones constructed from seashells, the mourners already recruited from local lifeguards.

The city is a metaphor for defeat. It is not rejuvenating. Palmetto bugs scatter about leisurely and in no particular direction. And this is true of its human inhabitants, too. Life on Miami Beach is always unhurried; it is the ultimate sanctuary for the underachiever. Surrounded by water on all sides, this is where people come to accept their lot as big fish in the smallest of ponds.

Hell, what do you think I'm doing here? My time in television's sun started to fade, and I covered up a career crisis by exiling myself to the only place I knew where I would get one last chance to feel relevant. Miami Beach is where such pacts with the devil get sealed. But, alas, a tan is just a temporary disguise. True colors eventually return. Being canceled last year by CBS was the unkindest cut of all. What, *et tu*? What, you didn't think I knew any Shakespeare? I helped build CBS, which they now call the Tiffany network. *Me*, Gleason, the Great One! And now the suits are all salivating over *The Carol Burnett Show* and *The Sonny and Cher Comedy Hour*. Give me a fucking break!

Those of us who live here, we know not to be fooled. The sun is blinding for a reason—for our own protection. Better not to see so clearly. The piercing look inward is usually not a pretty sight. It can singe the soul, and the people from South Florida mainly seek to avoid such self-examinations. Everything is right below the surface on Miami Beach, like an eternal low tide. For all the talk of radiant light, darkness shares equal billing in this variety show of a tropical paradise. There's a lot of bait and switching among so many who had had no idea how to cast a line.

It is a city of secrets, with suntans as an impermanent disguise, quick to fade—all fickle and freckling. Holing up in Miami Beach is mostly about covering up. To the outside world it appears to be a place of unrivaled transparency—the solar microscope view of cloudless skies? Even our moonlit nights cast shadows of pale illumination. The secrets of this city are kept close to its shore, caked into the sand like blood that never washes away with the tide. They say whatever happens in Vegas stays in Vegas. Here we say: Whatever happens in Miami we will outright deny.

And we're a simple people, actually. In fact, Miamians who are not natu-ralized Cubans aren't all that political. Current events bore us. The space race is too distant and interplanetary to pay much attention. Besides, there's no sunshine in space—just black holes. Physics doesn't carry much weight here.

We're not the kind of people who stake out ideological positions; we don't debate politics. The presidential conventions couldn't be coming to a more neutral site this summer. We probably won't even notice all those delegates and hippies giving each other the finger. Nuclear Armageddon is science fiction in Florida. Encroaching skin cancer is all that can ever dis-turb the languid, lazy days of life here in Miami Beach. We'll be following the Olympics this summer because Mark Spitz is a Jew, even though our Jews here on the Beach are not such great swimmers. They mostly sink, or order drinks from the bar. How did he get so fast? That's what we want to know. The medal count with the Soviets won't matter much to us at all.

I'll tell you one thing that ticks me off. The City Council years ago named 41st Street, which cuts right down the middle of Miami Beach—drawing a line in the sand from ocean to bay—Arthur Godfrey Road. Every-one knows that Godfrey, a radio and TV star, was an anti-Semite who wouldn't allow Jews in his hotel, the Kenilworth, up in Bal Harbour. Here's a laugh: with a name like Kenilworth, he didn't let dogs in either. Imagine that: Miami Beach might be the only city in the country where the majority of its residents are Jews, and they name a street in the very heart of the city after the best-known Jew hater in the country.

And that's why this Arthur Godfrey thing . . .

"Mr. Gleason, I'm so sorry, but visiting hours are over now," an imperi-ous but stacked nurse walked in and said. She enjoys bringing down the curtain on the Great One's act from his private suite at Mount Sinai Medi-cal Center. "You'll have to ask your guests to leave. I was just over at Mrs. Posner's room next door, and I asked her guests to leave, too. The two of you, honestly—such jokers! Anything for a laugh—and in a hospital, no less. She had her guests in stitches, which nearly caused her to bust her own stitches. I had to call the attending to make sure she was okay. We've got two competing nightclubs up here, side-by-side on the top floor of Mount Si-nai. You both are lighting up this place like a Burning Bush."

"Really, that Jewish lady next door gets a lot of visitors and laughs? I'm sharing a floor with a comedienne? I've got competition? What's her act? Maybe I should have booked *her* when I had the chance. I think I'll wheel myself over there one of these days and say hello."

All right, you heard the lady: you're all going to have to leave. The nurse with the nice boobs wants you out. I got more stories in me about Miami Beach. And I think this is going to be a big year for this island. Such a strange and fascinating place. No wonder the Fat Man ended up here. For now I got this surgery, and I'll be here for a while. I'm going to miss a lot of the action outside. But settle in and like I used to say in the old days:

"And awaaaay we go!"

One

Lansky's Lady Consigliere

All grand hotels are grand in their own way; all fleabags, flophouses, and eyesores are hideously the same. The gems are distinguished by their fine touches and posh elegance—the ornate lobbies and gilded elevators, the stately rooms and majestic pools. By contrast, the hotels that occupy the other side of the hospitality management business are satisfied when the room keys fit and the guests don't have to deliver a left hook to the TV sets to get them to turn on. Seedy, decrepit, and downright painful to look at is the calling card of these abject establishments.

The Carib on Collins Avenue was just such a hotel. If you booked a room in this runt of the litter along the strip, something obviously had gone wrong with your vacation plans or your upward mobility had just nose-dived. When compared to the other swank art deco palaces to its south, or the hulking glass nautical modern high-rises to its north, all dotting Ocean Drive and Collins Avenue on Miami Beach, the Carib looked as though it was begging to receive permanent SRO status. Yes, it was oceanfront property, but only insofar as it was an affront to the ocean. The Atlantic snarled with all oceanic contempt as its waves stopped short of the Carib's beach in protest, never rolling up against the sand as if it refused to cross a picket line. Yet the hotel took no offense and had no hard feelings. It just sat upon the beach like a shipwreck, a barnacle-infested jetty, a sorry structure that shamelessly blocked the view of the Atlantic from Collins Avenue.

And the inside was even worse. The lobby had lime green sofas rubbed to the hair stubble of its cushioning. These threadbare pieces of Bauhaus, once upholstered in lush brocade, were now parlor games of Russian roulette. Every time someone took a seat the chance that the sofa would combust into a hailstorm of cottony confetti became a real possibility. A cigarette machine beaming with nicotine and alluring red letters bulged with translucent buttons that offered a wide variety of cancer-causing options. The Surgeon General's warnings were subordinate to a different army in these parts. The standing ashtrays were littered with the final flames of countless cigarettes, still smoldering in a pyre of bright-eyed, unfiltered butts. Other ashtrays, these resting upon coffee tables, were in the shape of tacky seashells that hadn't been emptied since 1966.

Barren was the running decorative theme.

The lobby was without the obligatory smoky lounges or spacious ballrooms that distinguished the other hotels on Miami Beach, with their seafaring motifs and zodiac ambiance—Aquarius sharing wall space with Neptune and his trident. All the Carib offered was a shabby candy store that sold tanning oils, toothpaste, beach towels, and assorted Miami Beach tchotchkes, *Playboy*, rolling paper—and, of course, playing cards.

Despite its many shortcomings, the Carib possessed one essential amenity that explained why it hadn't yet been condemned, demolished, or sold off to a hotelier with more class: each night its cardroom hosted the best poker game on Miami Beach. This was nothing to take for granted along the strip. Many of the art moderne hotels along Collins Avenue boasted top-shelf entertainment—show girls wearing pasties and festooned with peacock feathers, borscht belt comics serving up racier, less kosher material than what was allowed in the Catskills, and silky voiced crooners wearing shiny tuxedos and packing enough oil in their hair to start a fire on a sunny day. Of course, Miami Beach's resident crime boss, Meyer Lansky, who owned a percentage in a number of these hotels, including the Carib, and lived in the Imperial House, also on Collins, had been counting the days since the mid-1950s when gambling might finally be legalized on Miami

Beach. He wanted to do away with carpet-joint card games and replace them with actual casinos with their whirring slot machines, green velvet poker mats, and deep-dish crap tables where high rollers and big whales could leave their money and sulk away broke. Twenty years later, however, and Meyer was still counting the days like an odds maker, and the odds of his success were getting lower.

The original hope was to convert the sleepy peninsula of Miami Beach into a gaming Riviera. Las Vegas, with its desert Shangri-La and dry heat wouldn't be able to compete with the warm inviting ocean that caresses the beaches of this paradise tucked away at the bottom of the United States. With a sun so strong, fried gamblers would be forced to put down their tanning reflectors and return to the casino for more air conditioning and another turn at the craps tables. What happens in Vegas might stay in Vegas or get buried beside a cactus, but if something were to happen on Miami Beach, it might just get washed back out into the high tide and never be heard from again. Sin City stood no chance against the "sun and fun capital of the world," as the great Jackie Gleason used to boast on his TV variety show, which was broadcast from Miami Beach.

But after all these years, casinos had as much of a chance of doling out chips in Miami Beach as snow had of falling from the sky in August. Every election cycle the voters of Florida would beat back any statewide ballot initiative seeking to legalize gambling on Miami Beach. When it came to this issue, the whole of Florida actually enjoyed its tropical irrelevance; it had no desire to see the state become a Cosa Nostra cliché, a punch line for any joke that involved *The Godfather* gone actually fishing rather than "sleeping with the fishes." The citizens of Florida were quite happy with sunshine, oranges, and water sports as the state's signature attractions. It didn't want the dirty business of the mob to outshine its otherwise good clean living.

As far as most people were concerned, pari-mutuel betting, with its quaintness and summery charm, should be more than enough to appease those for whom no vacation is complete without a game of chance and a stack of winless tickets. Disney had just opened a theme park in central Florida; all those orange groves magically disappeared inside the Magic Kingdom. But Snow White seemed far too fair-skinned to survive in Florida.

Most residents of Miami Beach feared the crime that would ensue from casinos along Collins Avenue. The mobsters that Miami Beach had gotten used to over the years—largely bookies, race track and jai alai hangers-on, and low-level pimps—were avuncular and cartoonish, fun to gawk at around town with their fancy, heat-packing suits and reconfigured noses that were pointing in every direction but straight like at a boxing convention. Casino gambling was likely to attract a more dangerous breed of mobsters, degenerate tourists, shady characters, and the genuine articles in hardcore crime. Miami already had enough troubles with cockroaches and alligators. And that's why all those gambling referendums were resoundingly defeated no matter how many bribes and fixes Lansky set in motion.

With each of these electoral defeats, Meyer Lansky would be reminded how catastrophically his empire had crumbled, and how his dreams of controlling the swankiest casinos in Havana and Miami Beach would never materialize after all. And the irony that it was all being done by a democratic process was not lost on him either. In one country he was screwed at the election booth, and in the other by the haughty rock star rule of a communist dictator. In 1959, a revolution in Cuba brought Fidel Castro to power and toppled the graft-friendly dictatorship of Fulgencio Batista, who didn't mind the American Jewish Mafia managing its gaming interests in Havana. Castro nationalized each of the hotels and casinos that Meyer and his syndicate of partners had invested in Cuba. It was for this reason that Lansky's plans for gambling on Miami Beach took on new and greater urgency.

Time was not on Lansky's side, however. He had just returned to Miami Beach from Israel, where he spent a year hoping to make *aliyah*—renouncing his American citizenship and pledging his allegiance to the Jewish state. He was not a rabid Zionist by any measure. The federal government had been after him for years for domestic tax evasion. Rather than risk going to jail like his former partner, Lucky Luciano, he absconded to the Holy Land in search of holy rollers. Within a year Israel extradited him back to the United States. Its Law of Return carries with it the fine print that excludes gangsters with criminal pasts. So like Moses in a far earlier millennium, and for less redoubtable reasons, Meyer Lansky was exiled by his own people only to return to Miami Beach where he received a rousing homecoming from his *other* own people.

But things were now bad on Miami Beach for his old associates. Without Meyer's business acumen, organizational agility, math wizardry, and overall Jewish *kop*, the Jewish Mafia that remained in his absence was falling apart—from incompetence and obsolescence. Bickering elderly Jewish gangsters, stabbing their pudgy fingers in the air and insulting one another, had taken a well-oiled machine and made it resemble a failed industry from the Rust Belt.

"Who are you calling a terrible don?" Bernie Cohen, the hapless placemat Meyer had installed to run the family, asked.

"Look, you're not good, that's all I'm sayin'," said Morty "the *Mohel*."

"And you could do better?" Bernie countered.

"Of course I could do better. Since Meyer left and you took over, business is way down and new families are moving in on our territory." Before Bernie could defend himself, Morty shifted in his seat, searched for an underling and belched: "Now pass the fucking sour cream for my blintz. And get me a smear of cream cheese on this bagel. I'm starving here!" He then speared a dill pickle with a fork and much of it disappeared into his mouth.

The greatest criminal mind in Jewish history was fumbling with his Hebrew in the Holy Land, while these stooges were sinking the Jewish Mafia on Miami Beach like they were wearing cement shoes. It was true that as soon as Meyer left for Israel, several competing Cosa Nostra of the Italian variety attempted to muscle in on Lansky's turf, all under the assumption that, without Meyer, his old crew would never survive—killed off more from strokes, diabetes, and incompetence than from old-school whacking.

Now that Meyer had finally returned, the mess that had been created in his absence was bitterly revealed.

"What the fuck happened here?" he demanded of Bernie. "I leave you in charge and now we're a third-rate syndicate, dumber than the Italians up north on Mulberry Street and too lazy to keep up with the Chinese in Chinatown. It looks like you've accomplished nothing other than consume massive quantities of cholesterol."

Poor Bernie was taking this abuse while choking down kishka, which wasn't sitting well in his kishkas.

So while waiting for his federal racketeering trial to commence, Meyer set about the task of reestablishing his authority in South Florida and setting his affairs in order. Deprived of his properties in Havana, exiled from the Jewish state, about to face prosecution and a possible jail sentence in Florida, and with rival gangs smelling blood in the water, Meyer had never before had to overcome such terrible odds or had a run of such bad luck. In all his years mastering the underworld, never before had he hit bottom. Miami Beach, his de facto home, would now have to serve as the scene for his personal redemption. But truth be told, he feared that he couldn't do it alone, that without Lucky and Bugsy he was missing a crucial link in a chain that bound him to a life of highly profitable, unpunished crime.

Legalizing gambling in Miami Beach would have been a tremendous face-saver for Meyer. But given all these obstacles, Meyer's recent streak of poor luck, and a federal racketeering charge hanging over his head, keeping the action moving—even in places as decrepit as the Carib—was vitally important to Lansky's outside reputation and self-esteem.

Unfortunately, new tsouris was on the way from an unexpected source.

"Meyer, I think we have a problem," Morty the Mohel said. In addition to being the Mohel most in demand on Miami Beach, snipping off the foreskin of hundreds of eight-day-old Jewish boys since his arrival here in the 1950s, Morty was also one of Lansky's most trusted lieutenants or capos.

"Yeah, Meyer, we got a problem," Danny "Dumb Luck" chimed in. Danny had married into a wealthy South Florida family. He didn't need to work, but he liked palling around town with criminals, slumming with Jewish degenerates. What else was he going to do: sit in the air conditioning at his stockbroker's office watching his shares of RCA and ITT stagnate throughout the entire decade? Playing mobster was much more fun, except that he was useless, and most of the crew believed that he had serious mental problems.

"I just said that, you moron," Morty turned to Danny and said.

"Sorry, Morty. Just trying to help out."

"What are you both talking about?" Lansky asked. Small in stature but standing tall on stacks of money in his shoes, he was wearing a gray pinstripe suit with a red tie. His silver hair was slicked back with enough oil to make OPEC jealous. It was often the case that Meyer had trouble following the circuitous conversations of his crew. These were uneducated men, without easy access to ten-dollar words. Madison Avenue and Wall Street were beyond their comprehension. They were men of Lincoln Road, their speech all Woolworth five-and-dime. "Tell me what's going on."

"See that lady over there?" Morty replied, pointing over into the basin of the cardroom. "Over there, in the corner, the one in the dress with flowers on it."

"Yeah, so what?" Meyer said as he spied the woman, middle-aged, plump, attractive with raven hair and blue eyes that beamed like coral below crystal waters.

"Well, she hasn't lost a round tonight, not a single hand," Morty said. "And she cleaned up at the Shore Club the other night, and the night before that she wiped out the poker players at the Di Lido. Last weekend she ran the tables at the Ritz Plaza and at the National. She's on the kind of hot streak that you notice—even in this city."

"How much is she up?" the Jewish don asked.

"We don't know for sure," Danny Dumb Luck replied. "I figure two grand. Maybe *tree*."

"Don't listen to him, Meyer. The doofus can't count," Morty interjected. "His wife pays for everything. It's way more than that—probably five grand easy . . . figure six; that's if you count all the hotels."

"People are starting to complain," Danny added. "They're sayin' that something must be up, like we're not running a clean game anymore."

This Meyer Lansky could not abide. He might be losing his edge, and his empire, but never would he allow it to be said that Meyer Lansky presided over seedy clip joints. Up until now, whether in Vegas, Havana, or Miami Beach, his gaming establishments were always run honestly. Even as a kid on the Lower East Side, he never bait and switched the pennies he pitched, never once swapped coins for valueless Hanukkah gelt.

"She must be cheating," Meyer surmised. "Have you checked her out? Have you seen any dumping or whipsawing? Is she counting cards, dealing from under the deck, false dealing, marking juiced cards, hand mucking, or card sharping?" Meyer asked as he rattled through the litany of sins of the poker cheat.

"No, she looks clean, Meyer," Morty assured him. "Watch her deal. She's a pro. She must have been playing poker all her life."

The three wise guys observed the lady play from a distance, and such a vision it was. She shuffled the deck of cards with amazing speed and alacrity;

if you didn't know she was human, you'd think she was a cash counting machine. The playing cards were being put through yoga poses, bending and flipping, turning over and back. She rifled them into the air and then summoned the cards down back to Earth—one at a time. Once the deck was full, she constructed elaborate bridges and fanned them across the table before she sent the cards aloft once again, this time doing loop de loops.

"Jesus Christ," Lansky said. "This woman is a fucking ringer. We're being hustled. Somebody must have sent her our way for a reason. When I was in Israel, how many new enemies did you *mamzers* make?" Meyer stretched his neck like a periscope. "Where in the hell did this broad come from? She ever play cards at our hotels before? You know something, she is starting to look a little familiar to me."

"She should," Morty said, "because you've seen her before, Meyer. In fact, you've handed her your own money—sometimes two or three times a week since you've been back."

"What do you mean? I haven't played any cards—and not with her!"

"Think, Meyer," Morty said, smiling broadly. "This woman is always around money."

"I don't have a fucking clue."

"She's the cashier at the Jewish NOSE-tra, remember? She just started working there around the same time as when you came back. She's from New York, and she has a thick European accent—maybe from Poland. That was also when she started hitting jackpots at our poker games along the strip."

"No kidding," Danny Dumb Luck said. "That's the lady who gives us back our change after we eat corned beef, a knish, and a Dr. Brown's Cel-Ray Soda?" Danny thought it was important that he recite his standing order. "She's also a card shark on the side? And she's from Europe? Is that anywhere near Toronto?"

Meyer and Morty looked at Danny, shook their heads in pity, and remembered never to give him any assignment beyond making coffee.

The Jewish NOSE-tra on Alton Road in South Beach was widely regarded as the best delicatessen in town. In so many ways, Miami Beach tried to recreate the old-world shtetls of Eastern and Central Europe, and the Pale, by welcoming Jews to relocate to sunny Florida. There were many synagogues, Judaica stores, and kosher butcher shops—all catering to a captive audience of complaining Jews. A remote island along the southern Atlantic coastline, yet it had all the necessary accommodations for Jewish castaways. But not everything transferred so easily. The Jews of Miami Beach always kvetched about the absence of a good deli. Everyone had a Jewish restaurant up north that made the mouth water compared to Miami's deli drought. All the delis from afar were superior to the pretenders of Miami Beach—with their tough tongue, dry corned beef, flavorless brisket, and knishes that passed through the digestive system like moon rocks.

"You call this pastrami?" a familiar refrain could be heard all along Washington Avenue and Lincoln Road. "And pickles! A disgrace, I tell you."

Others complained that the smoked fish had the texture of chewing gum. "How did they smoke this, in a pipe? This place is an insult to the high art of succulent nova, sable, and carp."

It had gotten so bad that the Jewish Mafia was called in to rectify the situation. If good deli couldn't be had through the forces of the free market, then the black market would have to be relied upon. While standing on the street Meyer Lansky would receive teary-eyed appeals from starving Jews who swore that they had not had a good bagel with lox, cream cheese, onion, and a tomato since they left Shaker Heights. As a public service and to appease his people, Meyer decided to open up his own deli, like Caesar's bread and circuses, but this one was only for the Jews of Miami Beach—to keep them entertained and fed (and to stop the incessant complaining). No one was under any illusion that the Jewish NOSE-tra would become both a popular lunch spot and also a convenient front for the Jewish syndicate. Actually, no one cared. Who would begrudge Lansky a place to wash his money after he fortified the Jews of Miami Beach with a nifty display of manna from the deli universe?

Meyer brought in the best provisions, shipped directly from Brooklyn, and even enticed a few of the experienced deli hands from New York to relocate to Florida and teach the unsteady hands of Miami Beach how to slice nova paper thin. Morty the Mohel, not surprisingly, moonlighted at the Jewish NOSE-tra as a counter man. He was fearless when slicing off foreskin. Belly lox was mere batting practice for him.

When the Jewish NOSE-tra first opened, the *Miami Herald* and the local *Miami Beach Sun Reporter* heralded this southern miracle with the headline: "Hanukkah Arrives Early on the Beach With New Deli." Meyer Lansky's epicurean benevolence showed once again that he was a savvy and resourceful Jewish fixer, a man who always saw a need, answered the call, and put the right pieces together. The woman at the poker table looked familiar, and now he knew why. Yes, he paid her salary, but more importantly, as the Jewish NOSE-tra's cashier, she was the last face everyone saw as they trundled out into the unappetizing heat on Alton Road.

"I can't kick her out of here. She's on the legitimate side of our payroll," Meyer reasoned. "How would that look? But let's at least go over there and say hello."

The three wise guys approached the poker tables like they owned the joint, which they did, and chatted up the regular clientele. Finally they made their way toward the lady poker player from Poland.

"Hey, missus, don't you think you've had enough for tonight?" Meyer began indelicately. "Let these fine people go home with some dignity."

"Yeah, lady," Danny chimed, once more oblivious to his don's directive to keep his mouth shut. "You have to know when to fold."

"I never fold," the lady broke in without glancing up. "Okay, everyone—another round? Texas hold 'em—in Florida. You all game? I'll deal."

The other five players, all men and senior citizens who had aged drastically during this murderous night of poker, groaned in unison.

Meyer reached over and grabbed the woman's wrist. "I don't think you heard me. I know who you are, the cashier from the NOSE-tra. What's your name?"

"Sophie Posner."

"Okay, Sophie," Lansky continued. "As I said, you're done for the night. Now get out of here."

"Don't threaten me, little man," the woman replied, now finally showing the respect to at least look Lansky in the eye. "And take your hand off my arm before I break it, and then I'll go to work on your legs. I'll decide when I'm finished. It's still early," she said, knowing that it was 2:30 in the morning. "I have a young son and a sick husband to support. Working as a cashier in your deli is *pisher* change for me. This here," she said, floating her hand over her barricade of winnings, green paper stacked like hedges, coins so heavy, the center of gravity of the table had shifted in her direction. The pigeon sitting opposite her looked like a child trying to make a space for himself at the grownups' table. "This game here is how I pay the bills. Now piss off!"

With that fiery exchange, everyone at the Carib—hell, everyone in South Florida—believed that the Lansky crime syndicate was about to go to the mattresses. The other players quietly reached for whatever small change they were left with for the night. The Carib, never a place that chased after splashy entertainment, suddenly was the scene of the hottest show on the strip. Someone had just threatened to break Meyer Lansky's hand and legs—and it was a girl!

The Jewish don blinked his eyes and straightened his back. He let go of Sophie Posner's wrist, and she withdrew her arm slowly, turning it over, as if checking for a blue bruise. There was one, wholly unique, an old one. Lansky twitched as he noticed marks on his cashier's arm—not the sort that he might have caused by squeezing too hard, and not the kind of digits that get rung up on cash registers like the one Sophie operated. No, this was a series of numbers, etched on her arm, branded in blue, forever marking her as one of Hitler's cursed ones. Lansky withdrew in fright, frozen in awe, then taking a step back, as if he had just seen the face of God.

Meyer Lansky, of course, one of the legends of Murder, Inc., was not unfamiliar with the dead and was never squeamish around them. Although despite his avocation and reputation as a Mafia chieftain, he hadn't done much personal killing of his own over the years. And while he was a Jew, and Hitler's Holocaust took place less than thirty years earlier, Meyer, surprisingly, had actually never seen a numbered arm belonging to one of his own people up close. It shocked him. Transported him into another epoch of Jewish suffering, the twilight zone of genocidal possibility. Yes, he was a killer by trade, but he was a rank amateur when it came to the kind of killing that Sophie Posner had both seen and survived.

"Lady, I don't think you realize who I am," he said, jittery.

"I know exactly who you are, Lansky. But you don't know exactly who I am. You're not dealing with Salvatore Maranzano here. That guy would have dropped dead of a heart attack even if you and that Lucky Luciano hadn't arranged for him to go bye-bye. I am not so easy to get rid of, and you would be making a terrible mistake if you underestimated me."

"This is crazy," Lansky said, recovering his senses and balance. His voice kicked down an octave. "You know, people don't usually speak this way to me and expect to live long."

Sophie Posner stared into Lansky's bloodshot eyes and offered him a half smile. "Live a long life? Is that all you got to threaten me with?" Sophie then convulsed into laughter—deeper than her spoken voice, with a throaty tinge of madness—which prompted Danny Dumb Luck to follow suit with his own anxious rata-tat-tat machine gun chuckle.

He was the only other person in the room laughing.

Everyone else was scared that this moment would coincide with the end of the world. Some were transfixed by the spectacle of Meyer Lansky being dressed down by a woman in a floral dress. But this was no ordinary woman. Her kind also made their new home on Miami Beach, traveling from across an ocean, refugees not just from another time zone but from a different world altogether. They did not long for the lives they left behind. They were not sentimental about the past. They were nostalgic for nothing. When given the chance they left in a hurry. Unfortunately, they were not permitted to disconnect their memories and toss them away into some dustbin of perverted history. These memories were all too raw and the methods deployed in forgetting inadequate to the task. Card games would not be diverting enough. Drinking didn't do it, either. All modern-day distractions were remedies for ordinary moments of melancholy and boredom. Nothing about Sophie Posner was ordinary—especially her pathologies, for which at this time, in the tropical hamlet of Miami Beach, there was no diagnosis and surely no cure.

"Mister Gangster," Sophie continued. "I'm already living on borrowed time. I've lived a lot longer than I have a right to. I'm playing with the house's money. Most of the people at Maidanek were gassed and cremated— the Royal Flush of death. *You* can never beat that hand when it comes to murder. Do you seriously think I'm afraid of a short Jewish gangster? I already survived one short gangster—a monster, actually—wearing a mustache, and believe me: you are not in his league. You don't have that much blood on your hands, and you never will. Look at you: you're a Jewish accountant with a rap sheet. You've seen nothing; you've done nothing. So no, Lansky—you don't scare me one bit."

And from that fateful, frightful beginning, something happened in Meyer Lansky, something he couldn't actually account for: he was hypnotically drawn to Sophie Posner, and she was affectionately drawn to him. After grinding him down like the wife of Jewish husband, she felt the responsibility to build him back up—into a better, more confident version of himself. And a lasting friendship was made in racketeer hell.

A few days later, while paying his check at the Jewish NOSE-tra, he said, "You should come work for me."

"Here's your change," Sophie replied, counting off a few dollars and errant coins. "I already work for you," she said, looking him over like she disapproved of his suit.

"No, I mean my real business, not this legitimate front. This is not a place for someone like you."

"Why me? You keep a cash register in your other office?"

"Lady, I think we both know that operating a cash register is not where your true talents lie. I have a feeling about you—a feeling that you could be useful to the family. Besides, by keeping you away from the card games at my hotels, I'm actually saving money."

"I already have a family—a husband and a young boy."

Sophie's husband, Jacob, a partisan in the Hungarian forest who detonated bridges that sank German convoys, and learned how to handle a machine gun even though he was nothing but a bookish university student from Prague, lost his entire family in the camps. When it was all over—the guns and tanks, the shaved heads and the gas—he arrived to America a debilitated, broken man. He had seen many unnatural things, horrors that should disqualify his naturalization. Now, twenty-five years and three heart attacks later, he was a slow-moving old man, the putative head of a household actually led by a mentally unbalanced, uncontrollable wife. And together they had an athletic twelve-year-old son who was raising himself in a wasteland called Miami Beach.

"He must learn to live without parents," Sophie once said.

"But he has parents," Jacob goaded her.

"No, he's an orphan," she settled the discussion and created more mystery.

"He's our child," the father said.

"But he belongs to the wilderness of the world," the mother replied. "That's his true home."

"What, you want we should kick him out?"

Sophie became the family breadwinner after they moved to Florida, a year earlier. Jacob's manhood was manifested solely in cashing his Social Security checks. Aside from the fact that she was taking money away from degenerate gamblers, and hanging around with the most unsavory characters east of Las Vegas, she was doing a masterful job of feeding the family—even if that meant she was never home at night, often disappearing during the day, as well. She was not a likely PTA mom. She took no pride in baking. Indeed, she had once been among those selected for baking—but on the wrong side of the oven door. By 1972, ovens came equipped with all sorts of fancy dials and thermal gadgetry. Yet, she was among the select company that knew that Westinghouse was in a very different business from IG Farben. The ovens of the space age couldn't replace those other ovens in her mind, the ones not for cooking, the ones that left everything ashen and nothing unburned.

"It is difficult being the man in this house with a woman like you for a wife, Sophie," Jacob one day said. He was dressed in his tennis whites, a man who didn't possess a racket even though his wife was intimately involved with the rackets. He sat in a chair by the window of their apartment in a high-rise building, tanning himself through the glass, trying to avoid eye contact with his wife. He was a chronic squinter. "I'm not working anymore, and Miami Beach is like mold on the brain."

"It took more than a man to survive what you saw and lived through, Jacob," his wife said. "How much manhood does a person need in one lifetime? You're just bored in Miami Beach. You need an activity, something more than just walking. I have poker and the pari-mutuels," she said, smiling at the very thought of her nightly excursions, although she wasn't deluded into thinking that these relieved her of her own torment. "And it makes us money."

Jacob's mood darkened despite all of the radiant light flooding the apartment.

"I think you should spend more time with our son and less at the track," he said before darting out of the living room in a quest for cover.

At around this same time, Meyer Lansky was coming to terms with the reality that his Jewish Mafia was getting stale. His made men were dullards and second-rate bagmen. Where was Bugsy Siegel when you needed him? Dead for decades, actually. Meyer had an innate sense that this feisty Holocaust survivor, Sophie Posner, was a genetic female stand-in for his childhood friend Bugsy. Everything about Sophie reminded Meyer of Bugs. For one thing, they both possessed the same brashness, moxie, and mental toughness. And for another, they both conveyed a fearlessness that bordered on insanity. Truth be told: they were both crazy. Standing down was not in their anatomical vocabulary. When in their presence one had the sick sense that they could not be restrained, that ignitable rage was always simmering in their veins like embers inching toward lighter fluid. And while they were both unpredictable, they each also emitted a secure feeling that no harm would come once they were by your side. Meyer was desperate to reclaim that feeling again.

What best camouflages such unappeasable volatility is a gentle, generous nature and an affable personality. Meyer had little of that charisma and confidence that makes the *shtarkers* all that *shtark*. Bugsy had been a Mafia rock star; Sophie carried herself not like a cashier but as a warrior princess. That's one of the reasons why Lansky brought Sophie aboard: he hoped that this lady who had, indeed, survived Hitler's ovens could heat up his flagging enterprises in torrid Florida.

And what heat she brought. In due time Meyer came to rely on Sophie's judgment, street smarts, killer instincts, and tactical edge. After all, she was orphaned in the Warsaw Ghetto, and then survived two years in Maidanek, a death camp in Poland. It was there where she first got her period, was welcomed into womanhood: the cycling of life in a place of death—without irony, without hope. She confided in Meyer, told him things she could not speak out loud in polite company. Even Lansky's felons were not sordid enough as confidants.

"I'm ashamed of what I did, didn't do, and wanted to do," she once told him. "A trifecta of human failure."

Lansky listened in silence. He regretted nothing about his own life, and never felt shame.

Sophie Posner's tales from hell were not the sort of moral compromises and survival techniques that are easily explained—or explained away. If you were not present, you could not possibly know. Ordinary folk struggling through the banalities of life were abysmally ill-suited to appreciate the hellish conditions of the camps. All that Sophie had buried haunted her at night still. And yet she would have done it all over again in order to survive.

She may have felt shame, but, like Meyer, she, too, regretted nothing. Every movement—of coolness, calm, ruthlessness, emotional detachment, and unforgiving nature—had kept her alive.

"What, you think surviving a death camp is all luck?" she once remarked to Meyer. "Like a winning hand in cards? A death camp is no summer camp. Death is what is expected; death is why you are there. To survive is a full-time job! The lazy die, even if lucky. From when you wake up in the morning, all through the night, every day you have to look for the edge, find the angle, make the right moves—even in your sleep."

Meyer's shrewd business instincts made him believe that some of what she had learned might be transferable to his business. She was self-taught and battle tested in ways that gladiators, samurais, and Navy Seals might not make the grade. What seemed incompatible with the above-board world of the living might come in handy in his underworld of organized crime.

And so Sophie left the cash register at the Jewish NOSE-tra and gave up her nightly card games, too, and settled into a new career: an apprentice mobster with big ambitions in Meyer Lansky's crew.

On her last day as a cashier, Jackie Gleason was having lunch, a mountain of brisket on a kaiser roll with Russian dressing and pickles in his beefy hands. The Great One rarely ate at the Jewish NOSE-tra. He feared that it would be unseemly if he consorted with the wrong element on Miami Beach. Sinatra benefited from such associations in Sin City. Gleason didn't wish to promote that his "sun and fun capital of the world" actually had a dark side. Of course, that didn't exempt him from eating the food. The Mafia's own eatery was too tantalizing for a fat man to resist. Seeing Gleason sitting there on the day that Sophie was punching her last ticket, Lansky believed that the coincidence was kismet, an omen that business would get better all on account of his newfound Polish lucky charm.

"Here's your change and awaaaay you go, Mr. Gleason," Sophie sang.

"Thanks, toots," Gleason said and locked onto Sophie's face as if he had seen her before, or simply wished for another sighting.

At first Sophie started with the routine stuff—like collecting money from those who borrowed from Meyer the old-fashioned way. Sophie took to the task immediately, and was pitiless in shaking down anyone with a sob story. She put the hammerhead into the old loan shark model, a fish not altogether rare in these waters.

"I don't care that business is bad," she would say. "Have you heard of Auschwitz? That's bad. What you have is not enough customers, and lousy merchandise. Look, you borrow, you pay back. Mr. Lansky is not a savings and loan; he's a pay back or lose a thumb. *Kapish*? Now what's it going to be?" she asked, while standing there with brass knuckles in one hand and a leather sap in the other.

With each success she broadened her scope. It was like a rotating internship into the nefarious ways of the Mafia. Sophie made the rounds in counterfeiting, money laundering, extortion, coercion, the protection racket—even arson and insurance fraud. In fact, many of these jobs were not only pulled off by Sophie Posner—they were conceived by her, and she executed them in the high style of a seasoned criminal. Meyer beamed with pride over his new protégé, who was a regular gangland prodigy. She brought the wile and the guile back into what had become an otherwise stodgy criminal outfit.

"Sophie, how in the hell did you come up with torching the place and planting evidence implicating the Perpignano brothers at the same time?" Meyer asked, slapping his knee.

"I know a little something about fire, Lansky," she said. "The Nazis were expert arsonists."

The rest of Lansky's crew was envious over Sophie's lightning promotion to capo. Sure they admired her unique talents and endless energy, but this was 1972. Women's lib was in the air, but it was about equality in the legitimate workplace—not in the rackets of organized crime! The Mafia, after all, was old school. Chauvinism was *de rigueur*. Unlike the Cosa Nostra, Jewish gangsters never went in for *gumars*; they generally respected their women—but they expected them to stay at home! Made men wanted their wives to make dinner.

Sophie never made dinner. The Posners had no nightly dinner table. They ate like strangers waiting for a train to arrive, more out of boredom than hunger, eating alone.

"Meyer, I don't understand," Charlie "Nunchucks" began cautiously one day. Charlie supplied a lot of the muscle, a real goon, but despite his grandiose Mafia handle, the only black belt he possessed was holding up his pants. There was a rumor that Sophie actually had some martial arts training, which explains why Charlie always shot out of the room the moment Sophie appeared. "We never include our women in the business. Our own wives aren't even allowed to ask questions about what we do for a living. Hell, my kids tell their friends that I'm in the import-export business, whatever the fuck that means."

"We're doing business a little differently, fellas," Meyer settled them down. There was jealousy among his ranks, and a don's job is all too often about managing egos and putting out fires before they go wild. "Sophie Posner is a natural." Meyer then reversed himself, realizing that what Sophie learned in Maidanek was altogether *unnatural*. Who knew what she would have been like without the unwanted Nazi tutoring?

"Okay, let me say it this way: Sophie is no ordinary lady," Meyer continued. "She's some kind of savant about the underworld. Breaking the law is in her bones. She has one of the best criminals minds I've ever seen. Christ, she thinks faster than anyone I know, and her instincts are always right. Thanks to her judgment, suddenly I'm now making the right moves again. She's totally responsible for a twenty-five percent increase in our bottom line. What an earner she's become. It's like having Lucky and Bugsy back again—in the body of a Polish woman brought to us courtesy of the Third Reich."

Given the fact that Meyer himself was regarded as the shrewdest man ever to be wanted by the FBI, his crew realized that this was high praise, indeed.

"So what's going to happen?" Morty the Mohel wondered. "You gonna make her a made man?"

"No, made lady," Meyer corrected the Mohel. "Better yet, I'm about to make her my lady consigliere."

"Consigliere!" Morty barked. He always imagined that *he* was next in line for that job. "Meyer, how could you pass me over like that? After all these years . . ."

"Morty, I've always appreciated your loyalty. I never thought that the Mohel would ever turn into a mole. You're a good man. But I am going to ask you to respect my decision here. And that goes for the rest of you, too. Do you all hear me?"

These big changes in the organizational flow chart of the Jewish Mafia had implications outside of this crime family. Meyer's own wife, Trudy, asked about this wonder woman who had somehow insinuated herself into her husband's head.

"Meyer," she said in a high-pitched nasal voice while her frosted hair was wrapped up high like a pineapple. "Are you sure there's no hanky-panky going on between you and Mrs. Posner?"

"For God's sakes, Trudy, how many times do I have to tell you?" Meyer sighed. "She's married, and she survived a death camp. She's real damaged goods—good for nothing other than what I got her doing. She's certifiably nuts. I'm afraid she might go off and start her own family, steal some of my crew and put me out of business. I got to watch her all the time. The lady is the craftiest son-of-a-bitch I've ever seen. I can't believe she didn't take out Hitler all by herself. Me and her together? Please, I don't need that kind of stress. My blood pressure is up in the clouds right now anyway."

Trudy Lansky didn't seem convinced, and for good reason. Meyer *was* developing romantic feelings for Sophie. He was enchanted by her, believing that she was his felonious equal, a soul mate sent from that great penitentiary in the heavens. He imagined that she had survived Maidanek for a reason—and that reason had to do with her future in organized crime on Miami Beach. Had they met earlier, what resourceful, conniving, badass children they would have produced—a gang of real *goniffs*, the ultimate diabolical crime family.

Sophie was having to answer similar questions in her own house.

"When did Uncle Meyer become Uncle Meyer?" her twelve-year-old son, Adam, asked quizzically one day. "I mean, whose brother is he? And how come I only found out about him this year?"

"He's your uncle; what more do you need to know?" Sophie replied impatiently. She was the true head of her family, and she permitted far less back talk than Meyer allowed in his home and with his crew. "What's with all the questions, you little *pisher*? What are you now, the FBI?"

"But . . ."

"Enough, he's your uncle, be happy. He's a terrific role model. You watch and see. Actually, from now on call him Godfather."

"My godfather? I have a godfather?"

"You do now. See what happens in Miami Beach? Lucky you."

"Sophie, please don't confuse the boy with this dirty business you have gotten yourself into," Jacob said. Knowing the look of disapproval he was about to receive from his wife, Jacob popped yet another nitroglycerin tablet into his mouth, keeping a cyanide tablet tucked inside his trousers for a more special occasion. "You survived Maidanek so you can involve yourself with Jewish hoodlums—and God knows what else you are doing with them? And now a godfather you want to make Meyer to our son? Isn't it enough that he's the godfather for an entire syndicate? My son is going to kiss Lansky's ring whenever he sees him?"

"Yes, he will, but only on *Shabbos*."

Some mothers played tennis and then met for a ladies lunch. Still others volunteered at the Bass Museum, docents more interested in frigid air conditioning than modern art. A few worked outside the home. Absolutely no one's mother was a chief capo in the Jewish Mafia on Miami Beach—or any Mafia anywhere! Adam had to endure some teasing at school, but so many of the other kids at Biscayne Junior High also had parents with underworld ties. Did gender norms really matter amid all this abnormal degeneracy?

"What happens if you don't do all of your homework, Adam? Your mom going to whack you—but not with a paddle?" they teased.

The boy was well liked, even by some of the black kids who were only recently bussed over the causeway as a way of integrating the schools. Adam was a little shy, but a great athlete—the fastest runner at Biscayne Junior High, they say. He could stand the abuse at school; the neglect at home, however, was a different matter altogether.

Soon word spread all the way to Vegas that Lansky had found a consigliere with special powers, an X-Woman, a Maidanek Mutant with a highly developed criminal mind. Meyer half-wondered whether one of the other crime families might actually try to steal Sophie Posner away. And then where would he be? He assigned some of his men to keep an eye out on her at all times. "She's our biggest asset, boys," he cautioned. "Out of the crucible of the Holocaust came our very own Holy Grail."

Sometimes they bickered like a married couple. "Where's your balls, Lansky?" Sophie said only half-jokingly. "What's the matter with you? Is this any way for a Jewish don to act? Have some dignity, and stand up straight!"

Like Bugsy Siegel from an earlier era, she was filled with big ideas—some of them hairbrained and impractical, or too immense and convoluted to implement with Meyer's limited personnel. One scam that did meet with Meyer's approval was a plan to ensure that legalized gambling would finally come to Miami Beach.

"The next time it's on the ballot," Sophie said, laying out the plan like a field general, "we rig the polling machines so that even the 'No' votes get added to the 'Yes' column. It will be unanimous."

That idea failed disastrously owing to poor execution. Morty, Danny, and Charlie, calling themselves the Plumbers, were caught in the act, stowed away in the storage facility where the voting machines were kept. Flashlights beaming on their faces made them for Mafia. The tools hanging from their belts, and their fingerprints all over the machines, pretty much eliminated any alibi. Rocky Pomerance, Miami Beach's longtime police chief, anticipated that Meyer Lansky would eventually try to improve the odds on bringing casinos to Miami Beach by stuffing the ballot box. And so he kept around-the-clock watch over the machines until they were taken to the polling precincts.

The thing is: Meyer Lansky was given too much credit when the story broke and the paper reported the arrests.

"Not my finest moment, Meyer. I'm sorry," Sophie said.

"Hey, not even you can bat a thousand," Meyer reassured her. He didn't want Sophie to lose her confidence or tap the brakes on her always-fertile mischievous mind.

The ballot box caper wasn't Meyer's idea. It belonged to the new girl on the block. Consistent with his usual practice, however, Chief Pomerance didn't charge the Plumbers. He simply let them go. They were bungling and harmless, and he had a better idea for how these three Mafioso clowns could make it up to the citizens of Miami Beach, and the nation, by showing themselves to be American patriots rather than thuggish Jewish *paisans*.

Meanwhile, this minor hiccup—another foiled attempt to resurrect Lansky's Havana in Miami Beach—didn't dampen Meyer's faith in his peacetime consigliere. Sophie nearly took over the whole enterprise, all with Meyer's blessing. His luck had changed; now was not the time to take the die out of his consigliere's hot hands. In fact, Meyer's faith in her was so high, he even considered branching out further. Those Perpignano brothers, for instance, had just taken over the ownership of the Reef, an upscale hotel in Fort Lauderdale with sweeping staircases and a gilded mezzanine where some local high rollers liked to play. It was surely no Diplomat, but they were running card games that had siphoned off some of Lansky's regular clientele. Lansky considered making a move on those two Italians. The message needed to be sent that South Florida was Jewish territory—for both retirees and racketeers. On some fancier flights of Lansky's renewed ambitions, Meyer expanded even beyond the borders of the United States.

"Sophie, maybe we should consider putting out our own hit on Fidel Castro and getting our hotels and casinos back," he suggested giddily. "The Bay of Pigs was such a stupid idea. You're so much smarter than Kennedy's 'Best and Brightest.' No doubt you can devise a better way to knock off that commie bastard. What do you say, Lady Consigliere?"

"Meyer, I'm a Holocaust refugee, not a freedom fighter," Sophie said. "This is a job for the CIA. A war against the Perpignano brothers is one thing; setting off an international incident is something else. What, you want so that I might wind up like Ethel Rosenberg?"

"The CIA already screwed up the last time!" Meyer fumed. "A bunch of *goys* from Yale. What do they know from such down and dirty things? They're the reason why Castro is still alive and in power! I want you to take a shot."

"Forget it," she insisted. "If he was a Nazi, then you'd have me. But communists didn't kill my parents or put me in a death camp."

"I know I am getting ahead of myself," Meyer steadied his excitable voice, "but things have been so good for the family lately, the sky is the limit. We should think big. I mean really big! Maybe there's some money in sabotaging the Democratic or Republican National Conventions this summer? We're nearly untouchable since you got here."

"Worry about your racketeering case, Meyer," Sophie said. "And I'll handle everything else."

Meyer Lansky didn't actually realize all the big changes that were on the horizon for the American Mafia. Las Vegas was slowly being taken over by large and legitimate conglomerates, run by lawyers and business school graduates. The days of casino operators named Nucky, Lucky, and Ace were numbered. The Myrons, Mortimers, and Orins from Wharton were taking over the world. There was talk in New Jersey of legalizing gambling in Atlantic City. The old Atlantic City Boardwalk was being spruced up—gleaming casinos would replace the carnival games while real gun shots would supplant the shooting galleries. Without Sophie and a plan for the future, the Jewish mob, especially in Miami Beach, would soon probably cease to exist.

Occasionally, notwithstanding her colossal hot streak, some of Sophie's advice was too extreme—even for the criminal element. Meyer's entire crew convulsed in laughter after hearing one of Sophie's over-the-top plays.

"So you think we should just walk into the Reef Hotel, in the middle of the day, in broad daylight, with tourists checking in and out, and kill one of the Perpignano brothers just to send a message that we'll be coming back for the other one?"

"Yes, take him out," Sophie said emphatically. Her blue eyes were darting, and she paced around with a bounce in her step like she came upon occasional speed bumps.

"We can't do that," Meyer replied.

"Take him out," she repeated.

"No, I said."

"Slit his throat," she suggested.

"Absolutely not."

"Shoot him in the head,"

"Stop it, already."

"*Take him out, take him out, take him out!*" she belted out a creepy torch song.

"Jesus Christ, Sophie," Meyer said. "You're actually crazier than Bugsy. I swear. Even Bugs had his limits."

"Yeah, and he's dead," she pointed out. "Not a good role model. I think we should do things my way."

Sophie's rite of passage took place in a death camp and ended with a graduation ceremony where there was never any expectation of there being any graduates—only cremated corpses. The closest Meyer ever got to Nazis was back in the early days, in New York, when he and Bugsy and their crew broke up a German Bund meeting by busting heads and tossing everyone through the storefront window out onto York Avenue.

Meyer often pondered what Sophie would have been like absent the Maidanek interlude. Death camps bring to mind such nature versus nurture scenarios. The survivors proved they had the right stuff, but were they well suited to the camps—a test of the survival of the fittest on steroids—or did the camps make them survivors? Most of all, Meyer Lansky wanted to know whether Sophie Posner was a gangster at heart.

"Tell me what you were like before the Nazis," Lansky once asked.

"There is no 'before' after such a place as Maidanek, Meyer," she replied begrudgingly. "I don't remember having dolls, or imaginary friends, or tea parties with stuffed animals. All I know is what's engraved on my arm."

Two matters of some immediacy required the very best of Sophie's good counsel. The first was Meyer's tax evasion trial. The only witness to the alleged crime was loan shark Vincent "Fat Vinnie" Teresa. That's the best the feds could do—a mobster stoolie turning state's evidence. Meyer had kept himself so underground and undetectable all these years, moving his money around and washing it so expertly—like a giant game of three-card monte— the case against him hinged entirely on the testimony of a loan shark with his own criminal past.

But Meyer was taking no chances, and Sophie took this assignment personally. She didn't want to be the don should Meyer be convicted. She liked things just the way they were.

On the morning that Fat Vinnie was scheduled to testify, Sophie snuck into the kitchen of the Delano Hotel where Teresa was being held and watched over by US Marshals. She promptly stole a uniform from the closest, one reserved for room service attendants, and waited for Fat Vinnie to call down for his breakfast—a grotesque amount of food for so early in the morning, topped off with an ice cream sundae—which she then brought up to him. While in the elevator she laced the coffee and juice with three doses of Valium, her own drug of choice and necessity. At that dosage, Fat Vinnie would take the witness stand and either pass out or come across as completely incoherent.

Sure enough, later that day, with Meyer sitting at the defendant's table and Sophie occupying the first row of the gallery—glaring at the jury, tampering by osmosis—Fat Vinnie couldn't keep a single fact straight in his head. The judge admonished the federal prosecutor for leading his witness, which couldn't be helped, since Fat Vinnie otherwise couldn't be moved. His rambling, mindless testimony made Meyer Lansky out to be a saint.

Meyer Lansky beamed victoriously on the courthouse steps while chatting with reporters. A ray of sunlight glinted off one of his gold teeth. His crew was jubilant, palling on the steps like preschoolers. Sophie remained apart, in the shade, blending in, not wishing to stand out and be readily identifiable.

And there was still that other matter. The Perpignano brothers had to be pried away from their controlling interest in the Reef Hotel. It became clear that the Reef was their beachhead for greater gangland designs in South Florida. Either they would sign over their rights, or they would be rubbed out. Fort Lauderdale was technically Meyer Lansky's territory, after all. The rules of the underworld had to be strictly enforced. Crime families hewed to the letter of their own laws. And muscle was their court of justice. But Sophie Posner had another idea, one that played to her strengths in subterfuge and ingenuity.

"I'll wear my pigeon costume," she announced, "and take back the hotel all by myself. The Perpignanos are perps, and pigeons, so I will fool them easily."

She learned that one of the Perpignanos, Vito, was a degenerate gambler who played poker, lousily, every night at the Reef. The next night Sophie Posner walked into the lobby of the Reef Hotel dressed in a straw hat, an ill-fitting dime-store dress too loathsome for Loehmann's, cheap oversized sunglasses with red frames, and on her feet, pink flip-flops. In the unlikely event her attire wouldn't be seen as loud enough, she upped the volume on her accent, substituting her strong Polish with something sassy from Long Island.

"Here I am, make way for a great and glorious lady!" she announced herself three steps into the lobby. "I hear they play cards in this hotel. I know all the games."

She made her way into the card room and spied Vito Perpignano, who was betting heavily and downing screwdrivers as if he owned a hardware store. Sitting at a table near a window that looked out onto the pool, he looked miserable. Obviously, his poker face was cast in habitual defeat. Fortunately for Sophie, on this night Vito was winning.

"May I join your game, gentlemen?" she asked. "I love cards. All games— War, Go Fish, Old Maid. You play any of these?" She flung her seashell-ornamented purse on the table, toppling chips, which clicked against each other like dueling rainsticks. She then placed stacks of crisp currency onto the table and said, "What are we playing? You look like a bunch of fellas who roll higher."

A city awash in bait and tackle shops also attracts those schooled in the art of bait and switch.

The men all glanced up at Sophie, the self-proclaimed pigeon speaking pidgin English. Their eyes then drifted downward and settled on each other in unspoken consensus. Let the pigeon play, or tell her to scram?

"Lady, you know anything about poker?" a cigar-chomping, hairless homunculus of a man asked.

"I'm a fast learner. You'll teach me while we play."

"Deal her in," the others all agreed.

A woman carrying lots of cash and who had absolutely no idea how to play poker—what could possibly go wrong? The artistry of the con—whether it is long or short—requires the fierceness of pure conviction. "I am who you think I am. Why would I be anyone else?" The Sophie Posners of the world are professional posers—by necessity, instinct, and design. The survivors were an easily adaptable breed. They had lost themselves in the camps, and these are not the kinds of steps they could—or would even want to—retrace. A sucker is born every day; a survivor is of more rarefied birth. And they were liberated with a license to take as many liberties with their lives as they wished. Like a lady of the night, Sophie could role-play with the very best. Tonight a patsy at the poker table; on any other night the savviest and most savage gladiator of all.

Several hours later there were only two players left at the table: Sophie and Vito. Even among professional hustlers, Sophie Posner had everyone at the table looking the wrong way—she was right there and yet they still didn't see her coming. After a few early folds and mishandled hands, which only lured the men to bet higher, increasing the size of the pots, the tables started to turn, or shall we say tip, in Sophie's direction. It soon became clear to the players that they were being hustled in their own house. This woman *did* know how to play. And now it was too late. The pots were all hers and, perhaps inspired by the pool that twinkled from underwater lights and a full Miami moon, she raked in her winnings with a sweeping reverse breaststroke. All the other card games had already ended for the night.

Drowsy marks shuffled through the lobby to their wide-finned Cadillacs, lumps of beached colorful whales in the parking lot. The best action was always at Vito's table, and especially tonight. And he, too, as predicted, was starting to lose. For an Italian, losing hands is secondary to the greater indignity of losing to a woman.

"So, Vito, your money seems to be running out," Sophie said.

"My credit is good here," Vito said bitterly. "I own the joint."

"So you say," Sophie said. "Well, I don't work on credit. I need to see hard assets—chips, cash, stock certificates, bearer bonds. I'll even accept that *ungepatched* gold watch you are wearing."

"We're going to keep on playing until I win all my money back," Vito growled.

"I am getting tired," Sophie said. "It's late. I think it is time for me to pack up."

"Lady, you sure you're not some kind of card cheat?" Vito asked.

"I only cheat death," she snapped. "With cards I just play."

"No one has your kind of luck, lady."

"You'd be surprised," she scoffed. "I am alive today because of luck, and now some of that luck is paying off at the poker table."

"What will it take for you to play a few more hands?" Vito asked.

"Hmm, I guess we could raise the stakes," Sophie suggested.

"Like how?"

"We'll play one more hand. I'll bet all of my winnings from tonight against your hotel. Winner take all."

It was a good thing that Vito's brother, Carmine, was nowhere in sight, because he would have shot his younger brother in the head, execution style, no mercy, no family discount. The mob had their codes and rituals. It was a messy business, to be sure, but there was honor even among thieves. Vito's honor was on the line, and his word would have to be good. Of course he had no way of knowing that he was being cleaned out by a con artist of the highest order, and that she was Meyer Lansky's consigliere.

"Fine. We have a deal," Vito said.

"And I'll deal," Sophie said contentedly.

It was at this point in the evening when Sophie decided it was time to introduce these men to her otherworldly sleights of hand in shuffling cards.

She had saved this spectacle for the right moment, like a fireworks show at the end of an outdoor concert. Such a display of flashy dealing would throw ice water on whatever hot hand Vito was hoping for.

There was no point having to check and raise because *everything*, including the table on which they were playing, was all in, and Sophie dealt herself a five-high straight flush.

"How about that, a steel wheel," she announced. "What are you holding, Perpignano?"

Vito laid down his hand: two pairs, jacks and kings.

"Thank you for such a wonderful and enterprising night, gentlemen, but I think I will check in and get a good night's rest in my lovely hotel. What are the suites like in this place?"

"Not so fast," Vito said. "You think I am going to let you walk out of here with all that money? And this hotel, lady, belongs to my brother and me."

While their Trojan Polish horse was schooling the card players at the Reef, Lansky's gang had arrived a bit earlier, armed and ready. Nobody was watching the lobby because *everyone* was in the card room. By the time Carmine showed up, Meyer began reading him the riot act about how the Reef was changing hands. Charlie Nunchucks held a gun to Carmine's head just to make sure he was paying attention.

"Game's over, Vito," Carmine conceded for his brother, knowing that no hotel was worth getting his brains blown out over. Lansky's crew was operating with renewed savvy and vigor. They just pulled off a masterful job, one that deserved wall space in the annals of organized crime. The crew that had gone stale was now reborn. With Lansky in Israel they had been rudderless and inept, a bunch of patsies, their mob ties choking in Windsor knots. Lansky returned and installed a ringer for a consigliere, a tough broad not quite right in the head but inventive enough to reconfigure his entire operation. Lansky now had more muscle, and he meant business. "The lady won the hotel fair and square," Carmine said, sweat beading on his forehead, his fine Italian suit now the sum of his net worth. We're done here in Fort Lauderdale. See you in Atlantic City, Lansky. And do me a favor: leave the lady in Miami Beach. I don't want to ever see her kike face again."

Charlie rapped Carmine over the head with his Walther PPK while Sophie kicked him in the balls just to make sure he never forgot her kike face.

The night, improbably, was still not over. There was so much to celebrate—an acquittal in federal court and a jackpot in Fort Lauderdale. Lansky and his henchmen returned to the Carib Hotel on Miami Beach, the place where their fortunes had all changed all on account of a street hustler of a Holocaust survivor. The Carib, with all its shameless lack of amenities, was now rich in history, like Schwab's drug store in Hollywood: it was the setting where Sophie Posner received her screen test for the mob.

The Carib never looked so festive. There was drinking and joyous dancing in the lobby. And then, spontaneously, as if this large minyan of Jewish gangsters was celebrating in a manner more befitting of a Jewish wedding, they placed Meyer and Sophie in separate cushioned chairs, hoisted them up where they were repeatedly bounced into the air as the men danced in a circle around them, arms linked, shoulders pressed forward, legs all tangled up in a grapevine. This congregation of former yeshiva boys gone bad was anathema to Judaism, repellent to anyone who believed that Moses the lawgiver was the archetypal standard by which all future Jews would be judged. Lansky the lawbreaker was not only deviant, he was the aberration, the outlier and cautionary tale, the standard deviation that if God actually existed would never gravitate toward the mean.

Everything about this wayward tribe made a mockery of their biblical forebears. Yet, at a tender moment of bliss, they reflexively fell back into dancing the hora. Not one of them had been to a cheder in over fifty years, and very few attended any of the local synagogues, but they managed to twist their hips and drape their shoulders like seasoned Hasidim, all the while humming repressed melodies from their days on the Lower East Side. They hummed with the rumble of an elevated train, the kind that used to clank and cough while pulling away from Delancey Street. Bobbing up and down Meyer and Sophie went, grabbing each other's hand when they could, smiling and laughing with all the anticipation of a bride and groom on their wedding night.

Of course, these flea-bitten lobby sofas didn't quite have the upholstery to withstand this abuse. The fabric was frayed and all this dancing was turning into a striptease. With nothing holding them together, the cushions burst like an unraveling pillow fight, launching a ticker tape parade of white cotton candy throughout the lobby.

All those who happened to be in the lobby joined in this frolic—attendants at the front desk, doormen, bellhops, and the kitchen crew, not to mention the sleepy guests who awoke to see what all the commotion was about. The concierge was especially enthralled by the consigliere.

The only one merely watching off at a distance was a young boy, no older than twelve, who came to reclaim his mother and realized, yet again, that she wished to be nowhere else but here. At one point, in a grimace that no one except her son noticed, Sophie touched her stomach from a pain she had never felt before.

Adam Posner, fleet of foot, had run the entire two miles from the apartment building where he and his father lived to the Carib, the home where, apparently, his mother lived. Jacob Posner, with three heart attacks stacked against him as formidable as his wife's earlier winnings, simply didn't have the heart to make the trip himself.

Sophie did not see her son standing there, the only one not celebrating at the Carib that night. Going unnoticed was, in fact, a familiar experience for the boy. So without even waving hello or good-bye, he turned, twirled himself through the revolving door, and started running all over again—in a full-out sprint. He ran away from the Carib swiftly, yet he wasn't so sure where he was headed, and when all this running was supposed to end. He even forgot to catch his breath. He was sprinting home, wherever that happened to be. And when he finally reached it, he kept running, wondering how far away he could get, how free of all this he would become, and whether anyone would notice that he was gone.

Two

Flower Power in Flamingo Park

onspiracies are sometimes hatched from the simplest of minds, and the least likely of places. Few involve high drama or world changing significance. Rarely is the stage set for a palace coup. Most are simply small conspiracies undertaken by small men. Some even spring from the minds of boys, the endgame based solely on ending a game, or preventing one from even getting started.

"I so don't want to play tomorrow," Adam Posner moaned his familiar game-day lament in an Irving Berlin, bugle boy singsong. He batted the alarm clock and whiffed, striking the night lamp instead. Not a good omen. Without that clock he would never awaken. He didn't have the kind of parents who would get him ready for school. The lessons they thought to be essential were not taught at school. Well, at least none of the schools on Miami Beach. There were such places, survivalist in nature, preparatory, but not for college. One was a variation of living out in the wild, in the most civilized nation of all: prewar Germany. That's where the Posners were at their most resourceful.

But in Miami Beach in 1972, they felt the best way to impart those lessons was to say nothing at all.

"Who taught us?" his mother said. "And we survived."

Her husband knew better, and wanted better for his son. But in the meantime, that alarm clock, and an Eggo waffle, was the boy's best friend.

Adam Posner detested getting up early during the school year. What he hadn't realized yet was that school busing was set to arrive in Miami Beach in the fall. The county's public schools would become integrated, and Adam would have to awaken even earlier to catch the school bus. Mornings would commence at an ungodly hour, earlier even than these dreaded summer baseball games. Even before Miami's segregated past caught up to the civil rights era, there were other, less socially redeeming occasions for the sounding of an alarm clock—such as Little League baseball games. Adam was no less enamored of that reason, either.

Yet it was still summer, and he had already reconciled himself to the rotten fact that Little League baseball in Miami Beach required sleepless children to throw strikes and swing bats like zombies at dawn.

Adam had always believed that summers should be set aside for sleep—especially in the tropics where scalding temperatures produced emergency conditions that drove people indoors, like an air raid for incoming humidity. Air conditioning was to Miami what fallout shelters were to the huddled, bombarded masses of London during World War II.

Apparently, however, as Adam came to learn, there was no rest for the weary Little Leaguer on Miami Beach. Little League in South Florida very much depended on alarm clocks, ironically for a sport played without regard to time. To prevent twelve-year-olds from getting sunstroke, the Parks Department required that the first pitch be tossed by 7 a.m., which allowed for double headers of six-inning games to be finished long before noon.

Adam Posner's first summer in Miami Beach would have him taking the infield just as the sun rose from beneath the blue Atlantic. Palm trees stood bowlegged and defiant in the morning light, surrounding the outfield, bleachers, and dugouts like Major League scouts. Adam began to feel as if the Dade County School Board and the high priests of Little League baseball were in cahoots in forcing him to become a perpetual, seasonal early riser.

"It's almost the playoffs," Brad, his wiry and bronzed friend reminded him. "Just two more games and then the city championship against the winning team from North Shore Park. You can hold out a little longer. You can sleep *after* we win the World Series."

"World Series" in Miami Beach? How grandiose, like a city suffering from a midlife crisis, pathetically showcasing a trophy wife sitting in a Ferrari Berlinetta Boxer.

It was a typically scorching summer in Miami Beach that year in 1972. The city's Little League program was in full swing—at the bat, and in its local parks. There were games played in the north end of Miami Beach, in both North Shore and Normandy Parks, by what was widely believed to be the better league, with the best players, which mostly included newly arrived Cubans who played baseball like men and should have dominated the city's Little League World Series, but they had inexplicably lost for the past several years.

The other league was on South Beach, at Flamingo Park—the largest public park in the city, which included Memorial Field, where the high school's football team played its games. There was also the Tennis Center, with its massive rollout of clay courts, parched and caked throughout the day like suburban tract housing on the moon, and the multitude of courts dedicated to shuffle board, handball, racquetball, and basketball, and the vast open areas that comprised the football and soccer practice fields, along with several baseball and softball diamonds, and the baseball stadium. A vastly nicer complex with weaker players. Comprising foursquare blocks between Lenox Avenue and Alton Road, Flamingo Park was large enough to host Woodstock, and it got very close to doing just that.

Adam and Brad played on the Butterflake Bakery Little League team, sponsored by one of the local South Beach businesses, a bakery that prided itself on its onion rolls and rye bread, strawberry shortcake, and wide selection of cookies. Inside the store little children left their fingerprints on windowed display cases, evidence of sweet teeth pining away for cupcakes of any kind. The blasting air conditioning preserved both the ladyfinger cookies and all those kids' fingerprints.

In addition to its business with baked goods, Butterflake also had the good fortune to field a winning Little League team. Three days each week during the summer, nine scrappy Miami Beach boys trotted out onto the diamond of Flamingo Park in their yellow uniforms and caps, a getup that made them resemble bobbing citrus fruit, a Miami Beach mirage visible from the bleachers and alongside the perimeter fences. The owners of Butterflake Bakery believed in civic engagement that involved America's pastime. Sponsoring a Little League team was also a strategically low-cost marketing strategy where local kids walked around wearing the merchant's signage like mobile billboards. The uniforms in those days were made of densely woven shirts and thick burlap pants designed to prevent strawberries—not the kind that Butterflake placed atop its cakes, but the ones caused by aggressive sliding into second base and home plate.

The team was firmly in first place in the Flamingo Park Little League, and much of the credit for its lofty perch in the standings belonged to Adam and Brad. Adam pitched and crouched behind the plate on days when he was off the mound; Brad played a nifty shortstop—and both were hitting near .400 for the season. The *Miami Beach Sun Reporter* printed the results of all the Little League games in the city, and the only two kids who didn't care about seeing their names in the paper were the very ones tearing up the league.

They were too busy plotting ways to avoid the morning games and sleeping in instead of sweating in the sun. They were fare more interested in reading the daily weather reports than the box scores. So grave was their sleep deprivation that it was not beyond them to pray for slow moving hurricanes in the Caribbean to pick up speed and hit Miami. Any extreme measure was something to consider if it meant the game would be called.

"I have this great idea," Adam said. His thick dirty-blond hair was worn long like an aspiring surfer or an accomplished stoner. The times were very obliging of such sloppy getups and appearances.

"We can't pretend we're sick," Brad said, anticipating the recycling of an excuse that didn't work the first time they'd tried it on opening day.

"A rainout."

"Is it supposed to rain tomorrow morning or even tonight?" Brad wondered, his freckled face always red in the beaming sun, casting him in an angry light even though his disposition was gentle and, like his skin, fair.

"No, they are not predicting any rain," Adam replied.

"So what gives?"

During the summer months rain was always in the forecast for South Florida. The low-pressure tropical air and all those low-hanging purple clouds—the breasts of a nursing sky—unloaded sheaths of rain in the shape of waterfalls. It was torrential, but also temporary. Within minutes it would be over, leaving behind flooded grass, newly sunny skies, and rainbows the color of summer popsicles. Rainouts are common in baseball, especially in the tropics where dark clouds appear out of nowhere and empty themselves like bursting water balloons. Baseball was one game especially ill suited to water.

"We can't play if the infield is flooded," Adam said with a sinister smile, knowing that water—regardless of how it gets poured—was the key to this conspiracy.

"But how can it be flooded if it isn't going to rain?"

"We don't need rain from the sky," Adam said, speaking like a medicine man who knew how to make rain. "All we need is water."

"Huh? I don't get it."

Adam Posner and Brad Isaacson were certainly not long shots to become best friends. The Posner and Isaacson families had each only recently moved to Miami Beach; the Posners from Manhattan and the Isaacsons from Long Island. Their relocation was more like a hasty exit or a midnight run than a planned departure. White flight from New York was common in those days, with rising crime, failing schools, and urban squalor. Miami Beach seemed pristine and naively innocent of all the upheavals taking place elsewhere. It was a safe remove from the blackouts, inner-city riots, racial tensions, and all that was infecting the newly radicalized youth with their garish outfits, promiscuous sex, hippie politics, and contempt for rules and the people who enforce them. Yes, Miami Beach was a bit boring, but thankfully all that distance from the Mason-Dixon Line left it cut off from what imperiled the rest of America. The New World had become the land of the lost, but Miami was in an even worse position. It had been left behind, all communication closed as if it had been denied admission on the grid. But it was only temporarily spared from all this unkempt contempt for the uniform middlebrow. Soon enough the Fountain of Youth would flood the city like a freakish high tide, and conformity would get washed away like a pair of sensible shoes.

The dramatic change of address for families like the Posners and Isaacsons symbolized more than mere movements along a map. This exodus to the Sunshine State was a form of self-exile. There was no return ticket; it would become a final destination, as if all the bridges had been burned and the boats capsized. The Posners, the Isaacsons, and all the other Jewish families were now grounded snowbirds, wings clipped and migration patterns forgotten. The lazy pulse of Miami's tropical locale suited their passive rhythms quite well. What had once made them anomalous New Yorkers now endeared them to a less ambitious corner of the Jewish universe. Yet, there was also a curious destiny in these beached landings. All those family trees were now solidly dug deep into the sand, like the ancient caravans of their tribal pasts.

Nearly everyone on Miami Beach in those days had to acclimate to a new environment. The temperature rose, the general IQ fell, and sunglasses, floppy tennis hats, and zinc oxide were suddenly the most indispensable items in summer survival kits. There was even another mother tongue, courtesy of newfound neighbors. Hot-blooded people who spoke with the syncopated patter of high-octane Spanish were lumped together with northern Jews who had worked assiduously to rid themselves of their native Yiddish. And they were joined by Haitians who held onto their Creole as bargaining chips, sensing that they might find themselves on the bottom rung of Florida's immigration ladder.

Adam and Brad bonded quickly as undersized Jewish boys with a shared love for the New York Mets, the team they had only recently abandoned for a city that was without its own team. After many years of futility, the Mets had won the World Series, which overnight made kings of the people from Queens. Another World Series appearance still awaited them, but Miami was many years away from the time when a marlin would become a mascot for America's pastime. The Orioles had a local single A affiliate in Miami, a team that played in an old stadium that clanked, steamed, and whistled throughout the summer months like a cast-iron kettle. Baseball has a way of capitalizing on local allegiances, and for two small New York boys suddenly finding themselves living in the sunny south, a winning baseball team was a great unifier.

Baseball also exudes a pastoral connection to the heartland, all those fields of dreams imbued with the values and traditions, innocence and essence of Americana. No sport is as patriotic. Unlike football or soccer, baseball rarely becomes riotous. It is a summer game that attracts cooler heads. A revolution is not likely to emanate from a baseball game.

Adam and Brad appreciated none of these nuances. They had the good fortune to play for a winning team. During the summer of 1972, the hottest team played in Flamingo Park, where hazy heat rose from the infield to such a degree that the bases resembled rising loaves of Butterflake's breads. The team, led by its pitcher and shortstop, was undefeated through nearly two months of play, and sat atop the standings in the Flamingo Park league, just waiting to face North Shore Park at the end of the summer. Too bad the team's ace pitcher was far more focused on sleeping in rather than racking up wins.

"So what's your great idea?" Brad insisted. "You can't have a rainout without rain. Where's the water going to come from if there aren't any dark clouds?"

"We don't need clouds," Adam said defiantly. "All we need is a few hoses."

The plan, as Adam explained it, would involve a bit of sandlot espionage and covert tradecraft. Mother Nature wasn't going to postpone the game, but good old-fashioned sabotage would. The boys planned a trip to Flamingo Park later that night, long after the park had closed. Fumbling in the dark they would roll out the hoses that are used to water the grass during those rare times when Florida's tropical weather goes dry, and by releasing the spigots, turn the infield into the Everglades.

"We'll leave the hoses on all night," Adam said. "By morning I'll need a canoe to get to the pitcher's mound."

"It's perfect," Brad said giddily. He was less loathe to get up in the morning than Adam, but no less pleased to participate in this delinquent summery behavior. "There's only one problem," he said resignedly. "We'll still have to get up early. I mean, like the rest of the team, we're not supposed to know that the field is flooded."

"I thought of that," Adam agreed. "But Coach Bertman always gets to the park an hour early to sprinkle the infield with water and then drag it until it's smooth. He'll see the field and call us all up to say the game is unplayable because someone flooded Flamingo. He's done that before when it has rained overnight."

"He better, otherwise we're dead because we'll be the only ones who don't show up in the morning," Brad said. "We'll be asleep and he'll know it was us."

"He'll call up the entire team and he won't think it was us," Adam reassured his friend. "We're his best two players. Why wouldn't we want to play? If anything, he'll think it was some of the guys on the bench."

The boys snuck out of their houses at 11 p.m. for their rendezvous on Lincoln Road, which was only a few blocks uptown from Flamingo Park. Adam's father, Jacob, was reading in the living room and didn't notice his son leave. Adam never feared anyone noticing him gone. He could have paraded out as a member of a marching band and his father would not have perceived the house as any less quiet. Adam's mother was nowhere to be found, certainly not that early in the evening. The Posners paid no attention to curfews. Contempt for authority was their family creed. They were lawless—no rules of the house, and few rules outside of the house that had to be adhered to either. Roll calls and bed checks didn't seem to them as the essentials of parenting. There were far better lessons, but they weren't teaching any of those either.

"What's the worst thing he could do out there in the world?" his mother once remarked as a way of justifying her neglect. "Better he should find his own way."

"What can we teach him?" his fathered conceded impotently. "Our knowledge is limited to pure evil. What do we know of this new world?"

The people who had survived a fire would surely have seen nothing wrong in their son playing with water. As a family they were a mordant jazz ensemble, sheet music be damned, play as you go, solo when the impulse strikes, riff away at will.

Adam and Brad pedaled down Lenox Avenue on their three-speed Raleigh Choppers—Adam's was yellow with a black banana seat; Brad's was an emerald green with white trim. Overhanging tropical trees formed a canopy above, which blocked the moonlight and provided safe passage on this most adventurous night.

The boys coasted into the park, and the clicking sounds of their coasting bicycles harmonized with nighttime crickets. Weaving around the bleachers and the backstop, they tossed their bikes into the dugout. The Miami Beach air that July, in particular, lacked any relationship to oxygen. Even the act of breathing caused the sweat glands to excrete as if working a double shift.

This summer night was especially harsh. While no hint of rain was present, the stranglehold of heat would have to let up somehow.

The night was begging for a cooling off period. Instead what it got was more heat—sweat upon sweat, skin sliding up against skin, a bacchanal of carnal pleasure, an orgy of sexual immodesty. The gyrating thrusts of the counterculture were very much in need of hydration. Flamingo Park was an open air hothouse catering to the most debauched desires of the counterculture.

Adam and Brad moved quickly, dragging the hoses out onto the infield as if uncoiling snakes. Next they turned on the spigots. The hoses expanded and straightened into stiff rods as a steady surge of water drenched the field. As the boys triumphantly danced on home plate and the pitcher's mound, they heard noises coming from the outfield. In spite of the dark, they saw flickering light and the shadowy outlines of bodies lying on the grass, silhouettes thrusting and grinding like spirits rising from the earth.

"What's that?" Brad wondered. "No one's allowed in the park at night. It should be deserted." Reacting to a sound, Brad asked, "Did you just hear that? It's kind of spooky."

Adam stared into centerfield like a pitcher trying to follow a fly ball.

The outfield was surrounded by towering nightlights that made it possible for the American Legion League to play their games at night; but now they were nothing but darkened sentries. No game had been scheduled for that night. Even if it had, it would have been long over by now, the cars departed, the fans gone off for ice cream.

"Let's go over and see what's going on out there," Adam said.

"I don't think it's a good idea," Brad cautioned. "It's dark and creepy. And I've never heard noises like that before. I just heard a girl scream, 'Yes!' Who knows what that means." His voice grew more fretful. "If something bad happens, my parents will kill me. I'll be grounded until next summer. First, we flooded the infield. Then I got kidnapped in the outfield."

No such worry entered Adam's mind. His parents would have expected him to march headlong into his fears.

"I'm scared," he once announced when, as a five-year-old, he awakened from a bad dream. The family lived in New York City back then. Washington Heights was noisy at night. It might have been a roving band of teenage thugs heading downtown to Hell's Kitchen to take on the Jets or the Sharks.

Perhaps it was the sound of a backfiring car. Adam approached his parents' bed looking for comfort, or, failing that, at least to crawl under their comforter.

"Go back to your room, you pussy!" his mother bellowed.

"Adam," his father said, offering the only sort of soothing accepted in the Posner household, logic delivered as love, "you had a dream. It's not real. When the truly bad men come, you will know."

Adam never got used to the shadows of the night. Even in Miami Beach, where the moon lit up the tropical sky with chalky streaks of iridescence, the night gave Adam the fear that something was always looming in the darkness. Yet what second-rate terror could possibly have awaited him in the blackness of the outfield of Flamingo Park at midnight? It sounded like some kind of rally, but surely not a Nazi rally. Such rarefied menace arises only once a millennium. Adam was merely the next generation; his tormentors, if they existed at all, would be of the ordinary kind.

"I don't want to go to school today," he had said that spring in anticipation of a social studies project he was supposed to deliver in class. All the kids were required to make a campaign poster in support of their candidate for president, and then to deliver a speech accepting his party's nomination. Biscayne Junior High School had gotten itself into the campaign spirit early; election fever had come to the American tropics. Adam was shilling for George McGovern, but he didn't have the courage to get up and do so in front of the entire class. "I'm sure I'll throw up if I have to speak at the assembly."

"That's only natural," said Jacob, shielding his son. "But Adam, this is not something that people like us take very seriously. The Nazis didn't give us stage fright. I wish that was all they had in mind."

"What's wrong with you?" Sophie, his mother, entered the fray gently. "Nobody dies from stage fright. You are embarrassing me, embarrassing us! You have no idea what you should be afraid of. I got news for you: *this* isn't it!" she shouted, holding up the white cardboard campaign poster like a pane of glass she was about to slice through her son.

The poster read: "If you can't end a war in four years, then you're not entitled to four more."

Adam was no longer sure what war he was referring to, because the one raging inside his house had been going on a lot longer than four years.

"You have to go," Jacob said. "Besides, McGovern needs your help. Remember, Nixon has a house in Key Biscayne. He's a local. McGovern is from South Dakota. I don't even know where that is."

"Stop talking," Sophie shot back at her husband. Turning to her quaking son, she said, "Now take your poster and your speech and get out of this house, and don't come back until you convince those kids to get their parents to vote for McGovern. And if I find out that you threw up, I'll drop you off at Nixon's house with a suitcase and he can raise you. Our house is one where people know what's what."

The boy's stomach, unsurprisingly, was perpetually nervous; his overall nerves, a wreck. Adam traipsed out onto the outfield like a bather wading, as though waiting to step into an undertow. The madness of the war that had hobbled his parents' peace of mind—and kept his mother perilously close to true madness—was not being replayed in those sounds coming from the outfield. But he would have to see it for himself to find out.

Those strange noises of the night, apparently, also had little to do with baseball. No thumps and claps of balls smacking inside smooth leather could be heard. Instead came the sounds of bodies pounding against and riding on top of one another. Soft moans escaped from the mouths of bodies in recline. As the boys inched closer, almost holding hands, they saw other hands being held on the grass, fingers intertwined, in some cases clenched tightly. While barely visible, these players were without uniforms—without clothes *at all*, nothing but bare skin. The entire outfield was littered with condoms and covered in coitus. Adam and Brad's fears waned as their tiny dicks stiffened.

"There's fucking in Flamingo Park?" Brad wondered aloud in a whisper, not wishing to disturb the party. Nothing to fear; all this balling in the outfield of Flamingo Park was going into extra innings. A hailstorm of snowballs couldn't cool this place down.

"I can't believe it," Adam said. "Is it like this every night? Why didn't I think of this before?"

"Yeah, we're in the big leagues now," Brad noted correctly. This was very much an adult game, and true Little Leaguers were in the best position to know.

Bodies were everywhere—taking up every inch of grass, on top of sleeping bags and picnic blankets. The boys were still a year away from studying geometry, and this was a master class, with legs and arms locked in right angles, diameters measured by lining up diaphragms. Silhouettes were lit softly under the moon like candles melting into one another. The sexual revolution had come to Miami Beach in the guise of soft porn, and it appeared to be making its debut in Flamingo Park, which could now add yet another physical activity to its inventory of sports offerings.

"Stop drooling," Adam said and then swatted Brad in the face with his baseball cap.

"Hey, I don't see you looking the other way," Brad sulked. "Besides, no one seems to mind that we're here."

Adam observed the same thing. "I think they like it," he said.

"Thank God. I can't wait to tell the rest of the team."

An earthy flower child with long strawberry blonde hair that blanketed her small breasts, and legs that shimmied in the grass smiled at the boys and motioned for them to walk over. Brad suddenly felt the need to pee, while Adam took two steps backward and tripped over a fornicating couple who weren't even there a moment ago.

"Sorry," he said. "Excuse me. Keep doing what you're doing. Don't let me stop you."

"Love means never having to say you're sorry," giggled the girl, who was sitting on top of her partner's penis. Adam cocked his head counterclockwise as if to reorient the bodies to their proper positions. Such a strange intersection, he thought, where a man and woman were arranged like a centaur.

All this heat, but this time it had little to do with the mercury reading.

"I don't get it," Brad said as his eyes found a threesome, and suddenly he could no longer count. Blinking, he nearly passed out, as if he had just overdosed on the wettest of all dreams. Neither he nor Adam had received much in the way of sex education at school. Now it appeared that they had skipped a few grades. Sex was never mentioned at home, nor, he doubted, was it ever performed there. Even rudimentary biology would have leap-frogged over material better suited to *Hustler* than a page from the birds and bees playbook. "There's got to be a sign somewhere saying that fucking in the park is not allowed," Brad said, not that he was looking for one.

Yet no such sign existed. It wouldn't have made much of a difference even if it had. In that muggy and moonlit July night, nothing could have dampened these acts of openly free and promiscuous love. This was the Age of Aquarius, where no one seemed to age. Modesty was so middle class. Constraints on personal freedom, measured by hair length and hemlines, were to be ignored. The body could be painted or remain unclothed. All invitations for sexual pleasure were welcome and expected. Erections were like greeting cards. Wet loins made pickup lines obsolete. Miami Beach had become one big brothel. Flamingo Park was now a nude beach—at night!

"What's going on here?" Adam repeated. "Is this a secret?"

"Maybe Disney World has come to Miami Beach," Brad wondered, which was not so farfetched. The Magic Kingdom was still new to Florida, less than a year in existence. At the time very few on Miami Beach knew precisely where Orlando even was.

"This isn't Disney World," Adam surmised. "They don't have these kinds of rides. I think it has something to do with the conventions this summer. Everybody's talking about the election."

"Yeah, but they should be talking about all these erections."

Adam was right. Miami Beach had been a convention hotspot for many years now. Unions, teachers, the AMA, the ABA, the dentists, the Shriners—all made Miami Beach a winter destination for their annual meetings. Aside from the sun and surf, Miami Beach had posh hotels with nightly entertainment and swinging singles wanting a fling with married doctors, lawyers, or Teamsters, for that matter. The humid air was pregnant with hedonism. The city had every vice in a vise grip. The Jewish Mafia ran the action and gave the city its racy, risqué allure. Wife swapping and key parties took place around casual drug use. Most of its residents didn't pay much attention or partake in the fun, but tourists knew how attending a convention down in Miami Beach was a terrific way to break with convention.

Both the Democratic and Republican parties were holding their presidential nominating conventions on Miami Beach that summer. With Nixon ramping up America's involvement in Vietnam, swarms of antiwar protestors descended on their quiet city—the Yippies and the hippies; the flower children with their tie-dye shirts, body paint, LSD, and drugs that can't be bought over the counter but do take you to a place out of your head. The booze that Jackie Gleason swilled all over the city was suddenly, in this climate of tuned-out, plastered unconsciousness, nothing but a soft drink.

War protestors were the new greasers, without the white T-shirts and hair gel. Hair—long, knotted, braided and unwashed—was but one of their calling cards. They favored Camus over Kerouac. Politics was their theater, and the sixties their stage. Impassioned beliefs were delivered like tantrums.

This is what the Great One had to say about the rock music of those times: "That music! Don't get me started, but let's not confuse loud with tuneful. Music to your ears isn't supposed to break them and make you go deaf. I don't care what anyone says, you can't dance to noise. And everyone knows that I'm a great dancer. People are always surprised when a fat guy is light on his feet. It produces the same kind of disbelief and delight as a bear riding a unicycle. But what these kids do, spinning around in a circle, flapping their arms, and looking up at the sky and as high as a kite, that's not dancing; it's a séance that's gotten way out of control. And I have nothing against loud clothing either. Look over there, my orchestra leader, Sammy Spear. He wears brightly colorful suits that look like a Peter Max painting—but at least he's wearing a suit and tie, and my orchestra is playing real music!"

Gleason was among those on Miami Beach who could do without the flower children with their public nudity, pubic hair, pot brownies, contempt for authority, and pungent bodily odors. The Great One was of a different era, one of stiff drinks and even stiffer tuxedos. He liked Miami Beach the way it was: quiet and mindless during the day, louche and sordid after dark. The excitement of social upheavals and revolutionary change meant nothing to him. This was due to a healthy skepticism of the political process. Such are the prerogatives of kings.

"You want to know what I think about the conventions?" he joked with fingers curled into his best uppercut pose. "You really want to know what I think about the conventions?" he threatened mockingly. "I'll tell you what I think about the conventions—*pow zoom*, right in the kisser, to both the Democrats *and* Republicans!"

Despite these scattered reservations, these presidential conventions were going to be a big deal for Miami Beach. Jimmy Stewart, Sammy Davis Jr., and even Frank Sinatra were expected at the Republican Convention to support their man, Richard Nixon. Whenever Sammy Davis Jr. came to town, Jackie Gleason let loose on "that little black Jew who loves Miami Beach because it's like a homecoming for him, surrounded by all these short

Hebrews. Let me just say this: the Candy Man likes black-eyed peas in his *cholent*, if you know what I mean. He's playing on both teams, and he's married to a white woman."

America wasn't ready for that, especially in the South.

The eyes of the world were about to settle on this otherwise forgettable peninsula in the sun. The whole world was about to "come on down" to Miami Beach. It might have been too much pressure for such a pipsqueak city. The summer of 1972 was going to be a scorcher—for many different reasons. The world had many questions. Were people supposed to "turn on," "tune in," or "drop out"? Was America going to stay in Vietnam or get out? Will race relations improve or get worse? Will a country founded on the ideals of family, honor, and virtue be remembered only for pot smoking, bra burning, and wife swapping? Everyone around the world knew that, despite all the superpower bluster, America was in the toilet, and Florida was the very last sewer system before it all washed out into the ocean. After all, the entire state was shaped like something that only a plumber would carry around.

The convention would be watched on televisions around the world. The hotels along Collins Avenue were going to be jam-packed with suit-wearing delegates from the left and right, the donkeys and elephants, Dixiecrats and Libertarians—all learning to observe Miami's summer heat advisories, which for natives is as simple as staying indoors surrounded by the arctic blast of central air conditioning. Sultry may be Miami Beach's sweet spot, but it's also their very own tenth circle of hell, where Satan is sitting atop a palm tree handing out bottles of Coppertone. The delegates were destined to return to their states feeling burned by their experience on Miami Beach.

For the Democrats, the convention was set to take place in late July; the Republicans were going to kick off theirs on August 21st. President Nixon was running for re-election, bombs were exploding in Cambodia, there were antiwar protests at colleges across the country, bras and draft cards were being burned in public, psychedelic drugs were producing a generation of psychotics, and the musical *Hair* had just closed after a four-year Broadway run.

This feverish radicalizing of America was just getting started on Miami Beach, however. Men were showing more hair and the women were exposing more cleavage. Polyester patterns merged into one another like Japanese kites on Collins Avenue. Peace medallions swung from sunburned necks, replacing Stars of David. American culture was being countered at every turn. As if to pause from all the mayhem, both political parties decided to travel down to Miami Beach to nominate their party's candidate for President of the United States. But all the cynicism and degeneracy would follow them down to this beachside enclave.

The Summer of Love a few years earlier had missed Miami Beach, but now it was making up for lost time. The city was about to experience a summer of radical politics and reckless free love. Its Little League baseball games were now only the sideshow. The main act was an invading army of hippies camped out in Flamingo Park, an ominous Greek chorus in the political theater of American pomp.

The city that had embraced snowbirds, retirees, Holocaust survivors, and Cuban refugees was about to take on a new foreign presence. Delegates from voting districts across the country descended on Miami Beach like electoral locusts. The secret to Miami's magic was out; the insularity of this tropical hideaway was being overtaken by party delegates and members of the student body. These two groups had little in common other than a shared summer in Miami Beach. The delegates dreamed of the electoral college; the students were largely college radicals and dropouts. Both groups had their junkies, although they got high on different things.

Amid all the caucuses and backroom deals there was also carnality. In addition to the trysts and tryouts taking place after hours at the hotels along Collins Avenue, Flamingo Park became Miami Beach's answer to *Peyton Place*—with a whiff of Plato's Retreat.

That's where the antiestablishment protestors made their beds, right there on the grass, breathing in the humid air and kissed goodnight by the moon hanging over Miami.

Surrounded by groping hands, writhing bodies, and the multiple orgasms of college coeds who were less than a decade older than they were, Adam and Brad contemplated their good fortune. And just think: had Adam not minded getting up early to pitch in this very park, they would have missed everything.

"Will this be going on all summer?" Brad said with bedazzled, bloodshot eyes.

The field manual being used on this field could have been written by Linda Lovelace. *Deep Throat* had only just premiered in New York a month before the Democratic Convention, and so much of the film's central plot was being rehearsed, repeatedly, in the outfield of Flamingo Park.

"These are just protestors against the Democratic Convention," Adam said, wide-eyed and knowing.

"Will the Republican protestors be fucking outside like this next month?" Brad asked anxiously. "I sure hope so."

"I bet there's gonna be even more fucking in August for the Republicans," Adam predicted. "They all hate President Nixon, and they think he's fucking up the country."

"Thank God for Republicans," Brad said. "Orgies for Everyone! That's my platform. I wish I was old enough to vote."

A couple that had just finished copulating noticed, shamelessly, that they had been observed by two young boys. The male had a gruff beard, a helmet of curled hair, and the stick frame of a graduate student who lived off granola. His female partner had long and straight blonde hair, a stocky build, and sizable breasts. Her ankles and wrists were ringed with bangles the color of coral.

"You here to watch us having sex or to protest at the convention?" the young activist asked Adam and Brad.

The boys were silent, then stared at one another, as if this was a trick question.

"You both deaf?" he waited for his answer. "By the look of you two, I guess civil disobedience is getting younger and younger nowadays."

"Don't be ridiculous," the girl answered for the boys. "They're here just to watch us screw. They're not political. Just look at them! The only hard positions they are taking involve whacking off—if they are even old enough to do that."

Adam and Brad felt uneasy, not sure whether they had just been insulted. A ray of light from a kerosene lamp in the background illuminated the girl's face, which was sunburned from the limelight of her daily demonstrations.

"Actually," Adam began hesitatingly and truthfully, "we came here to flood the baseball field back there," he pointed behind him without removing his eyes from the still naked girl.

"You're here because of baseball?" the girl laughed. She had obviously forgotten that she and her lover had rounded the bases repeatedly that night.

"Our Little League team is supposed to play here tomorrow morning," Adam continued, "and we wanted to make the field unplayable so we could sleep late."

"You buying any of this?" the young man asked.

"If it's true then it's really cute," she replied. "Otherwise they're just a couple of perverted peeping Toms."

"Or budding radicals," her lover refused to give up, the ferment of protest always top of mind. "Giving the finger to their baseball coach, refusing to play by the system's rules, coming here at night like the Weather Underground. Rock on!"

The young activist was having another orgasm—this time without the assistance of his companion.

"Oh, please, Sheldon," the girl interrupted. "Leave them alone. Hey, I have an idea: come skinny-dipping with us."

"These kids are way underage, April."

"What, you're afraid of getting arrested?" the girl said defiantly. "We *came* here to get arrested."

"Yeah, but not for this."

From a different direction someone shouted, "Hey, kids, you wanna smoke a joint?" A stoner wearing a distressed army jacket and sporting a Fu Manchu mustache laughed himself silly.

"Flamingo Park is now occupied by the power of the flower child," April exulted. "All the old rules don't apply here. This is our place, our park. And we have nude swimming every midnight at the Flamingo Park pool."

The soul of the new left was sustained by aimless love and midnight swims. Radical politics required such erotic respites in those days.

"Okay, you two, off with the pants and let's see your peckers," the young man said. "We're going skinny-dipping."

Adam and Brad looked at one another, took another glance at the girl, lifted their shoulders, and dropped their gym shorts and underwear down to their Converse sneakers.

Having the flower children of the 1960s sexual revolution pollinating in Flamingo Park was not the idea of either political party. Even the old left would not have approved. Truth be told, the idea was merely to use Fla-

mingo Park as a safe harbor in which to congregate the convention protestors. The goal was always crime control, not baby making. In the end,
however, many babies were either created or aborted during those summer
weeks in which Flamingo Park hosted one of the largest open orgies ever
assembled.

When the Democratic Party held its last convention in Chicago in 1968,
youth activists and antiwar protestors descended on Lincoln Park, ostensibly
to listen to music and raise political consciousness. What happened was a
week's worth of skirmishes with the police and the National Guard, culmi-
nating in hundreds of arrests and well over one thousand injuries from beat-
ings and mace. The police wore riot helmets, chest-high plastic shields, and
masks for tear gas; and they were swinging three-foot-long billy clubs. TV
news cameras filmed Chicago's finest, dragging college kids by their long
hair while bashing in their heads at the same time.

Mayor Daley preserved law and order, but at great cost to his city. Mon-
sters of the Midway began to take on new meaning. Connecticut Senator
Abe Ribicoff, a Jew, referred to the Gestapo tactics of the Chicago Police
Department from the podium of the convention. It all played well on TV.

This is precisely what Miami Beach sought to avoid—a repeat performance of the riots that happened in Chicago—in hosting both conventions
in that summer of 1972. For most Americans Miami Beach was Gleason's
"sun and fun capital of the world." It was not cops dressed in riot gear
swinging nightsticks and making mass arrests of student protestors.

"I'm not going let that happen in my city: all that street violence for the
rest of the country to watch on TV during the evening news," said Miami
Beach's unflappable police chief, Rocky Pomerance, a bearish Jew with a
boxer's nose and a penchant for reciting Cicero and Shakespeare alongside
crime statistics. That nose was beyond the help of a cosmetic surgeon's tool
kit—and not because it started out as a Jewish nose. Long before he became
Miami Beach's top cop, he had, in fact, been a boxer when he was a merchant marine. By the time he became chief lawman in Miami Beach his
fighting weight had swollen to 275 pounds. Jackie Gleason became jealous.
He didn't like the competition, or ever being shown up—even when it came
to unflattering flab. Meyer Lansky, the mobster, wished that he had a goon
among his crew who could push that amount of weight around. Lansky was

always looking to recruit the best people, but Rocky was incorruptible. And he was never more masterful than that summer when heroics were measured not in shootouts but sit-ins.

"There will be no Chicago sequel in Miami Beach!" Pomerance boasted. Naturally, he was afraid of the sequel on Miami Beach, a premature Rocky horror show, or something like that. "I got an idea," he announced at a staff meeting of lieutenants. "I know it will sound nuts, but hear me out: I'll make friends with the hippies."

And he did.

"Here's my offer," he said, casting a wry smile and speaking directly to Abbie Hoffman and Jerry Rubin, the leaders of the Yippie movement.

They sat in his office dressed like several flavors of sherbet ice cream, pushing petitions and permits in front of Pomerance's face like petulant children. All the while Pomerance bit down hard on his familiar pipe. He sat beside them, having gotten up from his side of the desk. Hoffman and Rubin flanked the gargantuan police chief like colorful Japanese umbrellas. Surrounded by mementos and awards for his many years serving the city of Miami Beach, Pomerance believed it was wiser to show himself as an avuncular Jew rather than as a cop with a gun and a shield. His hope was to disarm the fight in them. These kids didn't possess any actual weapons, after all. They weren't anarchists looking to blow something up; they just didn't want their draft numbers ever to be called.

"No way, man," Hoffman said. "We don't trust anyone over thirty."

"We won't be co-opted by the cop, you dig," Rubin chimed in. "You can be all copasetic with us, but you're still a pig in our eyes."

"We'll have our people parading down Collins Avenue naked!" Hoffman threatened, shaking his fist at the former boxer.

"If you can get your people to walk naked on our asphalt in August," Rocky responded, "then I'll lead the parade, and you won't believe what I'll be using for a baton."

They all laughed. But Pomerance was serious. They were Jews from different generations. And yet there was symmetry to the positions they occupied, like a family feud that only they could stop. Remarkably, the immersion into the mainstream for American Jews had resulted in a Jewish police chief standing guard over the nation's presidential nominating conventions, and two Jewish student radicals leading the charge to end America's involvement in Vietnam.

"Here's what I'll do," Pomerance continued. "I'll give you Flamingo Park. I'll have the City Commission vote on it. You can camp out there—bring tents, sleep out on the grass below the stars. Play your music. Make speeches. Smoke pot. I don't give a shit. Do whatever you feel like so long as you don't get too close to the Convention Center or anywhere near the convention floor. I'll even set up a platform closer to the convention where you can bring your bullhorns and make speeches. You can engage in all the street theater you want. I know it's not Shakespeare, that's for sure, but you'll have to do it in the park and not at the convention site. I don't care what you do as long as it's peaceful. We'll refer to you as 'nondelegates,' which is a hell of a lot better than what happened in Chicago four years ago when you were known mainly as stoned degenerates and communists."

"No billy clubs and tear gas?" Rubin asked.

"I don't want that kind of publicity. You can hog all the press you want, but you won't have any pictures of Miami Beach cops pulling kids by their hair and beating on their heads."

And so it came to pass that in both July and August in 1972, Flamingo Park was transformed into a den of iniquity and political activism. Needless to say, Adam and Brad never went back to check on the hoses. In their nighttime journey they had found a far more interesting display of waterworks to admire. They also discovered serenity skinny-dipping in a pool filled with peace and love. By morning, after having spent the entire night in the park, they would be too tired to hurl a pitch or swing a bat.

"I'm dead when I get home," Brad said.

"My parents are already dead," Adam said.

They walked blankly toward the lake that had formed above the Little League baseball diamond, sat in the dugout, and waited for Coach Bertman to bench them for all manner of youthful indiscretion.

In the morning light when there was less public nudity and more social action, the members of the various protest groups that had commandeered the park assembled: Yippies, Zippies, Vietnam Veterans against the War, the National Organization of Women, the People's Pot Party, the Young Socialist Alliance, and Students for a Democratic Society. They were all handing out leaflets, drafting proclamations, and delivering speeches from ladders and makeshift podiums. Protest songs by Bob Dylan and Joan Baez blared from radios, which soon took the form of a chaotic concert as demonstrators strapped on acoustic guitars to sing along. Eventually, having gorged themselves on Pop-Tarts and Cap'n Crunch, and agitated themselves with the political pabulum of the morning news, they would leave the park and dart over to the platform that Chief Pomerance had erected a few blocks away from the convention site. There they would denounce the American government and call attention to political causes—racism, the environment, human rights, legalizing pot—that were being underserved or ignored by the Democratic Party. Vietnam veterans marched and chanted, "Bring the boys home!"

Meanwhile, as the "nondelegates" fucked in Flamingo Park and protested at their designated spot on 17th Street, the "actual delegates," and some of their Hollywood friends—and perhaps even some of the candidates themselves—found similar acts of depravity to engage in while sleeping on fine sheets and comforted by conditioned air in the hotels along Collins Avenue. Warren Beatty was in town, along with his girlfriend, Julie Christie, and his sister, Shirley MacLaine. In August, six weeks later, the Republican Party would, indeed, attract, as Jackie Gleason had predicted, his friends Frank Sinatra, Sammy Davis Jr., and Jimmy Stewart. Even Jane Fonda would show up after just having taken a two-week tour of North Vietnam and returning with a new moniker: "Hanoi Jane."

Pomerance kept true to his word all throughout. The police didn't bother the flower children that had gathered and fornicated in Flamingo Park. There were few arrests, and only thirty-three were injured. And very much unlike what happened in Chicago, there was no violence on the convention floor itself.

Miami Beach, with its charismatic police chief, was seen nationally as a progressive, sensible city that knew how to defuse a tense situation. The protesters largely got what they came for—and then some. They staked their public positions and made speeches with the cameras always rolling. Petitions were both passed out and voted upon. There was no shortage of social upheaval as the elderly of Miami Beach played Jewish grandparents to these malnourished, unwashed hippies.

"*Ach*, don't quote Marx to me," an octogenarian wearing a cabana outfit scoffed. "I had plenty when I was a student in Kiev."

"Do your parents know where you are?" a kindly, arthritic woman wearing an oversized hat and pushing her own walker said. "What kind of parents let their children sleep in a park every night, what with everything that goes on there?"

There was cause for alarm, to be sure, since there had been little preparation for survival in South Florida. All their readings on Marx and Marcuse, Buber and Martin Luther King Jr., left them woefully unprepared for the total solar experience of life on Miami Beach. What they most needed was far less leftist teaching and a lot more sun protection.

The sun in July and August left the hippies fried crispy. Pomerance realized that segregating the protestors in Flamingo Park would keep the peace, but it would also be the death of them. When Jim Morrison exposed himself several years earlier in Dinner Key Auditorium, at least he had the good sense to do it indoors. But these snow white, white-shoed, pampered and privileged middle-class college coeds and dropouts dropping acid didn't fully appreciate the consequences of going au natural in so cloudless a place as Miami Beach. Removing their bell bottoms, blue-tinted granny glasses, clogs, tie-dye T-shirts, tube tops, and jean jackets patched with peace signs, spouting Sartre while taking on the world with their principles and earthy ways, and dancing around nude during midday while mocking the sun god, demonstrated a freedom of spirit and a few loose screws. Many returned home up north and out west—to their dorm rooms and even to their mommies—broiled beyond recognition, sun poisoned and suffering from third-degree burns.

For the locals, the furnace that was Miami Beach in summer was nothing to trifle with. Miami was a city of endless possibility, but there were rules that needed to be obeyed. First, the sun is not your friend—especially in August. Yet, there was still some semblance of innocence to salvage by 1972, and who better to test the limits of Miami's Fahrenheit than the flower children running around naked in Flamingo Park.

Despite all the glamour that surrounded the two conventions, the locals were able to glimpse the end. These subdued riots and ardent protests, the celebrity delegates mingling among presidential hopefuls, the youthful, bearded activists shouting slogans in front of TV news cameras, were the final lap of the joyride that was once Miami Beach. For that summer of 1972, Miami Beach was the focus of the nation's presidential campaign season. With a war raging in Vietnam, racial tensions on fire in its inner cities, and the stoned youth of America running roughshod over everything that was once neatly pressed and pristine, the hopes of the entire nation settled on this small island city floating off the coast of Florida. Soon everything would fall—including the presidency. What happened that summer marked the beginning of that fall.

In a few years Miami Beach would no longer be a tourist mecca but rather a place only to visit aging grandparents. Retirees would go off and find new sanctuaries, and then die. A boatlift of Haitians and the mass exodus of Cubans from Mariel would change the composition of Miami and bring with it more crime and eventually the influx of the Colombian drug cartels. Jackie Gleason's TV variety show from Miami Beach would long be forgotten, his lovable loser Ralph Kramden replaced by Al Pacino's menacing drug kingpin in *Scarface*, Tony Montana. In the cultural imagination coke would morph from soft drink to hard drug. The strip of hotels along Collins Avenue would never again host rat packers or even Vegas-worthy strippers. And after all those referendums and statewide ballot initiatives, legalized gambling would still never come to Miami Beach.

An era was ending, but in the Posner household time was suspended in a state of perpetual unrest. A different kind of radicalizing was always in rehearsal. Adam Posner was an only child, but he was born with enough cynicism for an army of relatives—many of whom would have existed if not for the Nazis.

"These kids with the long hair and slogans are wasting their time," Sophie coached her son shortly before the conventions were coming to town. "The world doesn't change that easy."

"Yes, Adam," Jacob agreed. "The demonstrations won't make a difference. It will be a freak show masquerading as a peaceful protest."

"With teenagers looking like clowns," Sophie said. "Change comes from closed fists," she added, and then curled up her fingers on both hands gracefully as if putting up her dukes were second nature. "Screaming and holding up signs only makes you a target. It doesn't make you free. Real change comes from the underground, and it has to be done with force."

His mother's words washed over him, and he resisted the warning. Although only a pre-bar mitzvah boy, and untainted by adult disappointments, he wanted to believe that the deck of cards his mother shuffled so seamlessly was not stacked against the innocents. He held out hope that peace could come to those who asked for it, or protested loudly but peacefully. Jacob listened to his wife's lament, too, and wondered how difficult such a worldview was to maintain. Decades later and he was already exhausted from it. Not even the calming rhythms of Miami Beach offered a respite. Perhaps the life lessons from the camps would one day become obsolete—if not in his lifetime, then at least during his son's. But like his wife, he doubted that, too.

Before all the balloons and confetti rained down on the delegates, signaling that each party had finally selected its standard bearer, Police Chief Rocky Pomerance had one last maneuver to pull off. He charmed the radicals and made security for two presidential nominating conventions look easy. Perhaps he could salvage the presidency, too.

Operating on a tip he received from one of his undercover detectives, Pomerance learned that a few Republican operatives were planning to spy on the Democratic National Committee, which was holed up throughout the convention at the Octagon Towers, an apartment building across the street from the Convention Center. Apparently they had tried the same caper a month earlier in Washington, DC, at the Watergate building. That burglary was bungled and five men were arrested. The details were still very sketchy, including whether people in the White House were involved. With the Watergate break-in botched, and the entire Democratic National Committee situated in Miami Beach, the Republicans were going to try one more wiretap before the election in November.

"Republicans playing dirty tricks in my city," Pomerance fumed, chewing down even more firmly on his pipe. "Let's catch these guys in the act. What do they think: Miami Beach police are a bunch of rubes?"

Of course, the Miami Beach Police Department was stretched pretty thin that summer—the entire force only had two hundred officers. Pomerance had an idea who might be able to lend an assist.

Meyer Lansky, Miami Beach's resident Jewish gangster, was no fan of Richard Nixon. In fact, it was Nixon's Justice Department that had only recently extradited Lansky back to the United States from Israel. He was still awaiting trial for all sorts of raps that he would eventually beat.

"Jew-hating bastard, that Nixon," Lansky said when Pomerance called him into his office. The two Jews, one miniature, the other mammoth, one lawless, the other the guardian of the city, squared off, face-to-face, for a common purpose. "I just knew he was a crook. This is my business, after all. How can I help, Rocky?"

It was admittedly odd that a mob boss like Meyer Lansky was able to operate so freely and openly in an American city. Was all of Miami Beach Cosa Nostra? Not likely. Were the police on the take? Not at all, unless you count a free brisket sandwich now and then from the mob's wholly owned deli and hangout, the Jewish NOSE-tra. The truth was that local Miami Beach cops rarely bothered with Lansky's men. Few Miami Beach wise guys ever got arrested. Perhaps it was because they were all part of a larger tribal affiliation as Jews.

It was also the case that the police chief regarded the Jewish Mafia as just another Miami Beach tourist attraction. Pomerance saw them as more entertaining than threatening. They represented yet another provincial curiosity of life in South Florida, as essential to Miami as the Parrot Jungle and the Seaquarium. The city had its share of exotic birds, rare creatures of the ocean, and also the improbability of Jewish hit men. Yes, these Jewish gangsters of Miami Beach did have felonious sounding names like Morty the Mohel, Love Handles Levine, and Lenny Matzo Brei. But Pomerance knew that more people died from Hugo the Killer Whale splashing them with water at the Seaquarium than from these Jewish jokers with their bald heads and brass knuckles. They pathetically had very little in common with the golden age of Murder, Inc. The Miami Beach variety of wise guys was more like the senior center at Century Village—but not as tough. Bugsy Siegel would have been shocked if he had seen how soft Meyer had allowed his crew to become. The Miami Beach dinner crowd jostling in the mad scramble for the early bird specials was of much sturdier stock.

"I swear, they get tired from playing pinochle," Pomerance jokingly remarked about Lansky's crew. "They fall asleep every night in the middle of Johnny Carson with their cups of warm milk and Maalox chasers. Pepto Bismol is a dessert. That's the kind of tough guys we have here on Miami

Beach. No loaded .38 Specials but plenty of 'plop plop, fizz fizz' ready to hit water."

Pomerance always had more on his mind than policing these sciatic mobsters with their tall fish tales of how they became made men in New York, LA, and Vegas. The local crimes they committed nowadays barely qualified as misdemeanors in Miami. So at times he regarded them as assets of the Miami Beach Police Department, surrogate cops, auxiliary officers who just happened to have their own rap sheets, men who he could call upon to do the kind of dirty work that his otherwise clean police force wouldn't touch. And in return for their occasional, paradoxical services in crime fighting, Pomerance looked the other way as they stumbled about the city trying to recapture their confidence as once-revered confidence men.

"Remember those three bozos of yours who we arrested a few months back?" the massive police chief asked the diminutive mob boss. "You know, the guys who tried to rig the voting machines for the upcoming gambling referendum?"

"Yeah, Morty, Danny, and Charlie. They raided that storage facility at night—not one of my best laid plans, for sure."

"What did they call themselves again?"

Meyer laughed, then said, "I believe they went by the name, 'The Plumbers.' Who the hell knows why."

"Let's put those goons of yours back to work, Meyer," the chief said.

"Gladly," the mobster replied.

The trick was to introduce the Plumbers from the Jewish Mafia of Miami Beach to the Plumbers from the Committee to Re-elect the President, appropriately known as CREEP. Miami Beach was awash in plumbers during that especially leaky summer of 1972. It was a perfect time to combine two sets of criminals—garden-variety racketeers and high-level political crooks—one being used to set up the other.

Working together in ways that would have given J. Edgar Hoover a coronary, Pomerance and Lansky found out the identities and location of the three would-be co-conspirators, these lesser-known plumbers who were not the same as the ones apprehended at the Watergate building. They, too, would be charged with violating federal wiretapping laws.

Lansky's men met their counterparts one evening at Wolfie's Restaurant, its signage lighting up Lincoln Road with a cascade of flashing yellow and red lights. The spacious restaurant made it easier for harried waitresses to loop about as if in a game of roller derby. The tables were weighed down by pickles, coleslaw, and sauerkraut; baskets of warm assorted rolls with dollops of cream cheese and butter occupied the center of the table like floral arrangements. The aging Miami Beach mobsters squeezed themselves into a booth upholstered in shiny red leather. A cartoonish wolf dressed in a tuxedo devoured a hot dog on the main wall.

The Octagon Plumbers, four in total, sat at an adjoining table, their mouths mum and their heads pointed downward, staring into open-faced turkey sandwiches and a Reuben that bled Russian dressing. A side order of blintzes with sour cream and applesauce beckoned from the edge of the table like bait and tackle for the Jewish set. Lansky's men were boasting shamelessly that they were members of the local syndicate, a deliberate violation of the *omertà* ethos scrupulously followed by the Cosa Nostra. Keeping one's mouth shut wasn't so easy for Jews, however.

"I hear you guys are on a job," Charlie Nunchucks said.

"Yeah, something having to do with bustin' into an apartment building and wiretapping some phones," Morty the Mohel said.

"Piece a' cake. We got it right?" Danny Dumb Luck chimed in, always late, always superfluous—and then he ordered a slice of cake.

The Octagon Plumbers at first played dumb, not the hardest assignment they ever had. Then they dug into their food, which impaired their judgment even more.

"Love these little cheese Danishes," said one of the Plumbers, narrow face, square jaw, prep school pedigree, trying to find a fast track into the CIA.

"And the portion size," said another, a stocky Cuban with a thin beard and dark eyes, a likely Alpha 66 survivor from the Bay of Pigs. "Jews sure like to eat."

The other two remained quiet, professional spooks—wearing vests and keeping everything close to them—not giving anything away, not even what they ordered off the menu. By the time the frankfurters had arrived the co-conspirators had already spilled the beans to Lansky's men, who were all wearing wires—perhaps the only time in American history when organized crime cooperated with the authorities for no reason other than patriotism. Not to cut a deal or rat out another family, but largely to vindicate their godfather's personal hatred of Richard Nixon.

The next day the Octagon Plumbers broke into an apartment occupied by one of the leaders of the Democratic National Committee, not knowing that they were under surveillance. As the four of them rummaged through the apartment and concealed a listening device inside one of the phones, Pomerance and his men burst through the door and made the arrests.

It was a good day for Miami Beach's police chief. Rocky Pomerance shoved two of the handcuffed Plumbers in the back of his patrol car. As he pulled away from the Octagon triumphantly, local citizens cheered their police chief from street corners. Wearing an impish smile on his wide face, Pomerance cruised south on Washington Avenue toward the police station. Passing the Convention Center, he noticed a large number of protestors positioned across the street behind the barricade of buses that stretched all along the avenue. They were, of course, the very same activists from Flamingo Park, but they seemed to have grown larger in number on this, the last day of the convention and with George McGovern set to lead his party to what would become a historic defeat.

Rocky Pomerance slowed down as he passed by the demonstrators, many of whom were holding up signs, mostly against the war. Others were shouting into megaphones, their words garbled in the thick air, the sun melting sunglasses and sneering at any and all UV protections. The police chief allowed himself a moment of self-congratulatory peace. His Flamingo Park gambit resulted in him pitching nearly a perfect game.

And to top it off, the arrests at the Octagon might immortalize Miami Beach even further, depending on the outcome of the Watergate investigation. He checked his rearview mirror and spied the glum faces of the three CREEPS, and then his eyes looked left and settled on a young boy, not quite a teen, wearing a yellow Butterflake Bakery baseball jersey. The age of the boy and the color of his shirt no doubt drew the chief's attention. He was an uncommon sight even in a convention that drew so many freaks to Flamingo Park. The boy was standing in the front lines with the other activists— cheering among the peaceniks, feminists, and black power separatists—but he was the youngest one by far, and shouting even more loudly than the rest. He didn't even need a bull-horn. Dangling from his neck was a large gold medallion in the shape of a peace sign. And on the back of his jersey someone had drawn a green marijuana leaf. He was wearing blue-tinted granny sunglasses, and his face was painted with the rainbow hues of a true flower child.

Apparently, being the ace pitcher for the first-place team in the Flamingo Park Little League was not enough to keep him busy. He decided to join yet another team, to cover all of the bases. This was not a matter of an impressionable kid brainwashed with sixties agitprop; Adam Posner latched onto this protest movement as if it were a surrogate family. All those student radicals were running away from something. It wasn't all principle or common cause that brought them together. It was a longing for community in an unmoored America. And in 1972 Miami Beach offered ample docking. Yes, there was also a strong desire to change the world, and to find a ready supply of willing flesh and homegrown weed. But nearly everyone was also looking for mutual caring and connection. Adam Posner sensed that he was among friends.

The anomaly of having a boy so young, and a Miami Beach local, too, joining the demonstration triggered in Chief Pomerance the cop's instinct, and a father's concern, that perhaps the kid was there against his will. He was a man who kept abreast of all the goings on in his city. He knew that Butterflake was both a bakery and a winning Little League team. The boy didn't belong here; in all likelihood he was lost. Pomerance rolled down his window and said, "Hey, kid, you okay out here? Do you know what you're doing? Don't you have a game this morning?"

As the patrol car coasted toward the curb, the boy leaped up atop a police barricade, and with two hippies keeping him steady and egging him on, screamed a singular cry:

"Bring the Boy home! Bring the Boy home!"

The police chief rolled his window back up and continued on toward the station, now satisfied that he had his answer.

Three

Bullet Bob and the Jew Boy

The mottled Miami skyline at daybreak hangs low, like wrinkled laundry awaiting sunrise, all backlit in phosphorescent coral pink. A mosaic of purple clouds shadows all those oceanfront condos built to look like art deco birthday cakes, decorated with garish crowns and pointless spires. Hotels fit for lowly kings, greenhorns looking to change color. It was all for show, this sunny spectacle of a small beachside city, always trying to make an impression, to punch above its municipal weight, to showcase Miami as a revamped Riviera, a less carnal Cannes, a much poorer Monte Carlo—but impressive in its own blinding light.

Only seven miles long, a flat landmass of various man-made islands surrounded by ocean on its eastern edge, with Biscayne Bay to the west, and interlocking canals offering a water view for the otherwise landlocked. The waterways of Miami suffered from aquatic confusion, or perhaps it was just an optical illusion, the sun playing tricks on half-closed eyes already squinting from the sun. Blue waters actually looked green, the colors of glinting emerald, sparkling turquoise. It was a perfect surface for seafaring leprechauns, yet it largely became home for wandering Jews and anticommunist Cubans. And to add to the befuddlement, the Atlantic Ocean was altogether pacific, placid, and unthreatening—bath water warm, even in winter.

Muggy winds cut through pigeon-toed palm trees bowed sideways like tropical dancers. Palm fronds fluttered like seagulls, and sandpipers skidded on shimmering sand made smooth with each departing wave. The tides rolled in and out with a punctuality otherwise alien to laid-back Florida, with its Cuban castoffs, forlorn Haitians, smug snowbirds, and cowering Holocaust survivors. The footprints of nighttime lovers—toes marking their territory in the sand—by morning got washed away without a trace.

It was around this time each weekday morning when the boys stood outside in the predawn, their eyes still sleepy, bodies rocking in the wind, parted hair flapping—one moment combed, the next off course. They wore short pants to school like Swiss children in the summer Alps—except they wore them all year round and without all that yodeling. And they tanned like marooned castaways, shamelessly shirtless, skin peeling from their noses, third-degree burns on their backs, brown hair turned dirty blond from the highlighting alchemy of salt and sun. The wild children from *Lord of the Flies* had resurfaced in sunny Florida—equally unsupervised, but far less menacing. They were a gang of innocents, Florida bumpkins, wetlands between their ears, surviving in a misbegotten tropical paradise, not quite Caribbean, and yet not fully American either.

"Is the fucking bus gonna be late again?" Lee Kleinberg said, swinging his fist into the air, which was thick enough to take a punch. "We're the only people awake in Miami Beach," he growled. "Christ, it's still dark out. Even the lizards are asleep."

Heavyset with long blond hair and albino skin that was a forever shade of pink like undercooked meat, Lee was the kind of northeastern transplant who simply couldn't adjust to the climate. Organ recipients whose bodies reject kidneys have similar, albeit far worse, experiences. Lee's parents still wore the uniforms of Long Island commuters—long heavy pants and wool skirts. The cabana ethic had not yet overtaken their wardrobes. They were not alone. Many remained skeptical that Miami, with its surreal sun and transitional lives, could ever stand in as their true home. Emotionally they kept one foot in the marshes of Miami while with the other they stretched longingly toward the suburbs of the Five Towns—a difficult balancing act, indeed.

For them, Miami felt alien; the umbilical chord that connected the diaspora to certain urban locales was still very much tethered to the Northeast. Like so many other paradise agnostics and quality-of-life cynics, it was difficult for them to fully trust a climate that wasn't playing with a full deck of seasons. Endless summers are one of the world's great illusions, a ruse every bit as bogus as selling some nitwit a slice of the Brooklyn Bridge. All this played naturally to Miami's myth-making Chamber of Commerce. "See It Like a Native" was the alluring pitch: a topless, bronzed girl photographed from behind, wearing nothing but a bikini bottom and a snorkel. Such temptations of the Sunshine State were promoted on postcards, T-shirts, beach towels—even on stuffed alligators.

But the beach-bum ambiance wasn't for everyone, and Lee's mood often reflected his adolescent sense of Miami misery.

"Why don't we just walk to school . . . in the dark? Does anyone have a flashlight?" Ross Adler joked. He was tall, with shaggy-dog eyes and floppy dark hair. He walked with an athletic bounce, but also with an exaggerated stoop, like he was always looking down for seashells. Mostly, he was sensitive about his height, being so tall for a Jewish boy and so overly developed for a seventh grader. He compensated by thrusting his body forward head first, his upper torso always arriving early, at a right angle.

"Walk?" Lee replied. "Why not just have Adam sprint the whole way to school? He is the fastest kid at Biscayne Junior High—actually, the fastest kid in all of Miami Beach. No one can catch him."

"Yeah," Ross agreed, "Adam the Atom, as fast as an Apollo rocket."

Being compared to a NASA spaceship put one in pretty heady company in those days. Years later, hobbling on a bone-on-bone arthritic knee, when no bus would ever be worth giving chase after, he would longingly recall a time of much freer, painless mobility. It was the early 1970s, after all, when speed was the rage—and not just the drug, but speed in all forms. The space race was aptly named. It wasn't just how fast or how far American rockets could be launched; the *race* was to get them into orbit before the Soviet Union could get theirs off the ground. Cars were losing their oafish, wide-bodied designs, replaced with sleeker, faster models with horsepower the envy of any thoroughbred. Formula One and IndyCar racer Mario Andretti inspired even the old Jews from South Florida—many of whom were too short to see over the dashboards of their Cadillac Eldorados—to step more forcefully on the accelerators, racing to their gin rummy and mahjong games, hopefully without mowing down a retiree inching across Ocean Drive holding fast to an aluminum walker that doubled as a sun-tanning reflector.

"Of course, Adam might lose that title this year." Lee offered a second thought, even though no such actual "official" title ever existed. This was seventh grade, after all, and not the Millrose Games. The *race* was no more distinguished than a fifty-yard dash in the enervating outdoor heat of Miami Beach. "I mean, with all those black kids being bused in from Liberty City and Overtown, how's a Jewish kid gonna blow by them?"

"You kidding me?" Ross replied, sounding personally wounded. "Adam Posner's legs are like pistons. Just look at this guy," he said, opening up his palm as if he were presenting Adam for inspection. "Badass Jew, kick-ass kike. No way some black kid is coming over the causeway to our city and beating our local rocket in a race."

And so began a challenge he had no part in making and no interest in defending. Bold statements made so impetuously can end up defining a life. Failing to live up to childhood expectations is like having the weight of the world stunt your growth. A dare had been issued in the least mannered of places, and for a brief moment the pride of Jewish Miami Beach was weighing on his not-quite-teenaged legs.

"It really sucks getting up this early every day," Lee complained. "And all because of Martin Luther King."

"Not *because* of Martin Luther King, you idiot, but because of integration," Ross said with the conviction of a freedom rider, which he was too young to have been, although the memory of those "northern agitators" was still fresh on everyone's mind.

"Whatever," Lee relented, "but what's the point of living in this shitty paradise if we have to wake up in the middle of the night just to catch a bus to get to school—hours before school even starts?"

It's true that in 1972 they arrived at school each morning in desperate need of a nap. Even if they had wanted one, it was too dark to find a nice spot to lie down. At that time in the morning, the school was still officially closed. They huddled together at the front entrance of Biscayne Junior High, or walked over to 41st Street to an old drug store that had an oval-shaped lunch counter surrounded by a healthy supply of tanning oils, postcards, and assorted Miami Beach ashtrays and knickknacks. For most of them, it was still too early to eat. Other buses idled by the curb and then belched out their own allotment of resentful, sleep-deprived white children.

Who would have guessed that an almost forgotten stretch of America's Manifest Destiny, which had taken a sharp turn south courtesy of Route A1A and the Flagler Railroad, would serve as an improbable battleground in the struggle for civil rights? These children weren't worthy of the attention. Equality didn't interest them too much; they really weren't all that invested in the civility of rights equally shared. It wasn't that long ago when the Kenilworth Hotel in Bal Harbor, owned by one of America's most beloved entertainers, Arthur Godfrey, posted a sign outside the lobby that read: "No Dogs or Jews Allowed." It never occurred to the Jewish community to boycott the place. These transplanted Jews offered up no facsimile of Rosa Parks, with her tired feet and quiet dignity. They had no rabble-rousing Malcolm X who would spew venomous words of Jewish power in the face of white-Christian, anti-Semitic oppression.

They didn't seem to care. Why make waves on Miami Beach when the Atlantic Ocean had its own trouble foaming white caps? Fuck the Kenilworth. There were plenty of places that had a pool. Even their dogs didn't hold a grudge. Both outcasts were too busy working on their tans.

To live in Miami meant to not get all that caught up in politics—except, of course, when it came to Cuba and Fidel Castro's alliance with the Soviet Union. Missiles pointed their way had the very opposite tranquilizing effect that Miami Beach's Founding Fathers had hoped for. How did a region that never dipped below fifty degrees Fahrenheit wind up as a red-hot pin in the map of the Cold War? Compared with geopolitics, local politics was an afterthought. Even national politics didn't matter much until the Democrats and Republicans decided to hold their conventions in Miami Beach that same year. Busing came to South Florida with all the fanfare of a summer rain shower, which means it crept upon the locals fast and at first went barely noticed.

That's because somehow it didn't feel like it applied to them. They were

South Floridians, which was very different from those southern crackers that the rest of America had gotten to know—with the fire hoses, cattle prods, police dogs, and church bombings. Nothing like that ever happened around Miami. Most people could have gone an entire lifetime without encountering Lynyrd Skynrd, NASCAR, trailer parks, and chewing tobacco. Rednecks in Miami meant sun poison below the head; there were no unresolved Civil War tensions being played out that far south of Dixie. Red may have been lethal in global politics, but locally it was the shade du jour.

Racism was not in the DNA of Jews and Cubans. Grandparents came from Eastern Europe and the Pale; some were the human wreckage of the Third Reich. Many of the "northern agitators," as southern racists called them, were themselves Jews who had traveled down to the south to assist in registering blacks to vote. Some, like Andrew Goodman and Michael Schwerner, paid the price for doing so with their lives.

Cuban refugees dreamed of nothing else but reclaiming their island. And deep-sea fishermen casting for marlin were far too tired at the end of the day to suit up into a uniform consisting of a white bed sheet and a hood. Besides, a man would suffocate in such a getup in Miami. Bigotry wasn't worth all the effort.

It's for this reason that the Deep South always meant something very different to the people who actually occupied the southernmost corner of the United States. What's farther south than Miami, other than those dotting keys that tail the peninsula like a kite? There's no way to get much deeper south of the Mason-Dixon Line without tripping over a conch shell in Key West and splashing into the Atlantic Ocean.

Obviously, the Deep South was somewhat immune to geographical destinies, and they were not its natural confederates. They had far more in common with the Seminole and Miccosukee Indian tribes of Florida than they did with the xenophobic Klan or the born-again Crimson Tide. After all, they, too, had a ragtag tribal ancestry. And Florida proved to be such an accommodating state for mongrels like them, a safe haven for half-breeds, ex-cons, retirees, political escapees, boat people, and immigrants entering American waters floating on makeshift rafts. They were in no position to consign others to second-class citizenry. They were lacking in many qualities so prominent among the bland American upper-crust royalty; but one thing they had in abundant supply was a certain color-blind reflex, learned the hard way—from once being so hated themselves.

And, yet, while they were innocent of the crimes of the Confederacy, they were nonetheless perhaps unfairly required to atone for the south's segregationist past.

Busing in black kids from segregated neighborhoods and integrating the public schools in cities across America was the most prized legacy of the civil rights era. All those years of social upheavals; peaceful nonviolent resistance; the assassinations of Martin Luther King Jr. and Medgar Evers; the bus boycotts and the lunch counter sit-ins; the segregated swimming pools, bathrooms, and drinking fountains; had come to this: white and black would sit together in public schools—no matter how far black students had to travel to get to the better schools in white districts. "Separate but equal" was always a racist myth; true equality meant all races sharing the same public facilities, whether it came to writing on blackboards or drinking from the same water coolers.

Miami Beach, however, was, paradoxically, as segregated a city as there could possibly be. The blacks all lived over the causeway, in Liberty City, Overtown, and parts of Coconut Grove, in the seedier sections of Dade County. Across Biscayne Bay would lie the forgotten part of Miami, where an entire race of people lived among themselves—separated from white Miami on the basis of class, income, and the wide expanse of water. They traveled over the causeways to Miami Beach to work menial jobs as nurses, maids, and mechanics. But at the end of their shifts, back to the ghettos they returned. At least with respect to the public schools, however, there was now finally going to be integration—forced though it was, as in the rest of America.

Some cities, like Boston, protested these forced desegregation plans. Miami was not complaining. Their problem was not with busing but with the buses. They didn't have enough of them in all of Dade County to shuttle black students from inner-city Miami to the all-white schools on Miami Beach—where many of the best schools just happened to be. The causeways that linked Miami to Miami Beach, which hovered above Biscayne Bay like magic carpets—the beaches due east a gleaming, tropical Oz—were nearly five miles long. Transporting black students to Miami Beach schools in time for the first period bell meant that the kids living on Miami Beach, and who depended on those very same buses to get to school, would have to awaken at ungodly hours to catch a bus in pitch darkness in order to arrive at school in near darkness.

School bus drivers were suddenly working double shifts, racing across the causeways to retrieve the very students who were now the object of this national commitment to integrate the public schools.

They lived in a state with boundless natural resources and infinite space, but weak in tactical know-how; Miami's infrastructure was no better than a banana republic. Getting things done was not a priority for local officials. The state was known for its oranges, tourism, and siestas, and not for home-grown industry and initiative. Nothing ran on time in those days, even though sundials in their city would have given them the timepiece precision of a latter-day Zurich. So Florida satisfied the nation's forced busing plans by exposing itself to the great inconvenience of reduced sleep and surreal school-day mornings.

"Thank God the bus is here," Lee said as a great yellow behemoth coughed and jerked along Dickens Avenue like an animal exhaling its last dying breath.

The boys arrived at school in less than fifteen minutes (they could have walked; "Adam the Atom" nearly could have sprinted), owing to a short commute and a city far too unassuming to command a rush hour. On the streets strolled elderly Jews taking predawn walks in their white tennis out-fits, zinc oxide on their noses to protect them, at this hour of day, from the moon, and baseball caps and oversized straw hats on their heads. A few Hasidim wearing long wool black caftans and fur *shtreimels* were tempting a stroke. Their devout ways, originating in the wintry Polish and Ukrainian forests, would make no allowance for Miami's mystical heat index. Certain rituals are stubborn enough to withstand both time and feverish tropical climates. The only men or machines seemingly in a hurry at that hour were the school buses and their drivers, all fixated on desegregating the Miami Beach schools by integrating black and white.

"It's so quiet," Ross said one morning while they sat on benches in front of the school's entrance.

"We're sitting here in the dark," Lee complained, "that's why we can't hear anything. The whole city is asleep. And we could get killed; all this busing back and forth is gonna cause car accidents. The black kids have schools in their own neighborhoods—right where they live! Hey, I believe in equality and all, but what does the government have against sleep? Isn't sleep a civil right?"

The three pondered yet another right that the Supreme Court had not yet considered, and peered into the darkness as other students trudged in, barely lifting their feet, Keds and Converses sloshing through the dew that had collected on the grass. They all seemed to be arriving on instinct, emerging from a fog with tousled hair and sleepy eyes, looking stoned, which some of them actually were.

Soon the teachers pulled up in their cars. In this delicate dance of American pluralism and diversity, they were the second group to arrive. The teachers, however, were not spared in the grand plan to integrate the schools. Last year all of the teachers were white. Many lived on Miami Beach. But this year brought not only busloads of black kids to their once-segregated junior high, but also cars driven by black teachers, making their own safe passage over the causeways that linked Miami with Miami Beach. One tiny privilege of being a black teacher was that they were allowed to bus themselves.

That year took a lot of adjustment. Coke commercials featured songs of racial harmony, but such displays of togetherness didn't come easily on the front lines of forced busing. Color TVs, which were still new in those days, exaggerated the depth of the primary colors. Blue and green came across as harsh and uneasy on the eye. The Age of Aquarius looked like a palette of tie-dyed excess. Such promiscuous mixing was quite rare on the streets, however. Those slogans would take decades to be fully realized—if ever at all.

And so they all regarded one another warily. The black kids seemed bigger, walking with sturdy, long-limbed struts that could have easily uncoiled into a brawler's stance. But very few fights occurred. There were the early iterations of trash talk and smack downs. Turning a corner and seeing a group of black kids milling by their lockers might provoke the occasional, "What's up, white boy? This here is our place! You better go find yourself another hallway. You best keep walking or your honky ass will get a woopin'."

No one wanted to test the boundaries of these rites of urban passage.

Some of the Cuban kids also acquired a gangland pose, but it was tamped down and tamed whenever in the presence of their guests from Overtown and Liberty City. Menace was conveyed through an accepted hierarchy.

The Jewish boys deferred to their black classmates for good reason. The streets across the causeway were reputed to be tougher, which no white kid doubted for a moment. They understood, even then, what a charmed life it had been on this privileged peninsula called Miami Beach. They were sheltered from almost everything but the sun, and the threat of a late summer hurricane. There was no living on the wild side in Miami Beach in those days. Each block was a bastion of security. No one ever got beat up or mugged. The bullies were at the beach. Drugs had yet to become a Miami vice. Sniffing glue was, for many, the only hardcore pleasure.

The same could not have been said for the meaner streets of inner-city Miami, however. Those grittier urban street corners and alleyways offered a wide variety of deviance. The bused kids came from genuine hard-knock lives. They were living a very different Miami reality. Some fights broke out in the school cafeteria, and when broken up by a teacher, sometimes resumed after school by the school buses. The black kids from across the bay may have been strangers on Miami Beach, but while in school they made themselves very much present on the island.

The white students maintained the same guardedness in how they interacted with their black teachers. In some ways it was even worse. The teachers seemed even more resentful than the black students—forced to travel long distances to teach in white schools, punished because they, too, lived on the wrong side of Biscayne Bay. The teachers were as segregated as the students in polarized Miami. It wasn't a privilege to cross a causeway just to teach in racially diverse classrooms. If anything, it was an inconvenient reminder of how far they had to come just to be treated the same.

The social studies teacher H. T. Scott certainly felt that way. There was an ominous quality about him, a suppressed anger and a grievance in reserve, as if desegregation caused him to feel hemmed in by the circumstances, taken out of his more natural habitat. Even the initials in his name suggested a man who didn't wish to dispense with formalities. He wasn't a talkative man. Mostly he had his students read in class. Perhaps he was afraid of what he would say if he spoke freely, unscripted from the state-approved curriculum. Everything about him was unapproachable. For one thing, he stood out because of his size. He was gigantic. Well over six-feet two-inches tall and nearly three hundred pounds, no one had ever seen anything like him—a giant of human flesh, like a spearless African warrior dressed up to teach social studies to junior high schoolers. Miami Beach's police chief, Rocky Pomerance, a man of formidable presence, and a former boxer, too, would have thought better than to scuffle with this Othello sent over to protect Jewish children from racial prejudice.

There were no such role models in their lives, nothing that quite prepared them for this new teacher. The causeways over Biscayne Bay provided a most scenic, disarming buffer separating black and white in Miami. Such forced separations were common in those days. South Africa had its apartheid system, Berlin had its wall, and Miami had its capacious bay. The only African Americans they ever saw on Miami Beach were either busing tables or driving school buses.

In comparison to Mr. Scott, their own fathers were more like pale welterweights with expanding waistlines. Six feet tall was nearly a statistical aberration for the people on Miami Beach, as if Lilliputians had found a corner of America to call their own. These men were salesmen and shopkeepers, math teachers and stockbrokers. None possessed the physical gifts where making a simple entrance caused a roomful of people to gasp.

Biscayne's new social studies teacher had a military bearing and eyes that held one at attention. One hesitated to look away until being properly dismissed. His nose was wide, and the deep pores on his face could be seen even from the last row of the classroom. He had large, jagged, yellow teeth like the native stone crabs that were so popular, and so very unkosher, on Miami Beach. Black dress pants and a white shirt were his everyday attire, which he sweated through from morning to afternoon, as if teaching was, for him, a workout. Even the air conditioning feared getting too close to him.

The black students believed, mistakenly, that they would win his favor since they shared the same skin color and were, on this narrow island, in the same boat, so to speak. But in the true spirit of equality that commanded H. T. Scott to work so far away from his home, he resented the students all equally and favored none in particular. This was not to be a sappy *To Sir, with Love* Miami Beach postcard. The students lacked the courage, and the teachers resented the social engineering, which made it unlikely for either side to become too sentimental.

It wasn't until many months later that they learned that he had played college football at Florida A&M. This discovery came upon them quite by accident. Mr. Scott didn't want any of them to know.

Biscayne's physical education teacher, Michael Kesselman, like some Cold War spy, broke the news and dispelled any further doubt that Scott's body had once been put to good use. Coach Kesselman was a muscle-bound local Jewish kid who threw the shot put in high school and hosted his own annual bench pressing competition at Biscayne, an event that nearly decapitated one of the stars on their school's College Bowl team, who entered the tournament on a dare and defenselessly found himself with 110 pounds crashing down on his neck. The coach seemed to be on a mission to toughen up his young unwilling recruits—both white and black. Each gym class commenced with a six-hundred-yard run, followed by a gravity-impaired turn at the monkey bars, further slippage on the rope climb, and bicep curls of tin cans filled with cement as makeshift dumbbells. His charges developed more calluses on their hands than muscles in their arms. And their green gym shorts and white T-shirts with the Biscayne logo stamped on the front were drenched from all these exertions like sails in a rainstorm.

Coach Kesselman humiliated anyone who was falling too far behind. He would bellow into his megaphone, which seemed attached to his left arm like a *cesta* in a game of jai alai.

"What are you, a cripple, Cabrera? Come on, Wilcox, stop doggin' it!"

Only after these grueling warm-ups were they permitted to play the sport of the season. Bending over with their hands on their knees, they sucked up as much air as the humidity would allow. Phys ed sometimes attracted a crowd. The girls who shared the same fields during their own gym periods were coached by less sadistic women who felt that twenty minutes of volleyball was plenty of exercise in the scorching heat. Before heading back to the showers, many of them sat on the lawn and watched them play. But there was another spectator who seemed to be taking an interest in their games, too. It just so happened that Mr. Scott's free period coincided with their phys ed. And on some of those days he could be found in the outdoor hallway, facing the playing fields, drinking an icy Coke and wiping sweat from his brow. Instead of spending the hour in the teacher's lounge, and inviting those newly awkward racial tensions, he chose instead to spend his break watching flag football. And he was so discreet and silent about it; he never once mentioned in social studies that he had seen his students play. Sometimes they wondered whether he was some kind of scout for another team. But what other team would that be?

Those first few months of seventh grade, a sharing of a once all-white school with kids of another race, were challenging not just in the classroom and hallways, but also on the playing fields. Such a simple ritual as picking teams took on new sociological significance. Where to sit in the cafeteria was similarly fraught with confusions. The desegregating of the school didn't carry down to the cafeteria. Not only did the students sit at segregated tables; the cafeteria itself seemed to be partitioned right down the middle, with all whites on the left, and all blacks on the right, like they were all in attendance at a wedding and their seats depended on whether they were there for the bride or groom. This pattern of impromptu, color-coded seating continued throughout all three years of junior high school.

Such natural bifurcations, however, were not practiced during phys ed. There, more of a siege mentality influenced the picking of teams. American boys like to be winners. They didn't need a Jackie Robinson to break the color barrier at Biscayne. From the very first day of phys ed, the boys all took the measure of the best athletes and were brutally unsparing in making these assessments. Many of the black kids were simply better, and they got picked first.

And this meant that a lot of Adam's natural physical advantages had been neutralized by the hard truth that all once-segregated sporting leagues came to learn: you're only the best if you play against the best. Die-hard Babe Ruth fans know all too well that Josh Gibson of the Negro Baseball League would have made the 1930s a true home-run derby had he been allowed to play against white players in the Major Leagues. Adam Posner experienced a similar demotion on a much smaller scale. He was still good, but no longer great. The playing field had been leveled and then enlarged, and he was now just another junior high schooler in shorts. No more were his teams assured of winning, and he was no longer always the first one picked.

Busing brought equality in places where they never felt they had needed any. Those noisy, un-air-conditioned buses, and the physically gifted cargo they carried, may not have exemplified civil rights at its most exalted, but they sure taught white students lessons in humility.

But whether Adam was still the fastest in the school remained an open question in the early fall of seventh grade. And speculation around it hovered like fast-moving cloud cover. On various days and for no apparent reason, the question had its own momentum, circulating throughout the cafeteria, traveling ear-to-ear and table-to-table without skipping over any of the cliques that all seemed to take an interest: band members and potheads, Jewish princesses and soul brothers, jocks and student government leaders, and, of course, the largest circles in the Venn diagram of Biscayne's social hierarchy— whites and blacks. The intrigue and gossip would carry over to the yard behind the cafeteria, where they gathered after lunch while waiting for their teachers to claim them.

All that whispering was fairly one-sided. Clive Hankerson was widely believed to be the fastest in the school, and if the bookies for the local Jewish Mafia were taking bets in the Hankerson vs. Posner fifty-yard dash, Clive would have been heavily favored. He was three inches taller with thick thighs and well-developed forearms. And while he was only in seventh grade, he appeared to be shaving already.

"I think Hankerson has fathered a few kids," Ross said one day at lunch. "He must have been left back a few grades."

"Isn't that cheating then?" Lee asked. "If he's older, then he's bound to be faster."

"You think he's faster?" Adam asked his pals. His reputation was fading fast, faster than he could even run. Even his friends started to see him as slower of foot.

"I didn't say he was faster," Lee recovered quickly. "All I said is that if he is, then that's the reason why. He should be in high school already."

"No, he's our age," Adam said, in a resigned voice. "The guy's a beast. He runs like a racehorse."

Hankerson was sitting at another table on the other side of the cafeteria, surrounded by his own kind: black jocks, Richard Pryor cutups, and girls who wore their hair in the close-cropped pixie style of Dionne Warwick, looking back at Clive with the look of love. While he ran like a stallion, he dressed like a show horse—cool, dapper, with brown bell-bottom jeans, funky patent leather platform shoes, and a beige flowery shirt. His Afro had the Shaft-shape of dark cotton candy. His was the sort of hot dog, Mack Daddy elegance everyone came to associate with Jim Brown, Dr. J, and the Jackson 5. Most of the white kids wore their hair long and stringy as if Three Dog Night were holding open auditions, which would have been appropriate for the circumstances since the band had just had a chart-topping hit with the civil rights song "Black and White."

From across the cafeteria Hankerson and Adam would eye each other and nod. That was pretty much sign language between blacks and whites in those days: lots of head movements without actual spoken words. Occasionally, when in a friendlier mood, they'd pass one another and offer a low-hanging high-five or they'd say, "We cool, we cool." None of the white kids actually knew what that meant, and many felt uncool in saying it, as if they had been caught with an Osmond Brothers' album in their locker. In those early months of seventh grade, without crouching beside him at the starting line, that was about as close to Hankerson as Adam had gotten.

"Okay, huddle up, everybody," Coach Kesselman barked from a few feet away, and then blew his whistle as if they couldn't hear him the first time. At least he wasn't using his megaphone, gripped so tightly in his other hand like a billy club. After completing his torturous fitness ritual, they played a game of flag football, and Kesselman, who preferred bodies colliding to the finesse of merely pulling a flag, didn't like what he was seeing.

"You people block like pussies," he screamed. "Afraid to get your shirts dirty?"

He placed a salute on his forehead, squinted into the distance, and caught sight of Mr. Scott standing his familiar ground, sipping Coca-Cola by the edge of the playing field, the green wall of the school to his back, perspiration washing over him like a waterfall.

Lifting the megaphone to his face, Coach Kesselman announced to the world, "Hey, Scott, you want to come out here and show these punks how it's done? They have no technique, and they're afraid to hit! Come on, you and me, mano a mano—we'll put on a clinic. What do you say?"

Even all the girls, who were suffering through the heat and, given their age, possibly their first periods—during first period—heard Kesselman's open invitation to Mr. Scott to join in on the game, in full dress, out on the field. Already a man who was largely unmovable, Mr. Scott did not budge.

He waved away the offer with the same hand that was caressing the Coke, which jiggled free some Cola. The bottle all but disappeared in that black mitt until it caught a ray of sunlight that reflected back at Kesselman like a Navy signal lamp.

Now speaking to the boys, Kesselman announced, "That guy played college ball at Florida A&M—a black college, and he was an All-American tackle. Blocked for Bob Hayes before he went to the Olympics, before he was a Cowboy. What a waste. There's so much a guy like that can teach you. Instead he's filling your stupid heads with American history. Where does it get you in life memorizing dates, or how many electoral votes you need to get elected president?"

The phys ed class, flags dangling from their waists like Hawaiian skirts, and gasping from the heat, grateful for any time out, all glanced back at Mr. Scott. As they entered the huddle, their teacher was suddenly demystified. As quarterback it was Adam's job to call the play, but he was momentarily at a loss for button hooks, down and outs, and post patterns. All he could think about was Bob Hayes, and how his social studies teacher had opened holes and running lanes for a guy with such special speed.

Bob Hayes was known as the World's Fastest Man. He won the Olympic Gold in the 100-meter dash, setting a world record at the 1964 summer games in Tokyo. After that he played wide receiver for the Dallas Cowboys, and pretty much changed the way the game was played, mainly because before Bob Hayes entered the National Football League, wide receivers, and, in fact, most football players, were never that fast. Flankers were all lithe builds, good hands, and flat feet. No one had thought that running away from tacklers without ever being touched was a winning strategy. Bullet Bob Hayes, as he came to be known, redefined the potential of a man in motion. Hapless defensive backs were not equipped to cover the World's Fastest Man in the open field. Whenever he was playing, it was never a fair race.

"Wake up, Posner!" Kesselman screeched through his megaphone. "Where's your head? Is this how you plan on racing Hankerson—fast asleep at the starting block?"

Months later and with the misnomer of a Miami winter forcing alarmists to change from short pants to Bermuda shorts, the bell rang and social studies came to another mindless end. The class filed out of the classroom, and Mr. Scott said, "Adam, come over here for a minute." Adam had been lagging behind, and he wondered whether his delay in leaving the room now caused him to become an unwitting volunteer. Mr. Scott wasn't the type to spend much out-of-class time speaking with students. They barely ever heard his voice—even when he was teaching. The look on the faces of the class was one of utter surprise. Obviously, something was wrong.

"Yes, Mr. Scott," Adam said as he approached and laid his books on the metal desk.

"I've been watching you on the field these past few months," he began. "You move pretty well for a white boy," he said. "You got some real quickness. You know, that's better than having raw speed."

Adam smiled, but then wondered whether Mr. Scott was throwing him a backhanded compliment, as if he, too, knew that Clive Hankerson was flat-out faster, and remarking on the white boy's quickness was just his way of offering him a racial consolation prize.

"Thanks," Adam said, "but I think I've slowed down since coming to Biscayne."

"You mean that race between you and that Hankerson kid?" Mr. Scott said, smiling knowingly.

"Yeah, everyone knows about it," Adam said. "We should probably just get it over with already. Pin the medal on him now."

"Some races are not meant to be run," Mr. Scott said. "Best not to know the outcome. Don't need to know really." He paused for a moment and then said with some laughter, "I bet you never figured that busing black kids to Miami Beach would affect you so personally. There's no affirmative action when it comes to a footrace. It all comes down to the stopwatch. God, or the school board, put you and Hankerson together in this junior high school for a reason. Heck, Hankerson could have been bused to another school."

"I wish he had," Adam laughed. "Busing has ruined my life. I don't get any sleep, and I've lost my reputation as the school's fastest runner."

"That's one of the reasons I wanted to speak with you," he said. "I overheard you one day talking to your friends about the Dallas Cowboys."

"I'm probably the only Cowboys fan in the school. This is Dolphin country, you know," Adam conceded.

"Yes, but the Dolphins aren't in the Super Bowl, yet, and the Cowboys are—right here in the Orange Bowl."

The man who spoke so rarely as their teacher was now suddenly speaking—and he talked sports! No one was going to believe this. In the days before smartphone cameras, live tweets, instant updates, trending timelines on Facebook, and Instagrams, there was no way to record the unexpected moment. One had to rely on the word of strangers, and hope that what was being represented as an article of faith was not actually just a tall tale.

The Super Bowl was only in its fifth year, and Super Bowl V was being played in Miami. Today one can't tell what number the Super Bowl is without having taken Latin in college. Pro football was still new in those days. The National and American Football Leagues had only recently merged. The Super Bowl is now the biggest sporting event in the world, but in the early 1970s it was still possible to have the Super Bowl played right in your own city without everyone in town knowing about it.

"I know," Adam said. "I can't wait."

"Well, I can't get you tickets to the game, but I thought you might like to meet some of the players."

"How am I going to do that?"

"My college roommate was Bob Hayes. You know who that is, right?"

"Bullet Bob Hayes? He's my favorite player." Adam smiled. The mere mention of his name made the boy feel faster.

"I'm going to drive out later this afternoon to the hotel in Fort Lauderdale where the team is staying and see my old roommate: 'the World's Fastest Man.' Since you're a Cowboys fan, and no one else is, and since you're a sprinter of sorts, I thought it might do you some good to meet a guy who has run a lot of races in his life and won a lot of medals."

"Olympic Gold medals," Adam said.

"Damn straight," Mr. Scott said with a boastful air, "and he held world records in the 60-, 100-, and 220-yard dashes. Some of those records haven't even been broken yet. And man, you should have seen Bobby run with me out front plowing holes for him. He was a running back at A&M, and after I cracked down on the defensive end, I could hear him breezing past my hip, and he was gone."

The boy had never seen Mr. Scott so elated, so visibly happy to be at Biscayne. Of course, at that moment, he wasn't *at* school.

"You know, Mr. Scott, we see you sometimes out by the field watching us play football. You should come and toss the rock with us some time," Adam suggested.

"Nah, I'll just stick to my civics lessons and I'll leave the coaching to Coach K. He seems to be having a fine old time out there yelling at everyone and blowin' that damn whistle." Mr. Scott released a throaty laugh, originating in his stomach as a growl, which then gained momentum before escaping through his mouth with a different sound altogether.

"We heard you played at Florida A&M," Adam said. "We were afraid to ask you about it."

"Coach K. told you?"

"Yeah."

"Can't trust that man to keep a secret," he joked. "I think he was hit in the head with a shot put."

"You should tell people. Coach Kesselman said your team won the Black College National Championship."

"I sure never played against any white people, I'll tell you that. Just like you, I'm new to all this integration stuff."

"Coach Kesselman also said you didn't get drafted into the NFL, and that's why you became a teacher."

"Nothing wrong with that. As long as I wasn't drafted into Vietnam, I'm okay with not having my dance card punched for the NFL. Besides, teaching is an honest living. And I don't think I was good enough to go pro. You have to know your limits. Sometimes you reach the finish line, and there are no more finish lines in front of you."

Again Adam wondered whether Mr. Scott was sending him a message, letting him down easy, knowing that once the black students arrived at Biscayne Junior High, all former records and titles held by the home team were now up for renewal.

"So what do you say: I'll pick you up later this afternoon? But don't tell the other kids. They'll be jealous. It will be just our secret. Where do you live? And make sure your parents are fine with this."

Adam Posner's parents were virtually strangers to their own son. Their involvement in his life was minimal. How he spent his time was not their concern. There were no curfews or chores. The clothes he chose to wear, the length of his hair, what he ate, the turmoil of his intestines, was not something they monitored. He was the first latchkey kid where the home was always occupied by at least one, if not both, parents. Nothing was expected of him. He was free to do almost anything he liked except to leave—to abandon the family, replace them with a more suitable and qualified couple, to escape from their home into one where security blankets were handed out as a matter of course. He paid a high price to be their son.

All of twelve, on the eve of his bar mitzvah—that celebration of prematurely declared manhood—he desperately wanted overprotective parents, surrounding him like ambient air. There were parents who wouldn't allow their children to play tackle football. The helmets, pads, and jock cups were required for good reason. In order to play, parental permission was necessary. The Posners were always the first to sign the form. Just once Adam would have liked to see them refuse, to worry about his safety.

"I don't have to play this year, you know," Adam once baited them. "I was thinking that I might just skip the season and join some clubs at school."

"Like what, baking?" Sophie asked.

"Maybe I can learn to play the guitar?" he offered.

"Do whatever you want," Jacob said. "We rely on you."

But Adam so very wished to rely on them.

Adam was about to get into a car driven by the largest black man his parents had ever seen, driving off to Fort Lauderdale at night just so he could run around the lobby of a hotel to get the autographs of even larger black men. On sheer size and girth alone, the occupants of that hotel lobby would have scared the Gestapo and the SS into an immediate, unconditional surrender. That should have mattered to the Posners, who were Holocaust survivors, and who nearly thirty years earlier had been liberated from the concentration camps.

Liberation comes in many different forms, if it comes at all.

The upcoming Super Bowl was not something Sophie and Jacob Posner would have paid attention to, and even if they had, they would not have cared. When it came to men in uniform, there was only one team they took seriously, and it just so happens they had escaped from the tyranny of that team. All other uniforms were just colorful clothes—buttoned-down and unvarying. One thing they knew for certain: the game between the Cowboys and the Colts was wholly inconsequential. It would not result in mass murder. The worst that could happen was a concussion or a broken leg. It was just a game, after all.

"I thought it was Cowboys and Indians," Sophie said in a thick Eastern European accent that rendered her English almost as incomprehensible as that of a nineteenth-century American Indian. "And what is a Colt, a beer?"

The anticipation of this great event did not cause them to forgo all manner of parental good sense. The fact that their son was getting into a car that belonged to his social studies teacher gave them little comfort. He could have been a complete stranger and a pedophile. But they just somehow assumed that Adam would find his way back. The worst that could happen to them had already happened. They weren't likely to lose a son in sunny Florida after surviving the dark smoke that had once been the sons of other parents—without any chance of reuniting with their families. Even in a state that allowed pari-mutuel betting, what were the odds that Adam would be taken away by a black man, never to return again?

Most parents would not have taken those odds. After briefly meeting Mr. Scott, the Posners stood in the crescent driveway of their high-rise apartment building on Parkview Point, and watched as Adam got into the passenger seat of a blue Buick with a white top and white leather interior. Mr. Scott hurriedly retrieved the scattered eight-track tapes that were resting on the passenger seat—Sly and the Family Stone, Ike and Tina Turner, The Fifth Dimension.

"Hello," he said. "Get in."

He was not visibly menacing, of course. Adam wondered whether he thought that his parents were afraid of him. This joy ride between a black teacher and his white student wasn't a Huck Finn reboot. It was not intended to be a demonstration that the races could, indeed, trust one another and get along. Mr. Scott may have been a social studies teacher, but this was no sociological experiment. He wasn't trying to prove anything.

But still . . . what the hell were the Posners thinking? They were a mysterious couple, for sure, uncorked from irregular vintage. They were possessed of an inventory of dark demons. Yet, of all people surely they were aware that entrusting children to the care of strangers was never without risk.

"He is driving away with a *shvartzer*?" Jacob asked. "And such a large one."

"It's Adam's teacher," Sophie reassured him. "He is not going to eat him. Maybe he will get Adam to do more homework? We never check."

"And where are they going?"

"To see other big *shvartzers*," Sophie explained. "They are all staying at a hotel in Fort Lauderdale."

"Is there a convention?"

They both laughed. This, too, was a rare occurrence, but the uniqueness of the night demanded a change in routine. Perhaps it was just nervous laughter. Everyone was getting used to thinking about blacks in a different way. This was the kind of prejudice that came from remoteness, not animus. Color blindness might never come. But the matter would cease being simply all black and white.

In the end the Posners knew that they had yet to be betrayed by a black man; whereas the line among whites stretched to infinity. The "master race" was white, morally abhorrent, and positively genocidal. All subhumans in the twisted German imagination were actually superior. For this reason Adam's teacher—as one among the persecuted—deserved all the benefit of the doubt.

"Don't worry, Mr. and Mrs. Posner," H. T. Scott said, "I'll bring your boy home not too late."

They shook his hand as if they were sealing a deal, handing their son over to his protective custody, knowing full well that he would do a much better job of raising him than they had done so far without Mr. Scott even trying.

Adam's mother, in a light blue tennis dress that fit her far too snugly, and his father, in his signature white shorts and white polo shirt, despite their tans, always looked out of place—glaringly standing out like dead giveaways. The Posners didn't wave good-bye as the car put distance between parents and child and they receded in Mr. Scott's rearview mirror.

The drive up to Fort Lauderdale was largely silent. The teacher and his student weren't friends, after all. And they certainly were not equals. Adam was not confused by the spirit of the times. The fact that Mr. Scott was required to bus himself over to Miami Beach to teach white kids didn't mean that he worked for the kids. The teacher owed his student nothing. Adam did not expect the easy manner of their earlier conversation to continue.

Mr. Scott commandeered the big Buick as if he were riding a tricycle, so overwhelmingly did his size contrast with other objects. Adam was amazed at how much of his body filled the space on the windshield, as if he were both driver and passenger. The boy's presence in the front seat barely registered.

Finally, somewhere along I-95, Mr. Scott began quietly, "I saw some numbers on your mother's forearm when we shook hands. I know what that means."

Adam's parents never discussed their past as refugees from Hitler's murderous Europe. And they deliberately chose not to associate with other survivors.

"It is better we should stay away from those who know what we know," Sophie said.

"Yes, better to blend in," Jacob added, which perhaps explained why he always wore white tennis clothes—the official attire of the aged and retired— even though he had never been on a tennis court and wouldn't exactly know what goes on between those rectangular lines.

There existed such communities of the once half-dead who believed that the rebuilding of lives was possible. Adam's parents, who would never buy into such rosy propaganda, remained apart—even from each other.

There was irony in that it had taken forced desegregation for Adam to find someone who also knew of injustice. No one else had ever remarked upon his unspoken legacy.

"Is that why you run so fast, Adam?" Mr. Scott asked. "Because if that's the reason, I think I understand."

"I don't know," Adam replied. "I just thought I inherited my parents' legs."

"Not only their legs," Mr. Scott, a college jock, said, "but the things they saw that made them run."

"I'm not sure I get what you mean," Adam said, although what he had just been told was probably true.

Mr. Scott didn't reply. It wasn't his place to speak so intimately about something so foreign to even his own peoples' pain.

They rolled up under the canopy of the stately hotel and an attendant raced toward the driver's side to park Mr. Scott's car. The Cowboys and their fans were apparently good tippers. Gargantuan men folded themselves out of rental cars like Russian wooden dolls, or surprises inside industrial boxes of Cracker Jacks. The car attendants were forced to ram the bucket seats forward so far, they looked like they had just hopped upon a child booster chair in a restaurant.

"Don't get lost," Mr. Scott warned, as they entered the lobby through separate sleeves of a rotating door. "I'll go up for a while to visit with Bobby, and then I'll bring him down to meet you."

Adam was not the only kid in the lobby. In fact, the place was swarming with autograph vultures of all ages, including groupies and divorcees looking to add their own monograms to a Dallas Cowboy's bathroom towel. Pro football players bulged out of pleated dress slacks and button-down short-sleeve shirts. They were ordering drinks at the bar, or just sitting in the lobby, or trying to fend off hangers-on with the same jukes used on Sundays for oncoming tacklers.

There were former pro football legends like Otto Graham, and players who had yet to become stars, like Roger Staubach, and players no one recognized outside of their uniforms but who still belonged in the lobby. There were porters, cocktail waitresses, media people, and guests staying in the hotel just to attend the Super Bowl. The racial diversity was apparent. Only a few years earlier this place would have been whites only.

Adam didn't come for signatures. Adam didn't want a memento. He knew he would never forget this day and no souvenir could make it any more memorable. Besides, he had already promised that he would never tell anyone at school that he was even on this impromptu field trip. What he came for would not leave evidence, and it didn't require that he bring anything back either.

One of the elevator doors opened and out walked Mr. Scott with two other black men of similar but not quite as hefty size. With their towering height and the color of their skin, they looked like three tall oil wells ready to gush. One of them was Bob Hayes, with his sprinter's strut, even fully clothed. Adam could tell from the wide mouth and expansive smile, the massive shoulders and biceps that bulged from a tight-fitting red polo shirt, that this was Bullet Bob Hayes. Even in his days as a track and field sprinter, he was always more muscular than the other runners at the starting line. And his explosive burst to the finish line, muscles twitching and striations rippling like an energy grid, gave new meaning to horsepower.

Mr. Scott pointed toward Adam and then he and the other fellow—

Hayes's roommate, cornerback Cornell Green—made their way to the bar as Bullet Bob approached Adam, slowly, as if he wanted the young boy to have a good look, as if he knew Adam was framing it all in slow motion—an athlete usually a blur in motion was suddenly arrested in time and held suspended in memory. The World's Fastest Man apparently had an arsenal of different speeds at his disposal, always ready with a new unexpected gear.

Nearly reaching Adam, he said, "You're one of Horace's students, right?"

"Yes, that's me. I'm Adam."

"You're that Jew boy?"

"Huh," Adam said, his face contorted as if he were sucking on a sour ball. "Yes, I'm Jewish. Why?"

"I didn't mean anything by that," he explained. "It's just who you are. I was once a black boy. Now I'm Bob Hayes. You know what I mean?"

"I think so," Adam replied, even though he really didn't.

"Horace tells me you're a football player and a sprinter, too. You're pretty good?"

"Well, I guess for a Jew boy," Adam replied.

Hayes laughed. His big teeth, the size of mahjong tiles and as white as bathroom tiles, brought a smile to Adam's tiny mouth filled with Chiclets teeth.

"That's unusual," he said. "I never heard of a Jewish sprinter before."

"There's Mark Spitz," Adam replied.

"I'm not talking about the pool," Hayes said. "On land. Where the brothers race."

"I think there was some guy in England who won the 100 meters at the Olympic Games back in 1924."

"What was his time?"

"A lot slower than yours," Adam conceded.

"Damn right. I'd woop his Jewish ass." Hayes grew a bit reflective, and then asked, "Any of your kind playing in the NFL?"

"I think Ron Mix is Jewish," Adam said, wondering why this game of Jewish Jeopardy was so fascinating to Bullet Bob.

"Yeah, that Mix is a big mother, but that's one slow white boy though."

He made himself laugh again. The muscles in his chest throbbed like water brought to a boil.

"If you're Bob Hayes," Adam said, "isn't everyone slower than you?"

"I suppose that's right," he said. "I hear you got some black kids in your class this year. Bused over from the other side of town."

"Yeah."

"You know, this thing between the races isn't over. And I'm talking about blacks and whites, not footraces. It's never going to be made right. Can't really force equality. You can bus kids over, but you can never bus away all those prejudices that were always there and will always be there—from both sides. It's just about the people coming together, getting to know each other. Hell, I didn't know that many white people until I went to the Olympics. Now I do. I like some of them. And I don't like some black people. You get what I'm saying?"

"I think I do," Adam replied.

"Jewish people helped blacks in the South. I know about that," he said, and then, with a plaintive look, he continued, "Horace and I had a Jewish teacher at A&M, Professor Leiblich. He taught us world history. He meant a lot to us, and we knew that he fought for civil rights in Montgomery and Selma, and he was with the Freedom Rides. Horace loved him; maybe became a teacher because of him. He was Jewish, Professor Leiblich was, from Poland, if I remember right. He was in one of those death camps. You know about those?"

"Yes, but not much," Adam replied, like a child of royal blood slumming among the unwashed riffraff—pretending that he didn't possess the lineage of the mass dead. He knew little of those camps even though he was born among the ruins and from the ruined.

"He died a few months ago," Hayes said. A tear rolled out of one of his eyes, and Adam followed it all the way down his face. "I didn't know about it. Horace just told me. That's sad news. He sent me a nice letter after the Tokyo Olympics. That was the last time I heard from him."

Adam was only in seventh grade, but he suddenly felt that he belonged in that lobby, even if he hadn't been a Dallas Cowboys fan.

"Blacks and Jews on the same team, isn't that something?" Hayes said, gathering himself and then searching for his two roommates—the one from college, and the one from the pros. "Now get out of here. I hope to read about you one day: Best Jewish Athlete in the World."

Adam smiled shyly. "That doesn't sound as good as the World's Fastest Man, but it would still be pretty cool."

Later that night, as they were driving back to Miami Beach, road signs on I-95 flipping by like a deck of shuffled cards, the quiet in the car seemed even more still. It had been a long day. Surprisingly, Mr. Scott didn't ask Adam what Bob Hayes had said. And Adam didn't ask him what it was like to see his college teammate who in a few days would be playing in the Super Bowl. Mr. Scott steered his big Buick in front of the Posners' apartment building just after 11 p.m. as the headlights from a circling van flashed his face and Adam saw his tired eyes and a melancholy expression that he had not noticed before. Adam was familiar with sadness. The Posners manufactured it in their home, and they worked around the clock. But they never thought to export it elsewhere. A monopoly is what they were after. Adam wondered whether Mr. Scott had accidentally gotten too close to his family, whether they were now somehow responsible for the decline in his mood.

It was for this reason that Adam opened the passenger door quickly. He still had time to get away, to spare his teacher from overexposure to the Posner pain. An unsavory whiff is all it took. As he got out of the car and before closing the door he looked back and said, "Don't worry, Mr. Scott. I won't tell anyone where we were tonight."

"Go to sleep, Adam," he said. "And say good night to your parents."

Adam's parents weren't waiting up. In the morning he told them that Mr. Scott had said hello, and that he recognized the numbers on his mother's arm.

Sophie seemed embarrassed, and instantly yanked her left arm and placed it under her blouse as if she had been caught stealing or the black man had caught a glimpse of her in the nude. She had hoped that Florida's sun would have long ago tanned over those digits, making them unintelligible. But a street savvy civics teacher had caught her, not red-handed but blue-forearmed.

Jacob, stroking the puff of a gray beard on his chin, said, "Of course he would. Numbers is how you brand cattle, and slaves—not people. This is the South. They know about such uncivilized things, and your teacher is black."

■

Adam was true to his promise: he never told his friends about any of this. But a few days later, after lunch while standing outside on the field waiting for their teachers to line them up and march them back to class, Lee had gotten himself in a fight with Tommy Jenkins, one of Clive Hankerson's friends. Adam ran over and helped separate the pile of white and black kids who had jumped on top of one another. Biscayne Junior High looked as though it had turned its experiment in racial integration into a violent game of pick-up sticks. An old-fashioned New York City rumble was resurrected in a Miami Beach schoolyard—minus the chain link fence, the barking dogs, and the obligatory Officer Krupke.

"Okay, let's settle this shit right now," Lee shouted, spittle flying from his mouth, his blond hair pasted to his head and a red welt on his cheek as a few kids pulled him away like an opened parachute.

"You think you're so bad, white boy?" Jenkins asked, restrained by his own friends in a section of the field where dust got kicked up and for a moment clouded his rage.

Whatever racial peace they had tried to make during the first few months had frayed badly. As winter approached, the heat was subsiding, yet, these heated exchanges became more common. The black kids began to feel more comfortable on the white kids' turf without permission. A turf war became inevitable.

Adam walked over to Clive Hankerson and pulled him aside.

"Let's race, fifty-yard dash—right here, right now, you and me. Come on."

Hankerson's puzzled look suggested that he found white people to be the most inscrutable race on Earth. "Why? Why now? Why here?" he asked.

Adam reached out and laid a hand on Hankerson's right shoulder, a gesture he wasn't sure he appreciated. "It'll be a lot safer for everyone," Adam began, "if we just race each other and get it over with. This is mostly between us anyway. It's better than everyone beating the crap out of each other."

"They're not fighting over us," he reasoned. "If they all want to fight, let 'em fight."

"Hey, it's time, man—don't you want to know?"

"Posner, I already know," Hankerson said, raising his voice. "What I don't understand is, What's in it for you? We don't have to do this thing.

We could just keep 'em all guessing. No one has to know. Shit, we already know how it is. The winner won't win anything. And I know, because I'll win."

Everyone gathered around as Ross Adler and Chad Johnson, another one of Hankerson's entourage, counted off the fifty yards and drew start and finish lines with their feet in the parched dirt.

All the students mixed in together to the left and right of this improvised track on this most impoverished of fields. Back in the 1930s, in the early days of Miami Beach, Biscayne Junior High and its surrounding ball fields was known as Polo Park, where the rich Gatsbys came to play before hurricanes and the Great Depression gave Miami Beach yet another mandate for a makeover. Along the perimeter of the school there had been a commemorative statue of a polo player leaning down from his saddle, about to strike the ball with his mallet. At some point over the years that arm with the mallet had broken off, as if to signal that this schoolyard now entertained a very different kind of ruling class. It also curiously gave the school a handicapped polo player as a mascot, which suited so many of the students, who came from either broken homes or who were themselves simply broken.

Ross yelled, "Ready, on your marks!" Chad screamed: "Get set!" And they both joined in to signal to the runners: "Go!"

Clive Hankerson and Adam Posner gave each other one last look before the locomotion of their legs dug into the dirt, their arms began to swing like slingshots, and they pushed themselves to sprint a relatively short distance for a race that would be over in less than seven seconds. The sounds of cheering junior high schoolers pierced through the heavy air, the very same air that Adam and his adversary sucked in like deep-sea snorkelers taking one final plunge. Right off the line Hankerson claimed the lead, his powerful legs churning and pounding the turf, but Adam caught up by the midpoint, only to fall back a few strides yet again.

The overhead midday sun was beaming down on them like a spotlight, and as Adam gritted out the final twenty yards, he saw in the young crowd the essence of what it meant to be easily swayed. Already their commitment to a side had lost its fierceness and energy. They were cheering for a blur. Adam glimpsed Coach Kesselman, megaphone in hand at the ready, smiling off in the distance. And there was Ross, his body always configured in a right angle, leaning horizontally at the finish line as if he were the true tale of the tape. Even from that awkward position he pleaded for Adam to pick up the pace. And in their final strides Adam observed Mr. Scott swilling a Coca-Cola in his familiar bleacher seat against the wall, kicking back in the blazing sun, nodding his head in approval, sensing the tide of history turn in this tropical backwater, another day closer to a more satisfying finish.

Four

Gimpel of Surfside

When walking upright began to define the human species, running—with fleetness and determination—was the mode of action that signaled urgency, whether it was hunting an animal, eluding a tackler, catching a bus, or outrunning a cop. Running was the very next step after shouting, "Fire!" the best physical evidence of leaving in a hurry. To run was to avoid crisis. Why else would anyone bother working up such a sweat?

In 1972, the running boom, as it was called, was still several years away.

Of course, in 1972 many acts of locomotion that would later come to mean something else hardly existed at all. Jane Fonda was known as an Academy Award-winning actress and as "Hanoi Jane," the anti-Vietnam War agitator—"aerobics" and "aerobics instructors," as terms of art, and her bestselling workout tapes, were very much unknown quantities back then. "Pumping iron" was the province of a future California governor and foreign bodybuilder who mangled his English while deadlifting barbells. "Cardio" sounded more like a wristwatch than something that was actually good for you. Cardiologists were the boogeymen of the medical profession, so no one would have thought that cardio was anything but a fateful warning.

"Gym" was a dreaded class at school. The gym teacher at Biscayne Junior High, Coach Kesselman, was the epitome of physical fitness carried too far. The man's chest arrived to every destination two minutes before the rest of him; his bullhorn, whistle, and other penal colony instruments served his ego to no end and cemented "gym" as a dirty word in the lexicon of a generation of Miami Beach boys.

A "gym" was also what Angelo Dundee, a fight manager, maintained on 5th Street, just off the beach on Washington Avenue, and it was used exclusively for boxing. Inside there were no treadmills, rowing machines, stationary bicycles, kettle bells, or exercise devices of any kind—just sweaty men punching body bags or each other in the head with great force. Occasionally, a boxer would fall and hit the canvas so hard, it was a wonder anyone lived to fight another day.

Dundee often barked at Muhammad Ali, who had only recently returned to the ring after losing his belt not to a fighter but to the United States draft board. If he could fight heavyweights for large purses, surely he could fight the Viet Cong for America. His refusal to do the latter resulted in him being stripped of his world championship belt. Ali never claimed to be an American patriot; he was a gladiator and mercenary—but the government took away his title anyway.

"Keep moving, Muhammad, keep moving," Dundee said from the corner of the ring. He was crouched down, forming his own cocoon as if it were he who was trying to avoid getting hit and not his famous fighter. "Let me see you rope-a-dope. That's it, now float like a butterfly, yes . . . then sting like a bee."

Dundee's 5th Street Gym looked like hell and smelled like, well, a gym—with socks and underwear that could nearly stand by themselves so pungent was the unsavory, unwashed admixture of sweat and salt.

Tennis was for many the exercise of choice on Miami Beach. One of the local rabbis, Sheldon Vered, a swashbuckling survivor of those German death camps, had a serve and forehand smash that sizzled over the net like asteroids from Auschwitz. He would usually hustle a few games against unsuspecting tourists who mistook his yarmulke as a sign of easy prey instead of the religious charade and sucker punch that it actually was. Almost everyone else played doubles, which drastically reduced the amount of running and any pretenses of a sport, where an hour of tennis became a foursome of friendly gossip.

Walking was what one did after dinner, but even that was done sparingly and not for too long. It was hot in Miami Beach, after all. All year round hot. Unwaveringly hot. Chokingly hot. Fucking hot! So relentless and unsparing was the sun on these largely northern transplants that they occasionally cursed their season-less lot, the blood red mercury temperature that made Miami nearly uninhabitable. Conversations all along Collins Avenue sounded pretty much like this:

"Our whole lives depend on air conditioning," a grumpy senior citizen would initiate the protest.

"It's either freezing inside or an oven outside!" came a familiar lament.

"And the humidity is like a Russian bathhouse. Who can live like this?" asked a snowbird who obviously had missed her flight back to Great Neck.

"What I wouldn't give for a pleasant afternoon in the Catskills where I used to vacation before these Sirens from Miami lured me down with their false advertising about paradise," said a wistful refugee, not from Europe but the Borscht Belt.

"Paradise, *feh*," replied his friend, who usually offered up words no more meaningful than "feh," because every Jew had a not-so-bright friend who contributed little to the conversation other than restating what had already been said. Pearls of wisdom rarely washed up on the shores of Miami Beach; the oyster shells were all empty.

"Paradise shouldn't require so much body armor—the hats, the glasses, the lotions, the bug spray, the constant reminders to drink more water. All this Miami *mishugas*, and for what?" came a remark from a retired year-rounder for whom overdoses of Florida's sunshine left him feeling like a survivor of nuclear waste contamination. Solar power was unknown at the time. The sun was an energy drain, not an energy source.

"Jackie Gleason—that lying bastard!" said the self-styled comedian of the bunch, who wasn't appreciably any funnier than the others. They were all a bunch of jokers, smart alecks, and kibitzers. "This isn't the 'sun and fun capital of the world'; it's the smoke and mirrors capital, where things aren't what they seem with all the squinting we do when we're outside."

There was golf, of course, but most Jews on Miami Beach were professional duffers. Like kvetching construction crews, they took to the fairways leaving moon-sized divots as evidence of their handicaps, which rose much higher than the anemic Dow Jones Industrial Averages of those days. A par five was an adventure in higher math; and all those strokes brought on too many actual strokes. When it came right down to it, golf in Miami Beach had very little to do with woods and wedges, putters and colorful pants. It was simply Jews being forced into taking a walk.

The Cubans, who had only recently arrived on Florida's jutting peninsula a mere ninety miles north of their beloved Havana, at least knew enough about the tropics to take afternoon naps to avoid the mind-numbing heat. Everyone else wore wide-brimmed floppy hats and slathered themselves with zinc oxide, Johnson's baby oil, Coppertone sun-tanning lotion, or whatever basting device was fashionable at the time. Some Cubans were adventurous swimmers, the desire to escape Castro's communism so great that they risked almost certain death by trying to float on inner tubes all the way to Key West.

The other water sports of note were surfing and water skiing. Surfing, of course, required big waves, and the tepid Atlantic Ocean that far south produced swells no more gnarly than what you get in a Jacuzzi. And since water skiing required a boat, there were few takers. Most people who owned boats on Miami Beach rarely allowed them to leave the dock. They were largely decorative, something to admire while sitting comfortably amid conditioned air in Florida rooms separated by Venetian doors. Boats were expensive baubles to Jews, floating trophies, more ornamental than oceanic. Boats on Miami Beach were a lot like swimming pools—part of the landscaping, but most people were apparently afraid to get wet. Very few Jewish boat owners knew for certain whether they had an inboard or outboard motor.

For all the pretenses of a city that celebrated outdoor life, much of the days, especially during summer, were spent serenely in ambient air conditioning. Actually, staying indoors, or inside a car, was a survival strategy, an art form, and a favorite pastime of the people of Miami Beach, most of whom, frankly, couldn't take the heat.

All except for Jacob Posner, a mild-mannered man of European refinement, silenced by circumstances that left him nearly catatonic, who took to the outdoors and its fiery temperature like a guileless wilderness survival guide—fearless of both melanoma and sunstroke. His daily uniform was simple and practical for the climate: white shorts, a white polo shirt, and white shoes that were on the far side of a sneaker. He was the sort of person who believed that a human being can never get enough camouflage in his life. White was the color of choice for those wishing to blend into the bleached palette of the tropics.

He was a slight man with a beard on his chin and thinning dark hair that retained its color despite his advanced age. In his short pants the contours of his calves extended from his shin like satellite dishes. He was nearly seventy years old in a city where the temperature and the average age of its senior citizens lined up like algebraic equations. Nearly everyone was retired and at life's twilight. Social Security was the meal ticket du jour. Wizened was a local fashion statement. Early bird dinners were so ubiquitous it was pointless to announce them. The city's night owls were comprised entirely of tourists and gangsters—the locals were long asleep. At times it looked as though the entire city couldn't hold down a job.

Jacob Posner's skin was a baked brown, with liver spots on his forehead, deep-ridged crows feet that resembled a plowed field, and a bald spot that gave the sun a moving target whenever he was outside. And he was always outside—a walking man, regularly in motion and on the move. He would bound the city streets of Miami Beach like an absent-minded beat cop who couldn't keep to his own beat. For all that purported forward motion, he generally went nowhere in particular, making odd pedestrian patterns, crossing over those small walking bridges that served as canopies for the canals, then making abrupt turns as if eluding a tail, keeping his watchers off guard even though no one was watching over him. He was his very own Venn diagram.

Jacob was a walker on a small island where outdoor excursions were regarded as foolish. He seemed to be the only one who ventured out willingly, longingly even, staying out as late as possible—even after dark. And if this wasn't enough to distinguish him from the card playing, mahjong clapping, porch and terrace hugging, frigidly air-conditioned crowd, there was the matter of his locomotion, which barely qualified as movement at all. Babies took more elongated, ambitious steps. One of Jacob's strides followed by another advanced him so little, and in such slow motion, it was as if he weres moon walking in Miami.

Jacob moved as if he were walking a plank, as if each tiny step brought him closer to his own execution. And at times his movements had the markings of reckless abandon. Cars honked as he crossed streets, unmindful of red lights. Those who knew him waved from their car windows, even calling out his name, and yet received no reply. Standing right in front of them he nonetheless appeared to be elsewhere, which was probably true. Where he was, however, no one could possibly know.

He squinted through eyes that had already seen too much, which only magnified the fuzzy, wary impression that he perceived in the people around him. In fact, perhaps as a protective device, his eyes were locked in a permanent squint, as if he were always in a plausible state of denial. Unseeing is, by definition, uncomprehending. Honking cars could blow a gasket for all he cared. Those offering him rides were better off without him, he felt. They just didn't know it. How could they?

He walked through summer downpours that were brief in duration but positively ferocious in their tropical fury. Rain pellets struck sidewalks and windshields as if Miami Beach were under gunfire. Thunder shook the sky like Apollo liftoffs from Cape Kennedy. The skies blackened with cloud cover that hung low overhead. Petrified Little Leaguers dressed in thick gray cotton pants stood motionless in the outfield as if the clouds were close enough to suck them up into the sky. Such downpours and hell raisings in heaven had the effect of bridging the distance between man and nature. They were awe producing, and they were also so close, which made them appear very much of this world, unlike volcano eruptions and earthquakes. Purple nimbus halos of rain and streaking bands of thunderous light rippled through the sky with the brashness and drama of a Hollywood premier.

Jacob walked right through those weather patterns fearlessly while everyone else properly knew that it was time to find shelter. Perhaps he more than anyone knew that for lightning to strike twice in the same lifetime would violate the laws of nature and upset all the random odds that occupied his wife, a part-time gangster and gambler. After all, he survived the forests of Europe as a partisan and escaped from a concentration camp as a mere number; what could a little rain and a bolt of lightning add to what was already a formidable survivalist résumé?

Yet, the better question to ask, the one that most people on Miami Beach wondered aloud was, What kind of fool would voluntarily walk desolate, baking streets, without a hat or sunglasses, and with all sorts of friendly motorists slowing down to offer him a ride? What kind of fool doesn't know when it's time to come out from under the rain, that lightning foreshadows thunderous booms for a reason: it's too dangerous to be anywhere within its electromagnetic sight? What can be said of such a person other than that he is, in fact, a fool?

No one else in all of Miami Beach maintained the same habits or displayed a similar un-tropical quirkiness. And that's why in time "The Walking Man of Miami Beach," as Jacob Posner came to be known, began to blend into the scenery like an iguana camouflaged within the wild foliage of Florida. After a while everyone simply took it for granted that Jacob Posner was making his rounds, or figure eights, or alternating right angles, or down and outs. It was all too hard to follow and even harder to comprehend, so senseless were his walkabouts on Miami Beach. Jacob Posner became just another fixture of the city, a curious old man with a most unusual South Florida gait, best left alone. There was no reason to notice him anymore, and even less reason to pity him.

Which suited Jacob Posner just fine. After all, these walks, while they kept everyone else guessing, were not without meaning, despite what these sun-poisoned provincials wanted to believe. The walks enabled a flowing rhythm to Jacob's inner world, a runway that kept his thoughts moving freely—even though his actual steps were glacial by comparison. Walking was like truth serum; that which can't be said behind closed doors found freedom on the road, even if it functioned as yet another attempt at covering up.

He didn't share any of these thoughts with others, not even his own family—particularly his own family. Adam, his son, must never know. Sophie, his wife, was beyond the capacity to take in more bad news. And, as he long feared, she was already insane; it's just that no one on Miami Beach had figured that out yet—least of all that lecherous Meyer Lansky, who was using his wife's brain and steely spine to help him win back his criminal empire. The contents that Jacob had been storing in his head, those relived and yet sequestered memories, were most definitely not for public consumption. The only person who ever heard his survivor's lament, his brief filed against God, his recitation of memories that could scare away any ghost, was I. B.—his literary confidante, unofficial shrink, truth-teller, and like-minded refugee.

There was so much to think about, after all, and so much to repress. There wasn't enough time in the day, or enough navigable streets in all of Miami Beach. It took work to train the mind to consign those memories to the very back of the recall line, to create a new hierarchy of remembrances, to essentially manufacture new memories just for the sake of keeping the old ones at bay. Imagine the stamina and self-delusion required to put strategic space between what is best forgotten and what must be remembered. It's an exhausting enterprise, and an island seven miles long and a mile wide doesn't offer enough *lebensraum* to finish the job. No wonder Jacob Posner never bothered to notice the people saying hello to him, or trying to avoid running him over. The Walking Man was busy—and not just with walking.

His son, Adam, was, by no small coincidence, a runner. The running boom had not yet sounded, but that didn't stop freakish joggers in their tracks from running around parks, along the beach, or, in some extreme cases, right on the streets. Both father and son had little in common, spoke very few words to each other, and yet shared this one Posner compulsion—stay out of the apartment, and on the streets, in motion, as long as possible. They each took a set of keys, nodding to the other, and then out the door. Moving at different speeds, they headed to the exact same indeterminate destination. Neither had a map in their minds, just escape plans. Adam relied on the road to clear his own head of things that twelve-year-old boys should never have to think about. Running seemed to be a panacea for all that silence within the Posner home—the damaged parents, the nightmares that awoke the household, and even the dead, and all that strange behavior far too extreme to qualify as merely idiosyncratic. Weirdness everywhere else was downright conventional by comparison. Silence was the family tongue, avoidance the shared obsession.

Father and son moved on parallel tracks while crisscrossing different avenues. They made abrupt turns, but not toward each other. They circled one another without either of them knowing it, but yet never intersected. It was a game of tag without the touching, hide-and-seek without any apparent hiding. They were the only two people out on the streets using their legs for transportation, and yet they improbably never ran into one another. It was as if their destiny was to remain apart, each maneuvering the same Miami Beach maze without the slightest sense of wonder about how they never managed to collide. Two magnets in a constant state of repelling one another.

Adam ran, but never left the island, never pushed himself to pass over into a neighboring peninsula. How could he? He was only twelve, after all. He was mature enough to be trusted to raise himself, to nearly be the head of the Posner household. But the world doesn't credit hard knocks as a basis for legal emancipation. And his parents, who never noticed him, still depended on him. They needed to be reassured that, unlike what had happened to them on the European side of the Atlantic Ocean, Miami Beach would protect them from the murdering kind. South Florida would become a safe haven by default. Whatever they loved could not be taken away from this beach. They were refugees who had finally found refuge.

Of course, they didn't really believe that. Their son, however, was determined to fool them with all manner of false assurances. And the best way to accomplish that was to stay put. Running away from home was not an option because he could not be the cause of any further loss. Each day as he took to the streets and headed toward a causeway or a bridge, he ended up turning around and returning to the site of all that shared misery. The roads that he ran never brought him to any forks, only a series of U-turns.

Jacob Posner, however, did have a route in mind, although a ridiculously circuitous one. It had an end point, but he changed the coordinates each day. Changing the pass codes and covering one's tracks was the specialized tradecraft of the partisan fighter. All trails must be untraceable—even on Miami Beach.

And, yet, on most days they ended in Surfside, that small township at the northern tip of Miami Beach. It was there that Jacob Posner's slow moving feet came to rest, specifically, at Danny's Restaurant on Harding Avenue, a nondescript coffee shop only a dozen years removed from its more glamorous days as the Brook Club Gambling Casino, which was owned by the Jewish mob. Jacob knew that his wife would have been interested in the joint back then. Mediocre deli meant nothing to her; high-stakes craps did.

Danny's Restaurant had become Jacob Posner's hangout in 1972, the meeting place for his rendezvous with a baked apple and with Isaac Bashevis Singer, the world's best-known Yiddish writer, future Nobelist, and overall Jewish raconteur.

It was only with I. B., known by his initials, to whom Jacob spoke. Not a word was uttered elsewhere on Miami Beach. But once over the border into neighboring Surfside, Jacob Posner sang like a paid confidential informant. The otherwise mute Walking Man, upon his arrival at Danny's, became a regular canary in a mineshaft called Auschwitz.

I. B. and Jacob sat at a booth, but it might as well have been a confession booth. Jacob would order his baked apple, or raisin pudding, and wipe off his drenched forehead with as many napkins as he could rip out of the dispenser. The sidewall of the booth was mirrored, and he checked his reflection quickly as if his very existence was always in doubt. He had long known that Miami Beach was one great optical illusion. Perhaps its cousin, Surfside, was worse.

By then I. B. had usually already ordered. He was a resident of Surfside who spent hours at Danny's each day in the same manner in which he used to inhabit the Garden Cafeteria in the Lower East Side of Manhattan, where a community of Jewish intellectuals once existed, arguing over everything from the political virtues of socialism and Zionism, to the literary comparisons between Tolstoy and Proust. So much of the fare on Danny's menu was *trayf*, in keeping with a very different set of kosher principles that I. B., as a strict vegetarian, lived by. But he, too, enjoyed a baked apple, or a cheese strudel, and multiple cups of hot tea—even in the Florida heat—a sugar cube placed between his teeth as a filtering, sweetening device.

He ordered little, and yet he reserved the most scenic booth and occupied it throughout the season for much of the day. The owners of the establishment had considered charging him rent. But there was value in having such an esteemed man of Yiddish letters sitting in their restaurant cautiously avoiding the alphabet soup because of its chicken broth. And so there he sat much of the day, with a notepad and fountain pen, scribbling notes like a detective, observing the apparently famished faces in the crowd.

But Jacob Posner was his favorite subject, and so I. B. invited him to sit at his table, a courtesy he extended to no one else. It would become almost a daily ritual for the both of them—a codependency between artist and subject. Despite what they jokingly referred to as a secret pact—Indian brothers bonded in Jewish blood—Jacob didn't seem to mind that his darkest truths were likely to resurface as plot points and character defects in I. B.'s fiction. In fact, it was all but guaranteed that Jacob had become a stand in for so many of the male Jewish refugees that I. B. had conjured for his many novels. I. B. politely borrowed from Jacob's uncensored testimony, and spun it into literary gold.

I. B. was a small, owlish man with a prominent nose and forehead, long boney fingers, and an all-knowing smile that was both devilish and endearing. His skin was a milky shade of translucent white, very uncommon for a man living in Surfside, but not for someone who barely went outside and never without a hat. His eyes were a rough cobalt blue that softened and changed color in the light.

Jacob Posner was a most complicated, morally compromised Jew, which was I. B.'s métier and stock-in-trade. Fallen Jews, foolish Jews, corrupted Jews, unflattering Jews, Jews with dirty thoughts—were the *only* characters that interested his literary imagination. And for this reason many serious-minded Jews speculated why I. B. was the best-known Yiddish writer in the world. In 1972 the film adaptation to Philip Roth's raunchy and hilarious novel *Portnoy's Complaint* opened in theaters, and anyone sizing up the literary scene in those days could have properly wondered why only perverted Jews seemed to be of interest to the literary elite.

"So what do you have to tell me today, my good friend Jacob?" I. B. said, as he usually did at the beginning of these sessions. It was his gentle way of luring him in. The Yiddish accent was dense and unmistakable, with w's that were transformed into v's. Most sentences were punctuated with up-lifted shoulder blades, as if all periods merited a shrug. "Vhat are you valking avay from today?" is what I. B. said, and how it sounded.

I. B.'s stories were translated from the original Yiddish into English beginning in the early 1950s. Prior to that his readers were dwindling with each passing year, as the birth of the State of Israel elevated Hebrew as the language of the Jewish people. Without English translations of his work, I. B. would have disappeared like so many other writers and poets who had the misfortune of writing in a language on life support. It took a few decades before he became widely known in America. At that point, *Playboy* started calling, not for his physical body but for his bawdy fiction. This Polish Jew was absolutely filthy—X-rated, indecent, unfit for a chaste readership. He worked almost entirely in blue like a burlesque short story writer. And he fit in so nicely in feverish, hot-blooded Florida, which proved to be a most hospitable breeding ground for degenerate Jews—whether they were adulterers, mobsters, or borderline pornographers. With a magazine known for its naked women and lewd centerfolds solidly behind him, it was only another six years before he would be awarded the Nobel Prize for Literature.

What were the Swedes thinking? If that isn't winning the Jewish jackpot, then what is?

While Yiddish speaking and artistically inclined men loathed I. B., he did have an expansive readership among Jewish women. Indeed, married women were especially infatuated with him, largely because of the sizzling sex he depicted and the license he seemed to be granting Jewesses to be as sinful as their newly liberated American counterparts. In his stories fidelity was faithless, and sex among the refugees was so plentiful and enticing, one would have thought that the migration to America—with all that sacrifice and hardship—was undertaken only so as to offer these young Yiddish-speaking, traumatized Jews an easier way to get laid than they had ever experienced back home.

There was no getting around the paradox that of all things on God's greenhorn Earth, it was sex that I. B. was peddling in translated Yiddish—not the purity of Judaism, but the depravity of its people. The *mamaloshen* of the Jews was being exploited by the master of the Yiddish short story in a way that vaguely suggested a mother's tongue could be used for something other than speech.

"Any new thoughts on the dark demons and dybbuks that won't let you sleep?" I. B. asked slyly, like tossing chum into a shark tank. "Tell me, Jacob. Tell me everything you had to do to survive, which now shames you to no end. Last time we met you told me how many men you had to kill, and how you remember all of their faces."

I. B. was not a survivor. He couldn't have known the inner world of the concentration camps or the moral sacrifices of the survivors. I. B. was a refugee, for sure, but the other kind—those who came *before* World War II, which was a very different world, indeed. The immigrant's tale before the war was an Ellis Island opportunity grab—rags to riches and eventually, in the imagination of I. B., corruption and smut.

After World War II the Statue of Liberty got a good look at the *truly* wretched—the survivors of a genocide who cried out for both asylum and a sanatorium. I. B. belonged to the first group, but was fascinated by the second one. He knew that literary luck had spared him; had he remained in Warsaw rather than follow his older brother to New York, he would no doubt have been killed in the ghetto or in a death camp. He possessed the skills of turning sentences around and observing humankind in its most debased state. But that skill set would have been useless in Treblinka where wile and fortitude were essential elements of a survivor's repertoire. Short stories were useless amid all those shortened lives.

The violinists, poets, and painters all died—and died almost instantly. I. B. saw in Jacob Posner the quick instincts and short fuse of those Jewish toughs whom he recalled from his childhood in Warsaw. They walked along Krochmalne Street with the fearless self-assurance more common to Odessa's Jewish gangsters. The Polish Jew was a less volatile breed. Most would not have allowed themselves the swagger and cunning that Jacob would one day turn into a means of survival. And that's how and why he remained alive. But did he survive? I. B. was obsessed with the damaged lives of such "survivors." He saw in them the greatest defiance of God's warped sense of humor. And he came to realize that preserving sanity in the aftermath of Auschwitz was, in some ways, a trickier undertaking than surviving the camps themselves.

"And how is the boy doing?" I. B. asked. "Still not speaking to him, forcing him to find out the family history all by himself? There is cruelty in that, you know. You are his father, and he should know where he comes from—a family legacy written in smoke."

I. B. wore a suit and tie in sunny Surfside, one of the few who maintained the look of a Yiddish intellectual, even in brain-dead Miami Beach. He luxuriated in the dissonance of refined Europeans coexisting with all the beach bums and platinum blondes. He was often seen wearing felt hats— fedoras and porkpies—and holding on to a cane or umbrella, which he used as a walking stick, something for his hand to grab onto when not clutching a pen. Not adopting the cabana uniform—those long patterned bathing shorts fastened with a draw string and matching jackets—so fashionable in those days was yet another example of I. B.'s eccentricity. Who wears a suit in Miami Beach? Even the lawyers adopted more casual attire. Re-creating life from the Lower East Side, or Upper Broadway, would be tough sledding in snowless Miami. And yet each day I. B. reported for duty as chronicler of the chronically miserable, dressed for the occasion, as if he were a mortician who had wandered into the wrong landscape painting.

One of the reasons for Jacob Posner's misery was the absence he felt in South Florida. The life of the Jewish mind on Miami Beach was dead. So much of his time with I. B. was spent describing the origins of his Miami laments—the shallowness of people surrounded by deep waters. Jacob was learned but unlettered; words didn't come easily to him—for various reasons. So much of what he had witnessed was truly indescribable—appropriately unspoken, ineffable by tragic design. And here he was, trapped in the tropics and rendered mute by Miami's cabana culture and coconuts for brains. The smart ones had stayed in New York; the empty headed retired and resettled in Miami Beach. It was, in 1972, a city without bookstores. *The New York Times* was nowhere to be found—even the Sunday edition! The Magna Carta was more available. The *Atlantic* had a better chance of being surfed than read in any of the Miami zip codes. Yes, Jacob Posner barely spoke, but part of the reason for his silence was that he had no one to speak to—except for I. B.

"I agree: it is a wasteland we have here, Jacob," I. B. said. "All the *meshuganahs* moved to Miami. What can I tell you: we're alone here—just you and me, and our books, and my Yiddish Remington typewriter, and your sticky memories. So tell me more."

In addition to the sartorial anomaly of his daily wardrobe, there was also the matter that I. B. couldn't swim. What they say about fish being out of the water was true of I. B. in Surfside. He never ventured into the ocean or the pool at his apartment on Collins Avenue with its water view and blinding morning light. Instead of swimming like that Jewish boy with the Chippendale body who would go on to win all those Olympic medals in Munich that very summer, I. B. spent much of every day holed up in a restaurant where he couldn't eat the food because most of it had once been alive. What he was doing in South Florida no one could quite understand. All that Miami Beach seemingly offered was material of the scandalous and racy kind. He was an able sponge and the Jewish refugees were bleeding with both nutty thoughts and naughty behavior. He had already milked the Jews on West End Avenue of Manhattan; now he would deplete the Jews of Collins Avenue in Miami Beach. What I. B. found in Miami Beach was a bounty of awkward mating habits, vapid vanities, moral mishaps, common corruptions, foul infidelities, and the most loosely gripped hold on sanity anywhere in the Jewish world. Miami Beach was a mental hospital for Jews, where everyone walked freely although their minds were securely restrained in straightjackets.

I. B. wasn't in Surfside to retire, but to follow leads and scope out the action. The vestiges of European Jewish life was fast succumbing to the obsolescence of a dead language in an America that demanded total immersion. They were his *landsmen*, but he took no pity in presenting them to the Gentile world in the bleakest and most unflattering of lights.

"You can't hide from evil in the world by walking around Miami Beach like a sunburned ghost, Jacob," I. B. said as he brushed the bowl holding the baked apple aside. "Sunshine doesn't make problems go away."

"What sunshine?" Jacob said. "You think I see sunshine? All I see are black clouds filled with smoke floating above Miami Beach. The rest of my family is up there; the wife and child I had before Sophie and Adam. This is a ghost town with everyone dressed in white. My picture of Miami Beach is not suitable as a postcard. Maybe Jackie Gleason was taken off TV because the people up north began to see what I see, and didn't want to 'come on down' after all."

"Nightmares?" I. B. asked, although he was quite sure of the answer. "Still they are haunting you?"

"Yes, of course."

"And the heart, your condition?"

"I take nitroglycerin tablets like no tomorrow, and sometimes I wish there was no tomorrow." And with that he popped another into his mouth, allowing it to dissolve under his tongue before searching for the water he feared the waiter had already taken away.

"I've been a vegetarian all these years," I. B. said, telling Jacob something that was already well known. "When people ask me why I eat no meat or poultry, I tell them I do it for the health of the chickens. But I also know that I will probably live longer because I eat healthier than these Americans."

"You think my problems are from food?" Jacob chuckled at the thought that something as mundane as eggs, butter, and sirloin could have sidelined him with three prior heart attacks. "My diet is fine. My cholesterol is low. I exercise, yes, slowly, but I exercise. What's not fine is my head and my memory, which, at night, brings me nightmares almost as bad as the real thing. They never list nightmares as a cause of death. But I'm sure that when I die, that's what the coroner will say. You don't need a heart condition to have a heart that is broken."

I. B. hurriedly sipped his cup of hot tea through a sugar cube gripped by his front teeth like a bit in a horse's mouth. This, too, was an artifact of the fallen Europe. He then licked his pen as if it were a vegetarian meal, and recorded what Jacob had just told him. "Cause of death: nightmares."

"I still can't believe it was six million," Jacob said. "That's the number they are saying. Your family. All of my family. All those families that the world will never know. I lost my first wife. And she was pregnant with a second child—an unborn child the Nazis took from me. When my son speaks to me at night, all I hear is '*tateh.*' Was the second one a boy, or a girl? Does it matter? I don't know. Even my dreams won't tell me." Jacob paused, his eyes moistened and he waited, perhaps for that child's voice to reveal itself in Surfside, in a whisper. "Fathers are supposed to protect their children, to make them safe. I failed with my European children—born and unborn—and I fail every day with the son who, with a different father, would be an American prince. They say that we survivors should carry on normal lives. The past must not destroy the future. Do not allow the Nazis to have the ultimate victory. So we start new families. We buy a station wagon. Take the children to Little League games and, after that, treat them to ice cream. Go see the circus. Clowns make everyone laugh, and it's important to learn to laugh again. Join the PTA. The PTA; Little League? I'm sorry: we Posners cannot do such things. There is something indecent about it. I won't be disloyal to my first family. And we've seen too much to join the clubs of ordinary people. Bake sales are not for me. Let the Americans do that.

"We are not from a *Normal* Rockwell painting. If anything, we are the screamers that haunted Munch. Show me a genocide club; now that's a group I can join. There I have something to contribute. But I can't watch my son play baseball. I hear he is very good, but I have no interest in *narishe* games. When I see someone shaking a stick at my son, I don't see fun and games.

"We are all such fools. We have all been so foolish. Pretending that suburbs can make it easier to forget, that sunshine can end darkness, that plastic places like Miami Beach can give survivors a second chance. Nobody can grant us that. And we wouldn't want it, wouldn't know what to do with it, and we wouldn't deserve it."

Jacob looked around nervously, as if he didn't have a passport for Surfside and was worried about getting caught by hulking lifeguards who doubled as the city's border patrol. As the roving bands of partisans in the forests of Europe knew all too well, it was often unclear whether one had accidentally crossed over into Hungary, Czechoslovakia, Poland, or Ukraine. In a time of madness, maps matter little. Everyone carries false papers. What does it mean to be a citizen of this world? Even the trees in the forests had seen too much that went against nature. Jacob didn't like to stay in one place for too long. He regarded it as unhealthy, unsafe—tactically stupid. To remain immobile was to tempt fate. Movement was always the survivor's most reliable defense mechanism; floating like one of Ali's butterflies was a very good insurance policy.

"Survivor as philosopher king," I. B. spoke out loud as he scribbled in his notebook, a leather bound, flakey brown block of secrets, rubbed raw from overuse. His pen was a silver Parker, the blue ink leaky, covering his fingernails, which were already blue from mashing the pen against paper, memorializing Jacob Posner's rambling, coded reflections. "Jacob, you have the prophetic voice! These are truths only the dead can hear. The living can never know from such things—otherworldly things that would dent their station wagons and melt their ice cream. I don't know how you carry this around with you so. And I feel such privilege that you would share it with me." Here, of course, I. B. failed to acknowledge how he was cashing in on another's suffering, mining his mind, the petty thefts of the fiction writer. I. B. was writing furiously like a court stenographer charged with capturing every syllable.

"And the missus? May I now ask about her," I. B. said. That was a sensitive subject in the Posner household. Sophie Posner was already so fully realized a character, she was beyond tinkering. Even the master fiction writer himself knew there was nothing to fictionalize when it came to Sophie Posner, no color to add to her outer life and inner world. She was a Queen Esther for the modern age, the mother of all Jews—the mother of all mobsters. For I. B. to recreate Sophie Posner would only diminish the high art she had obtained simply by being herself.

"I can't control her," Jacob sighed and lamented. "I'm not strong enough anymore. I don't think I was ever strong enough. Who is? She is involved in dirty business. Who would expect such a thing from a Jewish woman, a woman whose grandfather was an important rabbi in Poland? Consorting with a hoodlum like Meyer Lansky and his peasants. And, yet, who am I to talk? Obviously, she's attracted to men with blood on their hands."

"Don't say such things, do not talk such *narishkeit*. Those that you killed deserved it," the novelist reasoned. "Lansky makes bodies go away because he is a racketeer. He commits murder. What you had to do was morally just, and essential if one was to survive. It is the order of the universe, the first principles of the natural world. Killing is not all the same, after all."

"I didn't want the job," Jacob said, his eyes were now lost in both a full-on squint and a dead stare. "I shouldn't have had that kind of a life. I wanted to be a lawyer, not a lawbreaker. Now I'm no better than Lansky."

"Are you worried that Sophie hasn't been faithful, that her business with Lansky isn't strictly business, that there's been monkey business?" I. B. was getting to the crux of what for him was always a core theme—who is *shtupping* who? And when Jewish gangsters are involved, it was even better. Isaac Babel wasn't the only writer who saw the dramatic possibilities of Jewish thugs on the wrong side of the law but with the moxie of movie stars.

"I don't have the energy to care about that anymore," Jacob replied, his voice fading. "I'm not alive enough to feel jealous. I am too weak to have those feelings. And if I have such feelings, I don't notice the difference. We Posners are the laughing stocks of Miami Beach. We are a family of fools. And I feel no shame."

Jacob creakily slid out of the booth and rose to his feet. He then reached for his wallet to throw down a few dollars. I. B. waved away his friend's contribution to the meal. After all, Jacob had more than paid his fair share in bringing I. B. what he most wanted. It was a good day for the Jewish writer. A very good day, actually.

The two friends shook hands and Jacob turned toward the front entrance of Danny's Restaurant. It was there he caught the rare sight of his son, in full sprint, working up a ferocious sweat, tearing down Harding Avenue like a fire engine, a mere blur of a boy, his large shadow trailing, his heart pumping, his escape routes getting thinner and less dependable with each heavy step.

Five

Munich to Miami in Spitz Seconds

Sheldon Vered, Temple Beth Am's long-presiding rabbi, was widely known as the kookiest cleric on Miami Beach, and perhaps the entire western hemisphere—not that statistics on such secular matters are maintained anywhere. It was just generally assumed that he had no equal as a spiritual leader, what with his rare combination of ineptitude, irreverence, and overall vulgarity.

Vered carried himself about town with the swagger of a swinging playboy, equal parts Lothario and gigolo. Indeed, when not playing tennis, where he was quite an accomplished club player, he spent much of his spare time at the Playboy Club on Collins Avenue. Sometimes, shockingly, on a Friday night after services, he could be found making out with bunnies—two at a time—right in the middle of the lounge, easily noticed because of his considerable good looks and because he was the only one in the club wearing a yarmulke. Trim, tanned, tall, silver haired and square jawed, he was central casting's Hollywood handsome leading man.

He was also drunkenly screaming, "Good Shabbos, good Shabbos. *Shema Israel*, I'm about to fuck my brains out with a bunny!"

On other nights he was scoring with young fine things searching for sugar daddies to replace their own sour fathers, or with divorcees seeking vendettas, do-overs, and upgrades from their former loutish husbands who apparently were only interested in them as trophy wives anyway.

This was Miami Beach, after all, circa 1972. The sign of the times ran the gamut from the zodiac to free love. Hedonism was the new ethic. To be square was the worst of all geometric shapes. Ties that bind were suddenly seen as far too restrictive. Liberation was in the air—from old sexual mores and middle-class values, as well as from racial discrimination and unequal opportunity. Wife swapping and key parties had replaced bridge nights and mixed doubles as the fashionable way for foursomes to get together—or grow apart. Demonstrating personal autonomy and insisting on human fulfillment—at any cost—was the highest aspiration for the Me Generation.

Tourists came to Miami Beach for the sun, for sure, but also for trouble. Men showed a lot more hair, if not on their heads, then at least on their chests. And women revealed their cleavages with all the modesty of pole dancers. Polyester covered bodies like Saran Wrap, often with rainbow colors and pastels that made South Floridians resemble Polynesians. And tube tops accented shapely breasts in much the same way as thongs gave out way too much information about the male dong. Bodies moving toward one another in often confounding mating dances seemed as ordinary as the sound of clapping sandals on Collins Avenue.

And so the twisted pulpit of Rabbi Sheldon Vered was not a wholly unexpected phenomenon. He was a spiritual leader for a new era—Sodom and Gomorrah recreated in sunny South Florida. The times called for a different kind of Jewish cleric, a new model of rabbinic leadership—sleek, modern, permissive, desecrative, beardless, largely godless. This was rabbi as race car, a cleric who appeared to have never cracked a book or unscrolled a Torah his entire life. His rectitude defied the pious man of God. Nowhere could anyone imagine that an apostle of the divine like him could exist and have any followers at all.

Yet, paradoxically, filling seats in his synagogue was the least of his problems. Rabbi Vered's big-tent Jewish revival show was always sold out. Each service was like a command performance, standing room only, better attended than what was headlining at some of the biggest rooms and hippest clubs in the swankiest hotels along the strip.

The High Holidays at Beth Am were like tailgate parties for the Miami Dolphins. During a recent Purim, more people crowded into the temple to see Rabbi Vered's rendition of the *Megillah*—and his bawdy Purim spiel, replete with burlesque dancers—than they did to see Dean Martin at the Deauville on New Year's Eve. Jackie Gleason may have had the best show in town, but many believed that he was not the best showman on the Beach. There the competition tightened, because Rabbi Vered held his own against the Great One. After all, Vered was a rabbi by trade; he didn't have a Screen Actors' Guild card and he was not a member of Actor's Equity. His act was an accident of history, a mutation in a link of the genetic chain of rabbinic Judaism. He only stumbled into showbiz by making a diaspora detour and surviving a genocidal hiccup. Sheldon Vered emerged from Auschwitz with a punched ticket on his forearm, a radically revised view of the world, and a renewed purpose for his rabbinic ordination, which he received just months before the Nazis invaded Poland.

A rabbi like Sheldon Vered could never have existed in an earlier time and place. Pulpit rabbis were never conceived as rock stars. Their job, after all, was to impart spiritual comfort, moral guidance, and wisdom. Temple Beth Am's congregation received very little of that. Instead, they had to make due with shtick, courtesy of their *tumler* as rabbi, a pastoral mission that looked as if it had been hatched in the Borsht Belt. For this reason, many felt that Vered deserved extra credit in his side-by-side comparison with Gleason. Vered was still an amateur, an interloper slumming in another man's occupation, a rabbi whose holiness played second banana to star-lust, whereas Gleason was a five-tool showman who for many years had a national TV audience every Saturday night.

Many religious Jews of Miami Beach insisted that Vered shouldn't be considered a rabbi at all. His brand of Judaism didn't fit into any of the usual denominations—Orthodox, Conservative, Reform, and Reconstructionist. He was a radical rabbi without precedent—from any era. His authority appeared to be granted by Barnum & Bailey. What he offered veered so very far from the core beliefs of Judaism. Was it Jewish at all? A whole new category would have to be invented to describe where he was leading his tribe and whether this zany form of religious practice had any claims on the Chosen People.

After all, Vered's Judaism was unrecognizable to anyone who had ever once stepped foot inside a synagogue. For one thing, he didn't believe in God in any of the piously conventional ways. And, yet, paradoxically, as a way of demonstrating the conundrum of his conflicted faith and the sacred verities of his profession, he hated God's guts, and said so religiously and with little prompting. It was simply part of the liturgy at Beth Am. The rabbi derived no greater pleasure than seeing one of his flock openly taking God's name in vain—which included cursing God like a drunken sailor going down with his ship. Most religious leaders believe their pastoral mission is to turn their flock toward God. Rabbi Vered looked to turn his Jews violently against the Almighty.

For Sheldon Vered, getting Jews to blaspheme God in shul was the equivalent of the Jewish Rapture. It wasn't that the rabbi had his spiritual doubts, or sympathized with ambivalent agnostics, or that he was hedging his bets. On the contrary, Vered's belief in God was unshakable.

"Of course there is a higher power," he would say. "Who else do you think is intentionally fucking up the world and making life miserable for humankind?"

No one had a firmer belief in the actual existence of God than he. Rabbi Vered took God's presence as a given. Of course, that was the problem, he would say. Why would the Infinite be so callously withholding and under-performing? God's indifference to man's wretched plight was inexcusable. What's the value of being All-Everything—powerful and knowing—if it is a power held in reserve? How can Auschwitz and God exist in the same universe—in the same sentence? These were the questions that Vered offered as indictments. The rabbi had judged God and found him, or her, guilty—of dereliction of duty, of sins against man. No excuse existed for such neglect, and God was not worthy of man's forgiveness. There really was nothing else to say. To put it bluntly, Rabbi Vered wanted God to drop dead.

And, yet, there was a peculiar logic to Vered's madness. He was absolutely certain that his sacrilege was not going unnoticed. Without false modesty he believed that God had his eye on this renegade rabbi, keeping the channel tuned to Vered's loony synagogue on Miami Beach. All codependent relationships come to an end. And it's usually not a pretty sight. God would eventually tire of Sheldon Vered's transgressions. The two would go mano-a-Yahweh, and either the rabbi would be struck down by a thunderbolt or God would suffer a fatal heart attack from the anguish of such unremitting defiance.

Nearly everything Rabbi Vered did was *not* by the book. And he set the worst possible example for his or any other flock to follow. Jewish Hell's Angels would have roared right through Miami Beach and bypassed Temple Beth Am rather than pay Vered a visit. After all, when the time finally comes when a Jew needs to see a rabbi, you can't settle for a clown.

Even his associations were inappropriate. He palled around with Muhammad Ali, who, just a year earlier, had been defeated by Heavyweight Boxing Champion Joe Frazier at Madison Square Garden in what many had called "The Fight of the Century." In 1964, Ali, then known as Cassius Clay, became the Heavyweight Champion by knocking out Sonny Liston in Miami Beach, of all places. Several years later he was stripped of his title for refusing to serve in the military during the Vietnam War. The 1971 fight against Frazier was supposed to have been Ali's redemption. It was not to be. Ali spent 1972 training in Miami Beach, waiting for a rematch so he could reclaim his title. And when not sparring, he was out on the town with Rabbi Sheldon Vered.

As a show of support, the rabbi always sat ringside at Ali's title matches, blonde bombshells on both arms, and both hands clutching whisky at the ready.

"Muhammad, break his face!" the rabbi shouted from his seat, and then kissed the face of the starlet to his right. "Make it so he won't walk again! Make him go bye bye!" The rabbi then threw a French kiss to his left.

Ali was a regular on Miami Beach in the sixties and seventies—the only black man with any presence on the island. He wielded the kind of clout that allowed him to hang around at night on the strip—not as a waiter or busboy, but as a VIP patron. Nearly all the other people with dark skin made an end-of-the-day exodus from Miami Beach, leaving the nightlife largely segregated.

Ali's longtime trainer, Angelo Dundee, maintained his gym on 5th Street and Washington Avenue. One of the true special attractions that Miami Beach offered in those days was free access to Ali's workouts. Just one flight up from the street and the smells of men in various stages of punching something, or skipping rope, greeted visitors like a right hook. When Ali was in town, the crowds swelled inside the gym like the Atlantic Ocean on a choppy day. Ali sparred with chumps whom he ate alive like chum, working the speed bag, pounding away at the heavy bag with Angelo leaning in from the other side, like he was hiding behind a tree. A cigar was clenched in his mouth as he barked out words of encouragement. Sometimes Ali took his workouts on the road, where he alternated between running in full sweats on the beach at daybreak, and circling the ball fields of Miami Beach Senior High School in the scorching, ungodly August heat.

What a bronzed rabbi was doing carousing with Ali, a Muslim and a patron of the Nation of Islam, no one could quite understand. The friendship seemed bizarre—even for Sheldon Vered. It would have been bad enough had Ali still been Cassius Clay, but the rabbi was consorting with an associate of Malcolm X, who, like Vered, was another wayward religious figure—the former Detroit Red openly preached white racism and anti-Semitism. And Ali was a vocal supporter of the Palestinian cause for self-determination, which in those days was akin to believing that the world was flat or that cigarettes were good for your health.

"Take a picture of my rabbi and me!" Ali motioned to the paparazzi with his fully-staged bellicose banter. "People think I don't like Jews, but that's not true. Look at us here. Aren't we pretty?"

It could not be denied that Ali and Vered made for a very handsome pair—odd and inexplicable as the friendship certainly was. Vered stood tall with his sinewy and debonair James Bond looks and unnaturally white and wide smile. And there was Ali, still smooth faced despite the untold number of punches it had received, with an arm draped over the rabbi's shoulder, and a mocking fist pointed at Sheldon Vered's jaw. Ali's body was muscled and his black skin was aglow in the pop of each flashbulb, lighting up his self-possessed brashness, as if he needed any assistance.

"They say that Gleason is the Great One, but everyone on Miami Beach knows that *I'm* the Greatest!"

"He's the Greatest!" Rabbi Vered nodded wildly in confirmation, as if bestowing a blessing on his budding anti-Semite of a friend.

The A-list celebrities that Sheldon Vered cultivated over the years seemed to cleanse the scarlet letter A that he wore so proudly as a philandering rabbi. The rabbi never wanted for an opportunity to defile a woman, and almost never declined. Jewish women, however, were never his first choice—unless they were presently married and members of his congregation. Occasionally these assignations made the politics of other shuls seem positively Catholic by comparison. The rabbi's penance was achieved by his proximity to fame.

To his great fortune, it turned out that the rabbi was a Miami Dolphins fanatic, which in South Florida always counted for something. The Dolphins, like the city they called home, were a young franchise, one of the teams that merged into the NFL from the AFL. But in 1972 they became the only team in NFL history to have a perfect season, and then go on to win the Super Bowl.

A team that achieved the "Perfect Season" apparently demanded a perfect rabbi. Before each home game in the Dolphins' locker room, Rabbi Vered, along with a local priest, gave the benediction for the team. It wasn't until a year later that the Dolphins actually had a Jewish player, offensive guard and perennial pro bowler Ed Newman; but Joe Robbie, the team's owner, liked having a rabbi's blessing as the last words his team would hear before they ran through the tunnel and onto the Poly-Turf at the Orange Bowl. The rabbi would then be escorted to the elevator and brought up to Robbie's private suite beside the press box. There was no greater entry into Miami's high society than this: a Miami Beach rabbi treated as royalty—not as a pious sage but as the toast of the town.

From the gates of Auschwitz to the owner's suite in the Orange Bowl in less than thirty years. God does, indeed, work in mysterious ways.

Rabbi Sheldon Vered appreciated the role he was playing in the dynasty that the Dolphins were building. He returned the favor by several times inviting Don Shula, the Dolphins' coach and a personal friend, to deliver the *Devar Torah*—the insights that can be gleaned from the weekly readings of the Torah—at Saturday morning services. Shula wasn't Jewish, had never before been inside a synagogue, and as a man who was accustomed to calling the plays, felt grossly unprepared for this honor. Of course, the Devar Torah at Rabbi Vered's house of worship ran the gamut from matters that were not actually in the Torah. Some had little to do with Judaism at all— homemade recipes, last week's episode of *All in the Family*, the gambling referendum on Miami Beach. The Dolphins themselves were often the subjects of these discussions. The rabbi used to interrupt his own sermons to revisit his favorite highlights from that prior Sunday's games, or to predict the outcome of the game about to be played.

"I have no doubt that Bob Greise can throw a football much farther than God can," he once professed to a congregation too inured to react to these inane asides. "People always say: God willing everything will be okay as long as we place ourselves in God's hands. Now that's total nonsense. God has terrible hands! The absolute worst hands! He drops everything. In fact, God is a much bigger fumbler than Mercury Morris, and we all know how Merc can't hold onto the rock. When the game is on the line, you don't want to put the football in Mercury's hands, and when your life is on the line, you don't want to have to depend on the hands of God."

The congregation nodded its approval, which was the only way the rabbi would be guaranteed to stop and move on to something else.

At times Temple Beth Am resembled more a sports booking establishment than a synagogue. Don Shula would eventually relax and come to enjoy these occasional visits to the bima of Beth Am. He finally figured out that no one came to this synagogue for spiritual wisdom. So he stuck with the X's and O's, which is what everyone expected of their pigskin-obsessed rabbi.

Sports were on everyone's mind that summer of 1972—and not just in Miami Beach. The games of the ancient Greeks, modernized and globalized, were about to be played in Munich, Germany, the setting for the summer Olympics. The storyline most people were following was the aquatic wonder that was Mark Spitz, a California Jew who swam faster than any other human being on the planet. Even sea creatures were not especially interested in challenging him in their own waters. Spitz had already won two gold medals and one silver in the 1968 Olympics; but now, four years later, he was set to compete in seven events, and predicted to accomplish the unprecedented feat of winning seven gold medals in the same Olympiad.

The fact that Spitz was Jewish was merely a footnote for most people. After all, sports were supposed to transcend politics, to rise above partisanship, to simply be above petty bigotry and xenophobic nativism. The purity of the contest was all that mattered, not the race or ethnicity of the athletes. The nations could wave their flags, but the spirit of competition was far more important than national rivalries. Sportsmanship was a universal language, and the Olympics were designed to be a showcase for the splendor of the human form, and the embodiment of truth and beauty.

The world could not forget, however, the last time Germany hosted the summer games, a time irreconcilable with truth or beauty. The 1936 Olympics in Berlin provided a showcase for a very different set of values, as Adolf Hitler politicized the games by having the home team prove its Aryan superiority. The Olympic ideal of sports transcending politics was suddenly subordinated to Germany's vile racism. Fortunately, Jesse Owens embarrassed the diminutive Fuhrer with bursts of black explosiveness that put the lie to the "Master Race." Meanwhile, Jewish athletes from Germany, and athletes from other countries sympathetic to Hitler's ground rules, weren't even permitted to participate in those Olympic games.

Now decades later, this return to postwar Germany featured the just deserts of a Jewish swimmer representing the epitome of Olympic glory. Spitz and his single-finned demonstration of the Jew as jock enthralled people from around the world. Whenever the cameras were rolling they caught him gliding over the water like an airboat, standing tall and lean in his Speedos, and displaying his Wheaties cereal box smile. He even sported a mustache, as if he were unafraid of any water resistance at all. And sure enough, by the end of the first week of the games in early September, Spitz had claimed gold medals in every event in which he competed, shattering world and Olympic swimming records along the way.

The Jews from Miami Beach were giddy from Spitz's gilded accomplishment. It was for many on the same order of majesty as Israel's victory in the 1967 Six-Day War. During that brief campaign, plucky underdog Israel defeated three Arab armies—in spite of an enormous numerical disadvantage—and recaptured all of Jerusalem, taking the West Bank, Gaza, and the Sinai Peninsula, all in less than a week. It was a heady time to be a Jew in the world. The Israelis conquered three nations on land; Spitz defeated the entire world on water.

Given these massive headwinds of Jewish pride, the flexed muscles, the emergence from all those years of historical hiding, what a fortuitous alignment of the Stars of David that Adam Posner was scheduled to have his bar mitzvah on the second to the last day of those summer games. There was no more perfect time to proclaim one's connection to the Jewish people. It was suddenly hip to be Jewish. Adam's entry into manhood would coincide with Mark Spitz's historic Olympic moment.

The linking of one Jewish athlete's singular achievement to the bar mitzvah of another was not so farfetched—at least on Miami Beach. Although he was only twelve years old, Adam Posner was an exceptional athlete and rumored to be the fastest runner at Biscayne Junior High School. He and Spitz had something in common other than shared Jewish ancestry; each possessed the sprinter's mindset, where time is measured in fractions of a second. There was a finality to clocks and stopwatches that could never be suspended. Such people have a deeper appreciation of time—how it is to be used; how guardedly it should never be lost. Most important, it should not be wasted. There are too many finish lines, too many swimming pool walls. Staying out in front, or closing the gap, becomes second nature as the seconds tick away. Naturally, a Jewish boy with dreams of his own would see in Spitz's medals the possibility that speed can take someone very far away. Adam very much wanted to be taken far away, even if his own legs would be required to provide the transportation.

Of course, the Olympics had not been top of mind months earlier when the Posners met with Rabbi Vered to discuss their son's preparation for being called before the Torah. With the political conventions coming to Miami Beach that same summer and the tumult they were expected to generate, no one at Temple Beth Am had checked the calendar to see the thrilling company Adam's bar mitzvah would share with that other Jewish sprinter, Mark "the Shark" Spitz. There is a limit to how much excitement Jews can tolerate in the same week. A bar mitzvah is easily overshadowed by the Olympic games and the gold medals of an exceptionally buoyant and hydraulic Jew. The Posners would not have changed the date had they known. But perhaps it would have made those initial sessions less fraught had they realized that Adam's rite of passage would coincide with one of the brightest and most solemn weeks in Jewish history.

But first, the Posners had to decide whether they even wanted their son to become a man according to the laws of Judaism. A bar mitzvah was not a given in such a household, although the Posners were ideally suited as members of Temple Beth Am. Most of the actual members—as opposed to those who only attended out of a voyeuristic desire to see the deranged rabbi up close—often wished for an old-school rabbi who didn't bang married women and snort coke. This didn't mean they were clamoring for Hasidic or black-hat Judaism, mind you. All that these members wanted was a rabbi who wouldn't make them the laughing stock of Diaspora Jewry, a rabbi who was recognizably Jewish rather than messianic for a modern, iconoclastic age.

Was that too much to ask?

The Posners were among the minority minyan who believed that Sheldon Vered was an absolutely sublime spiritual leader—devastatingly good looking and with a healthy hatred of the Almighty. Before they moved to Florida a year earlier they had always hoped that a rabbi such as Sheldon Vered existed somewhere. Certainly nothing matching his description was seen at any pulpit in New York City. But here he was in Miami Beach, a wrecking ball of a rabbi—the rabbi of their dreams.

"No one would believe that such a rabbi could even be ordained," Jacob remarked one Saturday morning as the family crossed over a walk bridge on their way to Temple Beth Am. In their signature synagogue finery, they were toasting like Pop-Tarts.

"Yes, he is a godsend," Sophie said, swooning like someone with a schoolgirl crush on David Cassidy. "I am afraid that any day the *Herald* is going to report that Vered is a fraud—not a rabbi but some tent revival charlatan." As consigliere to the Jewish mob, it was her job to sniff out the con artists, scammers, and fraudsters. "Wouldn't it be funny," she chuckled, "if we found out that he is on the run from the FBI, and that he's not even Jewish?"

"In the meantime, we should be thankful that he's our rabbi even if he isn't *actually* a rabbi," Jacob concluded.

Like their rabbi, the Posners were outliers within the affiliated set. Theirs was only a tenuous connection to God. Yes, there were rabbis on both sides of their family trees, but what good are trees when two out of three European Jews were consumed in a fire? Thirty years before this bar mitzvah their entire families were either shot dead or gassed and cremated. For Sophie and Jacob Posner, God was placed on probation. Their return to him would be halting, if not backtracking. Keeping God at a distance suited the Posners' broken faith quite nicely. When it came to what they were looking for in a place of worship, they preferred an atmosphere of similarly ambivalent Jews with a bone to pick with God.

With parents like these, and a rabbi like Sheldon Vered, Adam Posner knew that his bar mitzvah was less than a sure thing.

"He doesn't need a bar mitzvah," Sophie said, squelching his son's manhood in yet another way. "What is it going to get him? Reading from the Torah won't make him a man—not in this century. And he already is a Jew. No one will let him forget. Hitler didn't ask for a show of hands from Jewish men who never had a bar mitzvah. He would have killed them anyway."

"You are absolutely right, Sophie. I can't argue with you," Rabbi Vered joined in. "In this day and age, a bar mitzvah is a complete waste of time. Aside from the party, the drinking, the dancing, what's the point?"

It was no surprise that Sophie Posner and Sheldon Vered would see eye to eye. They came from the same place from among Hitler's wretches, and naturally shared the same worldview—the unspoken language of the blue tattoo. Oddly for Miami Beach, they were the only two in the synagogue who had such markings on their forearms. Some speculated that those numbers accounted for the raw power in Rabbi's Vered's lethal tennis forehand. The fuzzy white ball screamed off his racket like it had received a nasty spanking. Others thought that the numbers explained why Sophie Posner rarely lost a hand in poker, as if those digits on her arm sparked the numbers in her head, which made her a particularly agile card counter.

As they sat across from one another and discussed Adam's bar mitzvah, their dueling tattoos were like shiny swords that could either kiss or collide.

"So you agree? So happy to hear that, Rabbi," Sophie said. "But I am not surprised. You are a wise man. Everyone says that. I don't understand why Jews still care about bar mitzvahs."

"Better he should be baptized," Rabbi Vered said, adding tinder to the provocation. "Even that would be a better idea."

"Baptized! My son?" Jacob finally spoke, and then popped a nitroglycerin pill into his mouth, wondering whether now was a good time to chase it down with that cyanide tablet he had been stashing. He loved the rabbi, but Jacob could tolerate only so much of the man's antics. Sophie, on the other hand, found Vered's irreverence positively addicting. She breathed it in like French perfume. "You want he should grow up a goy like you, Rabbi?"

"Look, don't get angry with me, Jake," Rabbi Vered said, hoping to calm his congregant down. He knew that Jacob's heart was long out of warranty. "I am just laying out your options here. There are many ways to enter manhood; there are various spiritual journeys. Judaism isn't necessarily the best one. I, for one, can't recommend it. Adam can choose from the many religions of the world"—he spoke like a used car salesman—"and there are even more tribal rites of passage. The Native Indian-Americans, for example, have some interesting tests of manhood where the boy has to survive all by himself in the wilderness."

"Oh, I like that one! Let's sign him up," Sophie said, smiled maniacally, and then shifted uneasily in her seat and grimaced from a sharp pain in her stomach.

"You see, Jake," Rabbi Vered said. "Sophie sees what I mean. Please, don't kill the messenger."

"*Meshuganah* messiah," Jacob muttered. "There has to be a limit to how much of a farce Judaism can become."

"Hear me out: it doesn't really matter what religion any of us follow," Rabbi Vered continued, obviously not trying to win Jacob over. "We believe in a higher power because we feel so powerless. It all goes back to the golden calf. We'll bow before anything if it makes the loneliness go away, if we can get outside of our heads and our terrible thoughts. We want to connect to something greater than the self. All religions are in the same business—not to save souls, but to give false hope and give meaning to the universe."

"I don't know," Sophie slipped in a hint of doubt. "I want him to be a Jew, but not like the Jews in America—with the big parties and the ice sculptures and the fountain pens. Such *drek*. I want him to be the kind of Jew who won't be pushed around. I want him to fight back. Bar mitzvahs do not lead to manhood; broken bones do."

"Hey, you are on to something there," Rabbi Vered nodded in full acquiescence. "It's an archaic ritual. Although who doesn't enjoy a large party?" said the party animal of a rabbi. "Maybe it's time to just skip all that Hebrew mumbo jumbo."

"No party then," she said abruptly. "There is nothing really to celebrate. We don't need to make Adam kosher in the eyes of God. God won't be watching this bar mitzvah. He's never watches such ordinary things. God only shows up for the fireworks."

"You said it, sister," Rabbi Vered said. "Fuck God," he said, raising the ante.

"*Oy vey*," Jacob said and out came another tiny pill that hopefully would temper his palpitations.

■

All throughout these indelicate negotiations, no one had bothered to ask Adam what he wanted. That was a familiar pattern in the Posner household. Adam, actually, very much wanted to be a bar mitzvah. He was not looking to sample how the various world religions and tribes treated their young men and marked their manhood. He wasn't shopping around; he wouldn't cast away his Jewish identity like a droopy tube sock. The rebellious, angry Jew persona with his disbelief in God was not as fully developed in him as in his parents. Deviating from the Posner party line, he wasn't looking to start a fight with the Almighty. He wasn't trying to make a statement. He just wanted to sing his haftorah, deliver a short *drash* without making a fool of himself, and perhaps lead the congregation through a bit of the musaf service before hurdling off the bima to race home, change clothes, grab his gear, and head over to Flamingo Park just in time to play whatever peewee sport was in season. By the time of his bar mitzvah, the summer would be over, and Little League would have ended, but Adam was always keen for the next sport and after-school practices that mercifully kept him away from his home.

Since neither his mother nor Rabbi Vered could agree on how best to observe Adam's bar mitzvah, they surrendered to convention and to Adam's own wishes.

"I don't want to do what the Icelandic tribes do," Adam implored. "I just want to be a regular Jew. Can't I just do that? It is my bar mitzvah, you know."

So his rabbi and his mother, with great petulance, acceded to a bar mitzvah of the generic kind—no flash, no extravagance, no sacrilege. The one consolation was the banning of chopped liver. For six months Adam practiced with Cantor Nico Feldman, formerly a professional opera singer who performed at the Metropolitan Opera House in New York City and even made an appearance on *The Ed Sullivan Show* before retiring from the stage only to resurface on the bima as the cantor for Temple Beth Am. Cantor Feldman was an owlish, Spanish gentleman with a creased face and a mustache of black bristles that would cause serious damage during a kiss. He was for many years the long-suffering sidekick in Rabbi Vered's crass sideshow, the good cop who exuded old-world class and new-world disgust with the rabbi who occupied the pulpit to his right. He smilingly shrugged off

Vered's wisecracks, and everyone knew that he was slumming it in the Sun-shine State as the straight man in a comedy act that was no joke.

But that voice! On Yom Kipper the tenor who had graced far more glam-orous stages never failed to summon forth all the ghosts of the Jewish past. The congregation succumbed to those tingling notes that turned their spines into tuning forks. Tears of atonement filled the sanctuary in the col-lective spirit of keeping the gates of heaven open until Cantor Feldman's last liturgical breath. Adam was drawn to Feldman, a grandfatherly sort, too tempting of a figure for a boy who had never met his grandparents and barely knew his own parents. Adam's home was broken—not in the way they mean it nowadays where families divided are deemed automatically broken, but in the truest sense of the word. The people in his home were intact in their marriage and yet completely broken as human beings.

"Come in, come in, my boy," Cantor Feldman would say and then he would wrap Adam in a baritone's bear hug. Adam was not especially famil-iar with affection. It wasn't the Posner way. His parents would not have dreamed of imparting the false sense of security evoked by way of the hu-man touch. The boy would have settled for any kind of hug—a pseudo hug, an air hug, even a cave drawing of a hug. Any embrace would do. As a for-mer opera singer, Feldman possessed a formidable physical presence; the thick body of a tenor houses a voice that erupts from within and resounds like thunder. The body becomes both echo chamber and acoustic sound machine. A musical instrument in such impeccable human form might have some extra space to house a small boy.

"What do you have for me today?" Feldman would ask, his study a shrine to his first love, with photos of him in various baroque costumes mounted on the wall. "How many new lines did you learn? Let's get to work."

Adam would sing, not knowing the meaning of the words but yet filled with a powerful sense of purpose, as if his chanting compensated for all that the Posners no longer believed in. Perhaps with these liturgical words and special melodies Adam could undo all the disrespect that his parents had inflicted on God by teaming up with God's greatest suntanned nemesis, Sheldon Vered. Adam sang in a pleading voice, as if trying to make contact with the unknown, the infinite, and the dead. His parents were already such Jewish apostates, on the verge of excommunication, Spinozan in both word and deed. He knew that God would be pleased to hear from him, as if to reassure the Almighty that not all of the Posners were AWOL. Some were marked present when religious attendance was taken.

Feldman looked on approvingly, smiling and brushing back a patch of Adam's blond hair that had fallen over his eyes while he sang.

"It will be a great day when you are called before the Torah—great for everyone," Cantor Feldman said, although he had his doubts. It was still only spring, after all. When it came to Temple Beth Am, anything could happen. Adam's bar mitzvah was slated for the second Saturday in September. Perhaps Feldman had spoken too soon.

As the days were narrowing and the bar mitzvah grew near, Adam was ready and even a little over prepared for his bar mitzvah. He was leaving nothing to chance. Chance was an article of faith in this family. His mother lived entirely by chance, a compulsive gambler for whom odds-making was a daily ritual. Like many children without siblings, Adam had a lot of spare time and a great deal of loneliness to fill. He spent much of that summer playing Little League baseball and practicing his haftorah selection, and, of course, awaiting the moment when Mark Spitz would take his historic Olympic plunge into the waters of Munich. A week later Adam would take the bima at Temple Beth Am.

In the topsy-turvy world of 1972, with the Cold War in full frigid force and the Middle East awash in oil and animus, it was hard to keep a date with any certainty. Spitz would have his golden Olympic moment, but Adam Posner was not destined to receive his day of manhood—at least not in the way such rituals are usually performed. The Olympics, dedicated entirely to sports between nations, suddenly became a blood sport between biblical cousins and geographical rivals. And instead of inanimate medals it produced Jewish casualties—in Germany, of all places.

On Tuesday, September 5, 1972, the Palestinian terrorist group known as Black September scaled the walls of the Olympic Village, burst into the rooms housing the Israeli Olympic team, killed several of its team members, and took the rest as hostages. During a two-day standoff, after the demands were not met and after Germany's snipers bungled a rescue attempt, eleven members of Israel's Olympic team were ultimately killed.

Jim McKay, who anchored the coverage for ABC's *Wild World of Sports*, announced at 3:24 in the morning, "They're all gone."

They were all gone? The Jews of the world were just getting used to having one of their own enshrined as the most decorated Olympic athlete of all time. Less than a week later, Jews would be remembered in Olympic history for something else entirely. The Israelis didn't medal; they were just murdered. Israel, which only a few years earlier shocked the world with its military commando prowess, now fell back into the more customary role as Jewish victims. Mark Spitz, and other Jewish athletes from other countries who participated in the games, were immediately sent home for their own protection. Fortunately, Spitz had already stunned the world and claimed his medals before the PLO brought new meaning to shock on the world stage.

"The Olympic games should have been canceled!" Rabbi Vered intoned at a hastily arranged meeting at the synagogue the day after the killings. He was reacting to news that the Olympic officials had decided that the games would go on. Instead of treating games as games should be treated, the Olympic organizers held a brief memorial service where the murdered Israeli athletes somehow went unmentioned. "The Olympic games continue?" Rabbi Vered continued. "How is that possible? This is not a time for sports. Where there should have been silence and mourning there is now track and field?"

The rabbi was apoplectic, a condition of incurable seriousness that was foreign to his state of mind and caused his footing to become less sure.

Many of the congregants at Temple Beth Am were surprised by Rabbi Vered's response. He rarely took *anything* very seriously. And as a sportsman himself, one would have assumed that he would have approved of the decision not to suspend the games. The Olympics should never be taken hostage—neither the games nor the competitors. Suspending the Olympics was tantamount to surrendering to terrorism. The aim of Black September was to instill terror by blackening the solemnity of the month. Cancelling the games was a victory to those who didn't want the world to feel safe while games were being played.

Rabbi Vered was taking this tragedy personally—actually, he was taking it as a Jew, which until now was not how he defined himself or how he responded to the world. For years his antics caused his congregation to howl; now here he was, clearly affected by the madness of Munich, which left him howling at the Miami moon.

"A synagogue is a place of silence and respect," he continued with a sermon that should have been delivered by a different rabbi. "Yes, I know in the past it was not normally the case at our synagogue. But since Germany did not think it was important to honor the dead Israeli athletes by calling off the games, something must be done, even if it has to come from Miami Beach. For this reason I have decided that Temple Beth Am will cancel this upcoming Shabbat, and we will spend Saturday in Flamingo Park hosting our own Miami Beach Memorial Games. The Olympic torch will pass through Miami Beach this Shabbat, and when it does, *we* won't forget the Israeli athletes. Will we?"

The congregation of Temple Beth Am, their mouths normally agape upon hearing the rabbi's harebrained schemes, performed double takes in one choreographed blink. There was already a good deal of shock to go around. But even for Rabbi Vered, this response to Munich was setting new Olympic records in lunacy. Flamingo Park had just survived hundreds of high hippies who camped out and detoxified during the Democratic and Republican National Conventions. The grass was pretty torn up in the outfield of the baseball stadium and at the fifty-yard-line of the football field. Rolling paper and roach clips were folded within the blades as if grass in Miami Beach were actually *grass*—easily accessed for a toke. The park smelled of pot even though the last of the long-haired, peace-loving, antiwar agitators had been gone for nearly a month. They left like a biblical Exodus, brandishing beautiful suntans courtesy of their copulations on Miami Beach.

Now an entire synagogue would be unleashed on that parched field, on Shabbat no less, where a day's worth of track and field events would be held in honor of the dead Israeli athletes from the Munich games. For the exhibition to take place, Shabbat services—and Adam Posner's bar mitzvah—would have to be called off. Rabbi Vered saw a more fitting use for God's day of rest—a group protest against those in Munich who were all-too-willing to forget. Flamingo Park would be hosting two political rebellions during the same summer. The one the rabbi had in mind was also a celebration of the body, but without the weed. Generally speaking, any opportunity to avoid having to chant Hebrew was a side benefit to this rabbi. But in this case, he was after something much greater than that.

Cantor Feldman, sitting on the bima in his high-backed, red velvet chair, stood up and walked over to his partner's pulpit. Shielding the microphone with his hand, the cantor said, "Sheldon, we can't do this to Adam Posner. I know you care little about disappointing God. But this is a boy we are talking about here. I'm sure these cockamamie Memorial Games you've got cooking in your head have the double whammy of insulting Germany and on the same day God, too, but there is a boy to consider, a boy who very much wants to become a man, right here, in your shul, on this bima, in just a few days on Shabbat."

Feldman stared out onto the congregation and glimpsed the Posners sitting near the back of the synagogue. The look of disappointment on Adam's face beamed across the sanctuary like a searchlight. Meanwhile, Sophie Posner's face betrayed a very different reaction—an excitable look and a wry smile. She may have been the only one in the synagogue gladly willing to go along with Vered's plot for vindicating the crimes of Munich.

Whispering to Cantor Feldman—while the congregation watched their brain trust decide the Posner boy's fate—the rabbi said, "I have a better idea for Adam Posner's rite of passage. I don't know how good his Hebrew is. That's your department. Yiddish, Hebrew—they're dead languages. Honestly, who gives a shit? But I do know what I have planned for him will show off some of his best talents."

Turning to the congregation, Rabbi Vered announced, "Now go home and we will reconvene on Saturday morning at 9 a.m. sharp—not here in the synagogue, but at Flamingo Park. Get a lot of sleep. Bring your tennis shoes and sneakers, and wear white shorts and a blue shirt in honor of Israel. Stars of David are welcome."

The Olympic Torch, desecrated and nearly snuffed out in Munich, was about to make a circuitous and unscheduled pit stop in Miami Beach.

By Saturday morning Flamingo Park had been transformed into a track-and-field Shangri-La. The rabbi recruited the track coach at Miami Beach Senior High to assist him. All the events were organized on the field with official timers and scorers standing at each station. Shabbat services were being replaced by Miami Beach's answer to the Maccabi Games. The grumpy members of Temple Beth Am were present and accounted for in a timely fashion. The rest of the Miami Beach synagogues had canceled their services, too, in solidarity with Rabbi Vered's inspired but impious idea of paying tribute to the fallen Israeli athletes. The ranks of Miami Beach Gentiles, and unaffiliated Jews, also showed up in uniform as either participants or spectators. Many were carrying Israeli flags. Others were singing Israeli songs. And off in the end zone of Memorial Field in Flamingo Park, a group of women were tangled up in the grapevine of an Israeli dance.

This Olympic tribute was not only playing to the locals. Word had gotten out to the *Miami Herald* that the Jews murdered at Munich were going to be honored in a most unusual way. The Jews of Miami Beach were not shutting down for Shabbat. The day of rest was being transformed into a day of just deserts. The whole town was getting caught up in this makeshift Olympic memorial. The *Herald*, local TV stations, and the UPI and AP all sent photographers, cameramen, and reporters to cover this splendidly conceived radical event.

Back in Munich they were staging the final two days of Olympic events, but the German newspapers—*Die Zeit, Süddeutsche Zeitung, Frankfurt Allgemeine Zeitung*—were bizarrely giving equal coverage to the goings-on simultaneously being staged in America—in sleepy but prideful Miami Beach. Even Jim McKay of ABC sports gave Rabbi Vered's Miami Beach Memorial Games a tearful nod. The world was, indeed, taking notice of how this tiny synagogue had decided to smack down the Munich Olympic organizers, delivering the message that the games should have been canceled. Now the actual Olympics had competition. The spirit of the Olympic ideal had been contaminated; the murdered Israeli athletes deserved to be remembered rather than forgotten faster than it took an Olympian to run the 100-meter dash.

These Miami Beach Memorial games commenced with the singing of *Hatikvah*, the Israeli national anthem, played by the high school's marching band, which had little time to rehearse since school had only just resumed after summer recess. And then Rabbi Sheldon Vered, standing on a platform erected for this special day's medal winners, spoke haltingly into the microphone, mournfully reciting the names of the Israeli dead. All of Miami Beach stood in silence as each name was read:

Moshe Weinberg
Yossef Romano
Ze'ev Friedman
David Berger
Yakov Springer
Eliezer Halfin
Yossef Gutfreund
Kehat Shorr
Mark Slavin
Andre Spitzer
Amitzur Shapira

When the rabbi was through, the games began. A shot rang out that caused quite a few pacemakers to malfunction and birds to evacuate palm trees like seasonal tenants. What a lively day it was. Sol Hardoff, one of the synagogue elders whose games of choice were usually shuffleboard and golf, received a bronze medal in the high jump. He joyfully lifted the medal to his face, which matched his tan. Ruth Goldstein, a fierce doubles competitor in tennis, took silver in the pole vault. Rabbi Vered himself won gold in the hammer throw, which many who knew him attributed to the mighty force he was able to generate in his left forearm. That bionic limb had been places and came with serial numbers branded in blue. Estelle Pechstein, who was in desperate need of two new hips, and was often kvetching about her immobile plight, gutted out the race walking event, uncomplainingly, on her way to gold. One ringer among the bunch was Michael Kesselman, one of the coaches at Biscayne Junior High School, who was a collegiate shot putter and who had always dreamed of having an Olympic moment. Here at the Miami Beach Memorial Games, with the bleachers packed solid and the TV cameras rolling to capture the "thrill of victory and the agony of defeat," he set records that would never be broken—for these games only. Nearly everyone, regardless of whether they were competing on the field or sitting in the stands waving Israeli flags, wore the white war-paint of zinc oxide on their freckled noses.

All the sprinting races belonged to the bar mitzvah boy: Adam Posner. He was already believed to be the fastest kid at the junior high school. Now he could prove it. At the Miami Beach Memorial Games, on the day that he was to become a man, he was as intrepid and imposing as Judah Maccabee himself. Yes, several of the runners at the starting lines were older than his parents. He was competing against a crowded field of senior citizens with feet problems. A podiatrist was standing guard at the ready. There were parking attendants for all of the wheelchairs. Four cardiologists stood next to a portable EKG as if they represented their own relay team. CPR and other resuscitation machines were in abundance. Regardless of the inferior competition, however, Adam Posner ran his races as if he were at the starting line of Olympic Stadium in Munich—as if his hero, Bob Hayes, was chasing him from behind. And the clock didn't lie. Adam's rite of passage produced a clean lane in which to run. And he responded with blistering times, even in the high heat of September.

Adam Posner made no appearance at the bima on the day of his bar mitzvah, but he made eight visits to the winner's podium, and stood proudly on the highest block, the one that signified a gold medal. Less auspicious, yes, of far less consequence, for sure, but he bested Mark Spitz with eight gold medals of his own. And the Jews of Miami Beach sent a message to Munich by honoring the dead Israeli athletes and celebrating the manhood of one of their own.

The following weekend, with the Olympic Village empty of athletes and spectators and security even more lax than when the Israeli team lost their lives, Adam Posner and his parents, and his rabbi and cantor, arrived in Munich for a very special purpose, one that had nothing to do with sports.

"What more appropriate place for you to become a man than at Munich?" Cantor Feldman said.

Upon their arrival on Saturday morning they took a cab directly to Olympic Stadium. Standing outside and holding the Torah brought along from the ark of Temple Beth Am, Adam chanted the blessings that would make official the bar mitzvah that had been postponed on Miami Beach. What took place on Memorial Field was the after party—played beforehand. A morning chill in the Munich air greeted the visitors who came from a much warmer, hospitable climate. Scattered litter whipped around in the parking lot. A few boys roughly Adam's age were skateboarding nearby, pulling off some nifty ollies, aerials, slides, and grinds as if they half expected the judges from last week to return to their scoring tables. They paused for a moment to eye these trespassers. No one needed to state the obvious: Jews never belonged in an Olympics held in Germany—whether it was 1936, or 1972.

With his parents observing him warily, his cantor smiling and his rabbi looking off distractedly, Adam Posner sang his haftorah for the gods of Mount Olympus, and the God of the Jews, and whatever god would accept him as a son.

Six

To the Moon, Sophie, to the Moon!

Jackie Gleason was known throughout the world as a multidimensional, once-in-a-generation talent. There were few things, if any, he couldn't do on stage or in front of a camera—as long as he was adequately loaded with Scotch, gin, or vodka, which made his blood run like leaded gasoline. As an actor he was equally adept at playing both drama and comedy; he composed original scores for his variety shows, and mood music that sold millions of records; he was a singular sketch comedian who brought to life a host of memorable stock characters, each one revealing a rare sensitivity to the human experience.

The fat man from Brooklyn was abandoned by his father as a young boy and ended up orphaned as a teenager. The street was his playground and institution of higher learning. He knew a lot about lovable louts, get-rich schemers, pool hustlers, and the armies of everymen who simply couldn't catch a break. He was, after all, a poor urchin who grew to become the most famous entertainer in the world. It was no stretch for him to lampoon the inebriated rich and the luckless schlub—he had been both at different times of his life. While his talents could run the table on the crap game called life, his heart was always pulsating with great compassion for the common man.

But he was a *terrible* hospital patient—just awful! The empathy he exhibited as a performer did not extend to his treatment of doctors, nurses, and orderlies. He discarded and dismissed them like bedpans, disobeying their instructions, which he ignored like the speed limit on Tamiami Trail. Jackie Gleason's stay at Mount Sinai Medical Center was beyond any hope of discipline, decorum, or good health, for that matter. He occupied the hospital like a sultan, and for those unfortunate enough to be inside—whether patient or staff—it was like sharing space with a hurricane. Such was the titanic force of his personality. But very much unlike a hurricane, he didn't just blow through town uprooting palm trees and flinging coconuts through car windshields. Gleason checked into Mount Sinai and stayed put, a fat man nesting, with no intention of ever leaving.

The Great One was given a suite on the top floor of Mount Sinai as if only he on Miami Beach could receive the Ten Commandments. Of course, once brought down to the lobby, he would have flouted them instantly, or simply dropped them because the two tablets required the use of both hands and each of his was always nursing a shot glass filled with Scotch and a smoldering cigarette. There were two such luxury suites on the penthouse of the hospital, neither of which resembled the cold, drab, metallic, antiseptic floors that were layered below and contained the terminally sick or surgically mending residents of Miami Beach. The two suites on the top floor—with their lush beige carpeting, chocolate brown felt wallpaper, soft leathery sofas, and La-Z-boy recliners, glass-encased Harmon Kardon stereo tuners with Pioneer turntables, and sliding glass doors that led out onto majestic, sun-drenched balconies overlooking Biscayne Bay—had more in common with the penthouse suites at the Playboy Plaza Hotel on Collins Avenue than with the other hospital floors with their blinking medical devices and infernal noise-making machines that make sleep impossible and cater to the elderly and dying. And, of course, Gleason's suite came equipped with a fully stocked bar sans medicine cabinet, with the finest Scotch, his elixir of choice.

The suite was Jackie's for the asking not only because he was one of the hospital's most significant donors and patrons. He was also a major Miami Beach luminary and the city's ambassador to the world. And naturally he had the money to pay for the best accommodations in the house. He always traveled first-class, even when sick. Aside from all that, the nurses and doctors felt that it was best to keep Gleason off the regular floors where the true business of the hospital took place. The penthouse, where Gleason held court, was reserved for monkey business, with medicine a mere afterthought. Better to keep the Fat Man sequestered, out of the way of the other patients who had checked into Mount Sinai on the dime of Medicaid and Medicare. These were the true inpatients, for whom horsing around was not the reason for their hospital stay.

With Gleason in the house there was the added pressure of his incessant needs and unpredictable whims. The other patients invariably received less attention. Worse still, Gleason might decide to either start a mutiny at Mount Sinai or ply the other patients with enough sauce to get them positively sloshed. Everyone would want his autograph, and in return they would receive his corrupting influence. The world was forewarned that Gleason was the patron saint of the fucked up—those who took nothing seriously and took lousy care of themselves. For these reasons, there was simply too much risk in allowing him to roam free among the sickly, who were no match for the Great One's appetite for life—even in times of near death.

Yet, the man who was always the life of the party didn't see why it should come to an end simply because he had checked into a hospital with a litany of life-threatening conditions. While he was still alive the party must go on; he was quite certain of that. In fact, a bad prognosis with death looming is the best reason to have a party. What's the alternative—a premature wake? He was told that his profligate lifestyle had brought on these various maladies. Many people in such situations would curse their fate and change their ways. The Great One had decided, instead, to challenge his body. No point succumbing to disease without a fight. He would not allow cancer the ultimate victory. He wanted to be like the Israelis who refuse to negotiate with terrorists. Cancer would not hold his body hostage like a repeat performance of the Munich disaster. Gleason would leave on his own terms and say goodnight to his audience for the final time without a gun to his back.

So he refused to modify his lifestyle even though his lifespan was shrinking by the minute. The doctors would have to work around his vices and behavioral addictions because the life of the party had no intention of shutting it down. They explained that he ended up in this hospital mostly because of a life lived large and always in extremis—with hard liquor, loose women, clogged arteries, the most sparing of sleep. He replied by insisting that he would not interrupt a routine that had worked so well for so many years, bringing him so much joy and personal riches.

Gleason was, after all, a top shelf, king-of-the-world, penthouse kind of guy. He was larger than life, and not in the vernacular of a cultural cliché—he was, in fact, larger than nearly everyone else, and he lived life large, on a scale that dwarfed the everyday crowd of working stiffs and trust-fund sloths. A hospital penthouse outfitted with the toys and amenities for the king of Miami Beach was precisely what the patient wanted and the doctors obligingly ordered.

Except for the two suites and a few nurses, the top floor of Mount Sinai was nearly empty of life. Gleason insisted that the nurses assigned to his floor not dress like, well . . . nurses. He, in fact, paid them double, out of his personal funds, with generous overtime, to dress like either Vegas showgirls or college coeds. The hospital administrators tolerated all this to ensure that Miami Beach's most famous resident would be both happy and less menacing. Even the Mayo Clinic would have found him a handful; no hospital was outfitted for such antics. When it came to the Great One, the Ten Commandments didn't apply—even when he was on the very top of Mount Sinai.

Such boorish behavior was the featured act in a variety show that offered no variation. "Mr. Saturday Night" performed every night as an inpatient and became a royal pain in the neck for beleaguered nurses, unsuspecting candy stripers dressed like strippers, and all those doctors out of their depth in treating a man of such outsized personality and presenting the most inhospitable bedridden manners.

"Mr. Gleason, honestly," an intern dressed to look like a Playboy bunny once said, "please take your hand off my ass! This may be the penthouse, but I don't work for *Penthouse*. I went to nursing school, I'll have you know, although look where it got me," she added, and then turned around to adjust her bushy tail.

"Mr. Gleason, you can't drink Scotch as a chaser after swallowing your pills," said an imperious head nurse who by now had more in common with a madam at a brothel.

"Mr. Gleason, you're scheduled for surgery in the morning and I simply cannot allow you to spend the night playing poker with your friends," said one of the Great One's severely diminished doctors. It's nearly impossible to have a God complex if your patient thinks *he's* God. "I am going to insist that you all leave instantly." At that command Gleason's glad-handers, hangers-on, and faithful cronies all broke out in laughter.

The hospital staff all saw a very different side of Gleason from what America had gotten used to, and that wasn't just because they had to turn him over occasionally to stick a needle in a man whose veins were as difficult to locate as a polar bear in the Everglades.

The suite was always his for the asking, kept vacant until his body would succumb to a relapse or a new disease. In fact, "The Great One" was inscribed right on the door as if the suite were a dressing room for the headliner at the hospital. He regarded it like a backstage dressing room ringed with light bulbs and a "Do Not Disturb" sign. One time Mount Sinai Medical Center turned down a visit from the Shah of Iran, who was having his own troubles—both medical and monarchic—all because Gleason was due for a tune up.

Miami Beach was an offbeat place to get sick in 1972. On the one hand, almost everyone was near death, so medical care—and the golden goose of Medicare—was on everyone's mind. The average age of the population was increasing every day with the arrival of yet another retiree complaining about the crappy kosher meal on the Eastern Airlines flight that had just landed at Miami International Airport. Grandparents who came to Miami Beach for their retirement, and to find a suitable location in which to die, took quality medical care very seriously. Doctors were local heroes. Cardiologists and rheumatologists made a killing.

On the other side of Miami Beach's demographic spectrum were all those residents who saw the city as a magnet for the forever young and the newly promiscuous. Degenerate gamblers, desperate divorcees, and serial swingers were always welcome. Since the 1950s those drawn to Miami Beach believed that Ponce de León had, indeed, discovered the Fountain of Youth, but it was much farther south along the Florida peninsula than he had originally thought. Like some mythical, tropical Eden, Miami Beach was so many things all at the same time: tourist mecca, cemetery in waiting, and party boat where swingers and seekers of Miami's endless variety of vices were all welcome.

South Florida was bathed in a special sunlight that everyone believed to be curative, a secret sauce savored by all. Sickness, actually, seemed so out of place. Disease wouldn't dare. No one feared the sun in those days, the leathery texture of a vigorous tan epitomized fine health. In fact, it was pale, milky skin that everyone believed to be the face of the sick. Liver spots and atypical lesions, even among the elderly, were signatures of vitality, not melanoma. Dermatology in those days was less respected than astrology, and cancerous skin was less threatening than the zodiacal catastrophe of matching a Cancer with an Aries.

Besides, who had time to worry about the sun's acceleration of old age? Miami Beach was a city of endless possibility. Free love and women's lib transformed middle-class values into the sexually open era of hippie chic. Hedonism was the new ethic. Divorce had liberated the divorcees and destigmatized the gold diggers. When it came to love, everyone was suddenly a Midas. Women pranced around with the red-hot letter "A" affixed to their bosoms—the inviting stamp of Availability. Men wore toupees, platform shoes, velvet vests, coiled perms on their heads, wide bell-bottom jeans, flowery shirts, and enough facial hair to qualify them for an earlier epoch of human evolution. It seemed like no one wanted to be taken seriously. In an age before microwave ovens, latchkey kids learned how to make Swanson TV dinners—like legions of teenage Suzy Homemakers.

This yin and yang of the city's wild nights and final days had cast an eerie aura on the residents of Miami Beach. The partiers along the strip refused to imagine that sickness could debilitate this sun-kissed island, and the aged population didn't want to be reminded of their lost youth. Neither wanted to shatter the delusions of the other.

For a man of such considerable girth, Jackie Gleason managed to straddle both spheres—he was both a living Bacchus and a reminder of what can happen when immoderation takes its toll on even the widest of bodies. The author of the pitch line for the Miami Beach Chamber of Commerce, "the sun and fun capital of the world," and the patron saint of all boozers who awoke the morning after with blurred vision, Gleason was also an anatomy chart containing everything that could possibly go wrong with the health of a human being. While partiers toasted him in absentia in clubs along Collins Avenue, a team of busy doctors labored on his many incurable ailments.

It was a miracle that he was still alive. There was no better boozer than the Great One, who had started drinking heavily as a teenager and whose tolerance for alcohol only improved with time. By his late twenties Gleason was routinely outdrinking even the legendary drunks at Toots Shor's Restaurant on West 51st Street in New York. His prodigious taste for Scotch was so great that many a bar bill was settled, and many an evening came to an end in the grand style of chivalrous drinking duels in which Gleason alone soberly managed to rise from the table without collapsing into a pool of slurred words and hungover heads.

It was there in New York at Toots's saloon where Jackie met his main posse of drinking buddies who, in the old days, often paid for his drinks. Years later they would all raise a glass in his honor—the world had finally recognized what they had known all along: Gleason *was* truly great. People were getting used to staring into a little box that featured the talents of their gargantuan friend. But in those early days at Toots Shor's, Gleason was famous for only one thing: drinking more alcohol than any other self-respecting drunk.

"Mmmmboy, that's some good coffee," he would swoon in front of the TV cameras years later while drinking out of a teacup on his variety show. Everyone—the live audience, those huddled around their TV sets at home, actors, dancers, and the crew watching from backstage—were well aware that the teacup was all a charade: Jackie was consuming neither tea nor coffee. The liquor was hard, and so was the laughter.

"Hey, Jackie—ring-a-ding-ding," Frank Sinatra, one of his old drinking buddies from Toots's, chimed as he entered his friend's hospital suite. He was buckled over in laughter. Such right-angled choreography was not unknown to Sinatra, but usually only after a three-day bender when standing straight was a real challenge. Sinatra was in Miami Beach visiting Gleason, his ailing comrade-in-mischief. He was no longer the skinny kid from Jersey whom Gleason met years ago at Toots's place. Frank had filled out a bit, as would be expected of America's silkiest crooner and tabloid heartthrob. His fedora and porkpie hats still tipped to one side, but now his body weight was shifting, which required a repositioning of his head to rebalance the hats. Hoboken was very much in his past; Frank was now considered old-school Hollywood, while his best friend, Jackie Gleason, was a Miami Beach mainstay. "The lady in the suite down the hall," Frank continued, holding his belly, catching his breath, his blue eyes watery from happy tears. "I swear, the lady almost made me bust a gut."

The one thing Jackie could never abide was being upstaged. In any social setting, his Irish storytelling bravura never failed to lure the spotlight over to his large frame. Rarely was Jackie ever in a room and not the center of attention. Back in his New York days at Toots Shor's, the joint was filled with Frank Sinatra, Humphrey Bogart, and Orson Welles, and yet all eyes were on the Great One, who was drunk early and often, which was precisely when his most raffish free associations would spring from his sloshed mind.

If he could command such crowds in Manhattan even while surrounded by an A-list of American icons—the Mount Rushmore of degenerate, juke-joint cool—how was he now suddenly reduced to an opening act on his own turf, right here in lowly Miami Beach? He should be able to kill in this hospital, in front of a sober crowd unburdened by a two-drink minimum. Who in the hell was headlining at the other end of the hall?

Frank said her name was Sophie Posner. Jackie now knew the name of the lady in the other penthouse suite down the hall. The nurses would occasionally goad him by saying that his neighbor had as many visitors as he had—they made an even bigger ruckus and seemed to be having even more of a good time.

"I swear, Mr. Gleason," an African American nurse would chide, "she's just the funniest thing. I says to her the other day: 'Mrs. Posner, you should have your own variety show all by yourself. That Gleason's got nothing over you, baby.'"

Jackie pretended he didn't hear—that he didn't care. What did the nurses know about talent anyway? You think they were sent over from William Morris? He may have dressed them up to look like cocktail waitresses, but these were not the kind of broads who went out for drinks at the Eden Roc, looking for a cock to keep them company for the night. They were respectable, ordinary folk, the type of girls who were in bed early and got a full eight hours of rest. Almost never would they fall under the influence of a drink or a drug in order to have a good time. They were only pretend swingers, paid for under his tab and for his own amusement. Yet, here was Frank

Sinatra, who, after all, knew good material when he saw it, wiping tears from his eyes and stomping his foot like a big band leader, pissing in his pants all on account of the lady down the hall with the sharp wit and salty tongue of a stand-up comic.

"Sophie Posner," Gleason recited her name as if he needed to vocalize the unbridled jealousy he was experiencing. "Who the fuck is this lady, and how come I never heard of her before? She's in my town. I know everybody, for Christ's sake!"

Ironically, these two patients who shared an entire floor on Mount Sinai's highest peak each attracted an entourage not so very different from one another. The people who visited Jackie were many of the entertainers on the strip—the old-timers and the up-and-comers; whereas the lady's crew, apparently, were many of the mobsters who controlled the action along the strip.

Sinatra had straddled these two professional communities since his big band days. After all, he brought Hollywood/Vegas glamour to the Camelot Kennedys; Camelot would have been only a Broadway musical had he not persuaded Chicago mob boss Sam Giancana to rig the Cook County vote in favor of America's very own King Arthur, John Kennedy. The Mafia and the movie stars, for Sinatra, were like Cosa cousins.

As it turned out, as Sinatra explained to his friend, Sophie Posner was one of them—a gangster herself, one of the top brass, higher than a capo. In fact, she was Meyer Lansky's trusted consigliere. Imagine that. A Jewish lady, no less, with a European accent and a row of numbers along her left forearm, was a major crime figure on Miami Beach. It's not how one usually imagined the postwar life of a Jewish refugee. Haberdashers, *shmata* salesmen, candy store proprietors, socialist poets, even slumlords—yes. But a *made woman* in a crime syndicate—and not even a lawyer? She must have walked away from those German ovens with very special knowledge, easily redeployed against a different type of heat, in the service of killers of a different kind.

Jackie Gleason had meant to drop by his neighbor's for a visit. Oddly, people who thrive in parties often come across as shy in more sober social situations. Jackie didn't want to just show up unannounced and find out that he and the Polish broad had nothing to talk about. Gleason, after all, was always on, always revved up at full speed, always loud and sucking up all the oxygen—even in a hospital where there are tanks and iron lungs for such things. He was unaccustomed to silence and awkward pauses. Besides, what would happen if she didn't drink, if she was the only patient on the floor who was actually following the doctors' orders?

What he didn't realize—what the Great One could not have imagined—was that Sophie Posner, the lady in Suite 2, his neighbor in lavish hospitalization, was every bit as much his showboating equal, his degenerate match, his spiritual twin.

As Jackie Gleason would soon come to learn, Sophie had come to this penthouse suite courtesy of Meyer Lansky, the Jewish mobster and kingpin whose empire extended far beyond Miami Beach's tiny den of iniquity. Gleason, of course, knew Lansky. They'd see each other around town—restaurants, the grand ballrooms of hotels, local bars, even city council meetings where Lansky was lobbying for legalized gambling and the Great One was just stopping by to claim yet another proclamation thanking him for his services to Miami Beach. Lansky and Gleason would smile at one another, tip a cap, or toss off a half-salute. It was actually they who ran this town, to be sure, and not the overheated suits parading around with their fancy municipal titles but no real influence or worldly calling card.

So any friend of Meyer's was surely welcome on Jackie's floor. He wondered, however, why Meyer Lansky didn't stop by to see him on one of his visits to his hospitalized consigliere. She wasn't the only sick patient on the penthouse. And everyone south of Tallahassee knew that Jackie was checked in on the top floor of Mount Sinai. Gleason pretended not to be irked by the snub, but privately he stewed like a basted ham. After all, who was the most famous sick person at Mount Sinai Medical Center—the Great One, or this Polish refugee with mob ties? It wasn't even close. The only thing to do now, Jackie thought, was to somehow team up with this seemingly powerful dame. But in the obscure world of hospital etiquette, who was supposed to make the first move?

First, Jackie wondered what the lady was in for? Was she really sick, like him, or was this one of those nip and tuck jobs that were becoming increasingly popular among women with money, where a lifetime of wrinkles suddenly, cosmetically, disappeared into a stiff, shiny sheen of face-lifted magic. Surgeons were no longer limited to the life-saving business. Some were into plastic, youth preservation; the Hippocratic oath now had more in common with the Age of Narcissism than it did with modern medicine. Perhaps Sophie Posner was at Mount Sinai not to receive revelation but to experience the signs and wonders of ridding herself of the ancient plague known as old age. When compared with a case of face-saving, Jackie Gleason could surely pull rank.

"It's not like I came here for fat removal," he thought, even though no such procedure existed at that time.

But Jackie didn't want to just trundle over to Sophie Posner's suite unless he knew for certain that the Great One was also the sicker of the two. Jackie always needed to be on top. What he didn't know, because the nurses were not allowed to say and Sinatra had not bothered to ask, is that here, too, Sophie Posner was able to match Gleason pound for pound.

"I'm afraid I have bad news for you, Mrs. Posner," the doctor said with deadpan delivery, a bedpan peeking out from below the bed, beside his shoes. "As we discussed before the surgery, I told you cancer was a possibility. Your symptoms of pain in your stomach and back were indicative of a gastrointestinal abnormality. If the tumors I located were malignant, they would need to be removed. They were, as I had feared, but they had also already spread. You have pancreatic cancer. I had to remove your pancreas, gallbladder, and spleen."

"Did you leave anything for me? Is there anything left inside?" she asked with a clenched jaw. Her eyes darted as if, although bedridden, she were looking to make a break for the exit. "Is anything still working?"

"The prognosis is not good. I think you should prepare yourself for a very difficult year."

"Okay, you've done your job. You can leave now," Sophie said, staring out the window, half-listening, plotting her next move.

"Do you have any questions?" asked the doctor, who was tall with wavy black hair and the stocky build of a Nordic skier slumming in snowless Miami. His doctor's coat was an immaculate white, which matched his cold, bland expression. A stethoscope clung from his neck like a shiny amulet. A ray of sunlight splashed into Sophie's eyes.

Now squinting, she said, "No, you've said enough. I understand. Please leave."

"I know this must come as a terrible shock to you. All of my patients react this way," he began stiffly as if reciting a script from his bedside manner playbook. He was a stomach surgeon, only casually in the death business and not very good at delivering bad news.

"Please, don't insult me."

"Pardon. I'm just trying to . . ."

" 'Shock'? That's the best you can do?" Sophie Posner scoffed. "You think I'm shocked by a little cancer?"

"It's actually quite a bit more than a little . . ." he said haltingly. He was unused to patients interrupting his God complex when it was in full magisterial stride.

"You think this is the worst news I've ever heard?" Sophie let out a demonic laugh.

"What could be worse than this? Your prognosis and survival rate is as bad as it gets." The doctor's demeanor, improbably, was downshifting into a lower gear of unfeeling.

"Is it worse than Auschwitz?" Sophie shot back with the name of the death camp that had become a universal synonym for hell. Her own particular brand of German poison had been dispensed at Maidanek. But that camp would have been less familiar to him, and she wanted to render her doctor comatose in a single blow.

The doctor blinked and then stared blankly at his patient. He wondered if there was epidemiological data on the association between blue tattoo numbers and the end stage of metastatic cancers.

"Cancer is just a disease," Sophie continued. "You think a tumor keeps me up at night? A little back pain, a shooting pain through my stomach? You think that's what brings on the nightmares?"

The doctor, trained in the building blocks of the Big C, believed that Sophie's questions were naively rhetorical. The answer to each of them, of course, was yes.

"You doctors are so in awe of the body's many mysteries. But disease is not the worst killer of mankind. Compared to Auschwitz, cancer is no worse than the common cold. Look!" she said, and then shoved her forearm into his face as if it were the only patient chart he would ever need to see. "These numbers mean that I am invincible. It will take more than a tumor to kill me. And, good doctor, unless your name is Mengele, there is nothing you can say that can scare me. This cancer I will survive, too, and not because of God's will or your skill. I will live because that's what I do. And I have already proven it. Nothing can kill me, not even this summer heat and humidity. So you do what you must. And not to make you nervous, but you realize I'm connected, right? Meyer Lansky is a personal friend. He wouldn't like it if something should go wrong, something that could have been prevented. I'm his lady consigliere, and Meyer never lets go of a grudge. Don't worry, the family doesn't believe in medical malpractice lawsuits. But you may wind up at the bottom of Biscayne Bay with your legs in cement shoes. Meanwhile, your family will receive a very strange package—gefilte fish all wrapped up in your white lab coat."

"I am very sorry if I upset you," the doctor said. "My bedside manners are lousy. But, honestly, I wasn't prepared for your response. I've never had a patient like you."

"That I believe," Sophie scoffed.

"Well, I'll be on my way," the doctor turned and retrieved Sophie's patient chart.

"Wait," Sophie reached for the doctor's arm. "One more thing: don't tell my husband this news. I don't want my son to know either. I need them to see me as unkillable."

"Whatever you think is best."

Well, at least that's the way Sophie relayed that conversation when Jackie finally summoned up the courage to walk over to her suite, introduce himself, and see if she wanted any company.

"What, you don't bring a Bundt cake?" she asked. "Who comes to visit a neighbor without bringing cake?"

Jackie smiled. He knew then that the woman with whom he shared the top floor of the hospital was not a competitor but a compatriot. They would make quite a mischievous pair of debauched patients in this penthouse of the tropically insane.

"Sorry, lady," Jackie began. "My suite down the hall is completely out of cake."

"But not out of the hard stuff, surely. Don't tell me the Great One doesn't have a bottle of the finest Scotch lying around somewhere—between the sheets, under the bed, stashed away in the lining of your robe?"

"Alright, you got me. I'll be right back," Jackie's face was flush, with his palms held up, caught red-handed. "Booze I have! The finest for my new friend. Coming right up!"

He then kicked up his right leg in a right angle and brought it backward like a braying animal only to thrust it forward in his "awaaaay we go" pose as he darted to his suite to retrieve the best bottle of Scotch he had—and two shot glasses.

And for the rest of that afternoon, with the "Do Not Disturb" sign dangling from the doorknob of Sophie Posner's suite, these two hopeless cases finished off that bottle, and then another. They had each lived sad, colorful lives, jazzed up and made fuzzier by washing it all down with the thick amber lubricant that makes unpleasant memories far less charged and unforgiving.

"What did they tell you about cigarettes?" Jackie asked as he puffed away lazily on a Lucky Strike attached to an elegant, ivory cigarette holder.

"Stop smoking them!" they shouted together.

"My doctors call these things killers?" she mocked, and then examined the puny tube of nicotine in her hand, which looked so otherwise harmless.

"How many did you smoke?" Jackie wondered.

"Did?" Sophie scoffed. "Still do! Five packs a day. Meyer sneaks boxes in here every few days as if it was Prohibition when he smuggled bootlegged molasses in from Canada."

"Same here," Jackie confessed. "I don't listen to my doctors either. What the hell do they know anyway? Soda jerks wear white coats, too, for Christ's sake. My pals haul cartons of cigarettes up the elevator like they're fencing the stuff. And then I go ahead and smoke them all like a chimney in Florida."

"You're not a chimney, Gleason, believe you me," Sophie corrected her new friend. "I've seen the real thing, and those chimneys in Poland were the true killers—and they never stopped smoking."

"Jesus, Sophie," Gleason said—her meaning was plain but the truth of it made Jackie shield his eyes as if gamma rays and not sunlight had just flooded her penthouse suite.

Despite hours of frolic and newfound friendship, neither of them awoke the next morning with hangovers. Their livers were long conditioned to handle such spongy responsibility. In fact, their prior day of drunkenness within a sanitized hospital only made their confinement all the more absurd. Maybe their doctors had it all wrong. Perhaps the alcohol and cigarettes were not the causes of their disease but the placebos that might ultimately cure them. In the screwball universe in which they lived their lives, these environmental factors might possibly be helpful rather than hazardous to their health. After all, what else was left to deaden the pain—to rewire their brains? The year 1972 was a high-water mark for marijuana, but it was still years away from being legalized for medicinal purposes. Tried and true moonshine was still the best medicine to distract the mind and disable the senses. All those chemo drugs were likely to kill them; Scotch was a temporary antidote that might actually keep them alive.

"Hey, neighbor, you up yet?" Jackie rapped on Sophie's door, which was open, by clinking shot glasses and a bottle of Chivas together. "You want to go for two?"

"Did you wash the glasses?" Sophie smiled.

"Of course, I'm always the perfect gentleman," Gleason boasted. "Even when I'm loaded."

"I'll give you that," Sophie said, lifting her glass in performance of a toast. "'Baby, you are the greatest' drinker I've ever seen," she said, borrowing one of Gleason's signature *Honeymooner* lines. "And I'm from Poland, so I know from drunks. The Christians from my childhood in Warsaw drank vodka like Floridians drink orange juice."

"You know, Sophie," Jackie said while the booze was fast oozing through his system and beginning to have its way with him, his defenses and discretion way down, "you're not my first Jewish friend."

"What, you're not a virgin when it comes to Jews?" she shot back, registering a look of total disbelief. It was early, and her graying hair was uncombed, which only added to the look of shock. "I can't believe—the most famous man in Miami Beach, the man who made his living on television for twenty years, with all those blacklisted commie Jewish writers, actually knows a few Jews."

"Hardy-har-har," the Great One shook his head and lowered it so that his double chin went through the gymnastics of a Lava Lamp. "I should have said you're not my first *best* friend who was Jewish."

"I'm now your best Jewish friend?" Sophie feigned even more surprise.

"You're kidding! After just a few days? The biggest star on TV isn't such a popular man, after all, I see. I have bad news for you, 'Mr. Saturday Night': I'll be dead by the end of this year and then where will you be? You sure Sinatra can't pretend to be circumcised?"

"Knock it off, Sophie. I was talking about Toots Shor, who was my best Jewish friend until you came along. And you won't be dead anytime soon. You'll outlive all the doctors and nurses in this joint."

"Gleason, if it will make you feel better, I didn't have many drunken, loud-mouthed Irish friends in my life until you came along either," Sophie replied ruefully. She was beginning to realize that, for one of the most re-nowned men in the United States, Gleason was a deeply lonely human be-ing. Hangers-on are only there for the cheap thrill that comes with proximity to fame. Gleason was rich in sycophants but quite poor in actual friendships.

The Irish lovable lout from Bensonhurst and the Polish Jewess from Warsaw were perfect for each other. But sometimes there would be actual bickering among all that playful banter.

"To the moon, Sophie, to the moon!" Gleason would ball up his fist and his eyes would bulge out just as they had when he had perfected this routine on *The Honeymooners*.

"Hey, Gleason," Sophie would retort, "don't you forget, unlike Alice who only scowled at you, I *will* punch back!"

They played cards on each other's balconies, inviting their friends to join them. Jackie Gleason, for the first time, really got to know Meyer Lansky.

Before then their meetings had been brief but entertaining. Meyer Lan-sky and Jackie Gleason had always been no more than distant acquain-tances, two local celebrities who catered to different Miami Beach crowds and who were notorious for excesses of a very different sort. Meyer never saw a law that he didn't want to break; Jackie never saw a vice that he could avoid. But they were nonetheless and unavoidably bound to each other by the city they shared. After all, as far as Jackie Gleason was concerned, the only other man of similar stature in Miami Beach was Meyer Lansky, the racketeer who proved that Jews with a head for business and a hair-trigger temper had career prospects aside from being lawyers and accountants.

Miami Beach had always had a thriving underworld, and not only be-cause so many old Jews came here first to retire, and then to die. Some of these Jews were bookies and number runners, card sharks and addicted gamblers, pari-mutuel parasites, and muscle heads for the mob. And for the whole lot of them, Meyer Lansky was the boss who ran all the action from Hallandale down to Havana, with Las Vegas as his very own Fort Knox.

Lansky had only recently gotten back from a short stay Israel. He was happy there and would have gladly forfeited his American citizenship if they'd let him stay. But he was forced to return to the United States to stand trial, so until Sophie devised a plan to spring him, he was cooped up in the Imperial House as he had been before. With all the dead bodies from the hits he had ordered over the years, the Feds were indicting Lansky for tax evasion?

"Fat chance they will be able to pin that rap on you, Meyer," the Great One said one afternoon on the balcony of Sophie's suite. They were cutting a cake for Meyer's birthday, the sun melting the frosting into a milkshake. He only wanted a thin slice. "You've got all those offshore accounts and money stashed away with people all over the world. Nobody knows how to hide money better than Lansky, I always say. I bet you don't have twenty bucks in an American bank in your own name. You were too smart for Hoover's G-men. You must have layers of goons between you and the crime, and then layers of lawyers between you and the Feds. You've beaten the system, and the odds, all your life, right?"

"Actually, Jackie," the modest mobster admitted, "my luck has changed all because of that lady right there," he pointed at Sophie, who was reclining on a beach chair wearing a red velvet bathrobe. "She's the one with the head for business and the brass of a brawler."

The Great One glanced back at Sophie, with not quite a double take, but the look of someone who was growing accustomed to hearing about Sophie's immense talents. A few of Meyer's henchmen waited outside in the hallway, guarding the penthouse suites like gargoyles, tilted wool fedoras and Italian-tapered suits cuffed at their legs. All these wise guys melted like winter gnomes in the brick oven of South Florida. Many had cut their teeth in Las Vegas and were now inserting their dentures on Miami Beach. In declining health and suffering from advanced age, they felt at home at Mount Sinai Medical Center even though they were not officially admitted.

Gleason was enjoying all this new company, courtesy of his penthouse roomie. "I've always thought it was much easier being a mobster in Miami," he said. "For one thing, there are no Italian neighborhoods here, which means there's no competition. Hey, did you fellas see *The Godfather* yet? It just opened in theaters. Everyone's now got the mob on their minds."

Lansky's made men didn't know whether to shut Gleason up or ask for his autograph. *The Godfather* wasn't good for business, and Gleason was a blabbermouth—a real BLABBERMOUTH! Even Sophie was getting uncomfortable. The Mafia, historically, likes to lie low.

"So, Meyer, you're like the Jewish Don Corleone?" Gleason chuckled, and then faked some *Honeymooners* fear, "Hamina-hamina-hamina-hamina. I may be the King of Miami Beach, but I guess it wouldn't hurt for me to kiss your ring from time to time. Heck, doesn't the actual mayor of Miami Beach have to do it, too?"

Meyer Lansky briefly considered having Gleason whacked, where he would end up sleeping with the whales, given his extra girth.

Before these hospital visits Gleason and Lansky were rarely seen together. But whenever they were, Gleason gave the gangster a big hug. And because Meyer was so short, it was difficult for Meyer to get his arms around the wide-bodied TV star. Lansky looked like he had just won the grand prize at the county fair and he was going home with an oversized stuffed animal. In the days before paparazzi, newspapers loved to shoot such unscripted photo ops—the bantam hoodlum and the Great One locked in a loving embrace, like Laurel and Hardy.

"So Gleason," Lansky once said, coincidentally having just shown up at Wolfie's Restaurant on Lincoln Road, "you still trying to make an honest living? I was prepared to give you the same deal I gave George Raft in Havana and you turned me down. You would have made a fortune and never had to work again. Instead, you made chump change from CBS. And how did CBS return your loyalty? They cancelled your show, WASP bastards! These 'legitimate corporations' are all thieves, I tell you, thieves. Real goniffs. And they call me crooked?"

Gleason enjoyed these chance celebrity sightings in his town. Lansky, of course, didn't mean what he said about the Great One's career on TV. He knew that Gleason had made out like a bandit in show business. He had the richest contract of any TV star for nearly twenty years. He made more money than Lucy and Desi combined! That fat face was known all over the world. He played golf every day of the week until he had to check into

Mount Sinai. Television had been very good to him, and he never wanted to become a Mafia stooge and owe Lansky and company any favors.

When the crowd at Wolfie's noticed them standing there and heard Gleason bellow, "One of these days, Meyer, one of these days, *pow*, right in the kisser!" the crowd erupted in laughter. Gleason rolled up his fist and continued, "To the moon, Meyer, to the moon!"

In jocular moments like these, Lansky would look up at Gleason with his bloodshot eyes, a cloverleaf of vein-tracks on his nose. He would then wag his finger, smile, and say, "Good one, Gleason. Baby, you are the greatest!" borrowing yet again from *The Honeymooners*, that saccharine bit of dialogue, lovingly reserved for Alice, that often closed out the show.

The two Miami Beach legends couldn't have pulled off that bit in a Vegas luncheonette to the same effect. No way. Bleary eyed and oblivious to the nuances of *The Honeymooners*, those suddenly poor, demoralized fortune seekers wouldn't have gotten all the inside jokes.

Here in Mount Sinai, Gleason learned to take even more liberties with Lansky's more hospitable temperament. In fact, he bravely took some of his money in poker and lived to tell people about it—lived longer than the doctors had predicted, in fact. Suddenly, all on account of Sophie Posner's pancreatic dilemma, these two Miami Beach *machers* were now friends. Meyer and some of his capos, in fact, continued to check in on the Great One after visiting with their consigliere.

"Aw, you shouldn't have, Meyer," Jackie blushed one day when Lansky popped into his room caressing a box of illegal Cohiba Cuban cigars. "Holy cow, I know this brand. This is the real deal. This is what Fidel Castro smokes! How'd you get it? It fell off a truck, or a raft?"

Lansky recoiled at the Castro connection, the matter of the future *presidente* and his running of the island a most delicate subject for Meyer. If not for that communist dictator, Lansky would be the richest and most powerful casino owner in the world. Castro cost him money and stole his hotels, something a criminal mastermind could never abide and certainly wouldn't forget. And for these and other reasons Castro was a marked man in Miami. The multitude of Cuban refugees who recreated *Cubano* culture in South Florida never lost hope that their island would be reclaimed and Castro eliminated. And the Mafia, specifically Lansky's partners in the gaming industry, had its own score to settle with that Soviet puppet in the Caribbean with his camouflage fatigues, long-winded speeches, bushy beard, and bearish manner. The casinos were nationalized, treated no differently than sugar plantations; the craps tables were upended and turned to crap, the dice now forever on ice in the tropics.

Meyer cringed when he imagined what those once-majestic hotels he had built in the 1950s now looked like in 1972, after twelve years of drab decorating by the *lumpenproletariat*. An industrial Soviet style had by now converted those posh palaces to look like Siberian prisons. So any mention of Fidel and his cigar fixations wafted over Lansky like a noxious odor. All the news out of Havana was, for him, bittersweet. He was obsessed with Castro's grand theft and with finding a way to give the presidente a grand communist burial. In the meantime, he begrudgingly kept cigar boxes of Cuba's finest around just for special occasions. He would have far preferred, however, to trade his Cuban cigars for a different contraband, something less evocative of the island but far more precious and personal to him. It was the loss of those hotels that broke his heart.

"Only the best for Sophie's friend," Meyer said, patting the Great One on his shoulder while Jackie lit a match, and soon a ring of glimmering ember surrounded the cigar like a halo. Lansky wanted Gleason to know that the local syndicate had their eyes on him—and not as an entertainer. His friendship with Sophie made him suspicious, if not dangerous. Mr. Saturday Night might wind up as the victim of a Saturday Night Special.

"What's with you and all of them gangsters?" Jackie asked Sophie as they baked on Jackie's balcony, eyes closed and heads pointed skyward with suntanning reflectors attached to their necks, vainly trying to add some color to their otherwise pale, sickly faces. "Honestly, Sinatra doesn't know as many hoods as you do, and they certainly don't take orders from him like the way these thugs hop to attention whenever they hear your voice. Not too long ago you're in a death camp at the mercy of Nazis; and here you are today, lounging on Miami Beach with all that Mafioso muscle at your disposal. That's quite a makeover if you ask me."

By this time it wasn't so surprising that Frank Sinatra and Sophie Posner could both be mentioned in the same sentence. Frank, it should be remembered, was the one who first introduced Jackie to the colorful other occupant on the penthouse floor of Mount Sinai Medical Center. And ever since that day these two giants in the entertainment industry were simultaneously courting this Polish refugee—not for romance, but for a certain inner respectability they could not manage to summon up themselves.

Sophie Posner spent more time with Frank Sinatra than any other Jewish lady in history, that's for sure. She became his spiritual Eva Gardner—a strong attraction but without the sex. Old Blue Eyes was drawn to this broad, whom he knew to be streetwise in ways that surpassed any of the neighborhood toughs from Hoboken and Vegas. The streets from which she had once escaped were not garden-variety ethnic gangs with their turf wars and rap sheets. She emerged from the unpaved, one-way street of Maidanek in one piece, without even a diploma to show for it. All she had was a numerical tattoo as souvenir. Whenever he was in town to visit Jackie, Frank would bring Sophie flowers, and even sing her a special song. Sometimes he would suggest something.

"How about 'High Hopes'?"

"Don't be ridiculous, Danny Ocean," she replied. "I'll throw you into the Atlantic. A very naive lyric if you ask me," she shrugged, passing on his suggestion. "How about 'Glad to be Unhappy' or 'Fly Me to the Moon,' or how about 'Dancing on the Ceiling'? I love to dance, you know."

Truth be told, Jackie Gleason would get jealous when Sinatra lingered too long in Sophie's suite while the Great One waited anxiously on the other side of the hall.

"That skinny Italian with the olive voice better not be trying to steal my girl!" Jackie once fumed to himself in his own gravelly voice. "You can't trust that guy with your women. They swoon over him. I think I need to lose some weight," he added, realizing that he had heard this recommendation before, in this very place.

Even Meyer Lansky was a bit put off by Sinatra's shine on Sophie Posner. After all, Sinatra only had "alleged" mobster ties. He wasn't himself a wise guy. Meyer knew that Sophie was turned on by the adrenaline rush that only a criminal syndicate could provide. Sinatra was like the hired help for the mob; he was no hired gun. Sophie was no groupie for some has-been singer. Bobby-soxers were not concentration camp material—they wouldn't survive a second. Sure, back in the day Frank had palled around with Sam Giancana, the mob boss from Chicago. But by 1972 Giancana had been hiding in Mexico for years. Sinatra's mob credentials were exaggerated; he was trading on the illusion of being a tough guy. Meyer, after all, was the genuine gangster article, and Sophie knew her own kind.

Jackie Gleason and Meyer Lansky were not the only two people in Sophie Posner's life who were distressed by the attention she was receiving from an American heartthrob. She still had a husband and young son at home who were none too pleased by the filled dance card of their wife and mother.

It got so bad that Jacob and Adam had to make a special appointment to visit with Sophie. They never knew her official diagnosis, and her prognosis was rendered positively unknowable by the party atmosphere that emanated from her room. Whenever they stopped by unannounced, there was a gangster, or a Rat Packer, or Miami Beach's Mr. Saturday Night holding court and commandeering her suite. At such moments Jacob merely retired into a corner, his flamboyant wife always overshadowing him. Now her larger-than-life friends were making him feel not so much a cuckold as a flat-out irrelevancy. What was he supposed do—fight off Jackie Gleason, who outweighed him by two hundred pounds? Frank Sinatra was called the Chairman of the Board for a reason; Jacob Posner, a man of modest means, had a decidedly weak portfolio by comparison. And Meyer Lansky, the most dangerous Jewish mobster in the world, was not the sort of man to challenge to a duel—even to avenge the honor of his wife. Jacob was already a sick man, after all. He was no match for these heavyweights—at least not at this time of his life, and perhaps not ever.

"Hey, Jake," Jackie Gleason once called out to him, "pull up a chair. Can I pour you a drink? What will you have?"

"No, no alcohol for him, Jackie," Sophie imposed her will, even from her sickbed. "His heart is bad."

"I guess I can't offer him a cigar either?" Jackie surmised, surprised that after everything he had witnessed during Hitler's Holocaust, Jacob Posner could now endure almost nothing else. This former partisan in the forest had become a fish out of water everywhere. Once a great risk taker surviving on grit and guile, now a virtual invalid waiting for directions from his wife.

"Does he play poker?" Frank Sinatra wanted to know. Frank tipped his hat and smiled weakly at Jacob in the corner, who had opened a book he had carried along with him, Proust's *Remembrance of Things Past*. Before burrowing down for another passage, Jacob nodded at Sinatra, not quite the

Summit's secret handshake, but at least an acknowledgment that he was well aware of the strange assortment of bedfellows that had gathered at his wife's bedside.

"He sure likes to read," Jackie said. "Doesn't say very much, though."

"That's because he's already *seen* too much," Sophie snapped back like an alligator from the Everglades. She was defending her husband in this bizarre, twisted love triangle where honor was cheap, virtue was nonexistent, and ego was about as sturdy as a soft-swirl Carvel ice-cream cone in the sweltering August sun. "What, you think he's like you bozos, your whole lives limited to booze, broads, and the applause from strangers? He's seen things, things he can't talk about, things that would cause you two to give up drinking for good."

Jackie and Frank stared at one another uncomprehendingly; then, after a few seconds, they appeared to be genuinely hurt, sitting there like children in front of a frowning principal, heads pointed downward with feet dangling, Jackie's jowls ballooning like a blow fish's and Frank's falsetto voice now whiny, his blue eyes ocean wet. Sophie's high opinion of them mattered; they would have to make due with a low opinion, if necessary. But they desperately wanted her to take the measure of them, to value them in some way, any way. Should she decide to start her own crew, a Polish Pack, a Slavic Gang, or even an Ocean's Eleven on Miami Beach, they wanted to be among its first two members. Jackie was beginning to feel less like the Great One and more like a second banana in her company. And he wasn't bothered by that at all. She was one of those addictions that are actually good for you.

She was real, as real a human being as they had ever known. No matter how far they had come from the gutters of their pasts, where guts, grime, and authenticity were abundant and where bullshit was exposed faster than a card cheat, these two would always value the real thing over the quick scam. In the VIP corner of the globe where celebrities dodge paparazzi and autograph hounds, and where groupies and fanzine writers serve as stand-ins for true friendship and intimacy, the appearance of a Sophie Posner, with a backbone fashioned in the crucible of the Holocaust, was a rare find. Gleason and Sinatra realized why Meyer Lansky treated her like a meal ticket. Her blood coursed through her body without stop signs or speed limits. Their interest in her was of a different sort, however. They desperately wanted her approval. They drew strength from her because these men of outsized reputation had no inner strength. In Sophie they had discovered a life source that wasn't in a bottle, this Polish Jew fueling the fragile psyches of American pop stars.

Would that were true of her own son, who had the very opposite reaction to his mother's presence—spare though it was. Sophie Posner's aura, which many of Miami Beach's most glamorous misfits wanted to have beamed on them with the warm embrace of Florida sunshine, caused in her son nothing but revulsion. Everything about his mother depleted him; she was not so much the mother ship as the krypton to his Clark Kent. To be in her orbit was to feel the slow dissipation of oxygen, the closing in of walls, the squelching of life itself. And since Adam was a runner who depended on a slow steady breadth, mothering of this sort was like a chokehold. This mother-son bond was about as frayed as a waterlogged coconut, and as buoyant, too.

While his mother's crew behaved as if they were receiving an audience with the Pope, and his father skulked in the corner of his wife's hospital suite like it was visiting hours in a zoo, Adam went off on a long run, far away from the smell of alcohol—both the rubbing and the spirited kind—the cigar smoke, the dirty jokes and cheap laughs, the shuffling of cards and the tossing of poker chips, and his sickly father, who would soon require his own hospital room, one on a lower floor, where medicine was actually being practiced rather than disgraced.

Soon the party on the penthouse of Mount Sinai would be called to a close. A busty nurse schooled in frat-house etiquette, who was specially assigned to this detail, drew the blinds, her skirt hoisted up to enhance the show. This was no work for a socially squeamish Florence Nightingale. The penthouse of this hospital required less medical training than usual. It was more like potty training for adults.

This party soon blended into the next one. There was always another one. Visiting hours were over, but the mischief was only now beginning. Jackie Gleason called his driver and told him to pull up to the side entrance of the hospital. Jackie and Sophie dressed for a night out on the town, provided they could sneak down the stairwell without being detected and slide past the emergency room filled with elderly Jews clutching their chests, then slip outside and into the waiting red Cadillac Eldorado without anyone noticing. Gleason put on a tuxedo, which didn't fit anymore, the cancer having eaten him away and slimmed him down. His neck had shrunk, too, which made him look like an especially well dressed tortoise. The extra flab under his chin dangled firmly, immune to weight loss. Sophie had similar problems with the elegant dress she picked out for this special evening. It was blue chiffon with flowery trellises, which dragged along the floor like a janitor's mop. And for jewelry she selected a three-strand pearl necklace that gleamed like a low-hanging halo.

The penthouse suites had been suddenly evacuated while the rest of the hospital functioned as normal.

A star-struck candy striper carrying a tray covered with dishes of Jell-O noticed them leave but didn't want to disrupt the fun. She winked at the Great One and he, knowing his fan base, threw her a kiss. She had heard rumors of the shenanigans on the top floor. Now she was an accomplice. For the several months that the penthouse was occupied by these VIPs (the "I," of course, standing for "incorrigible"), the hospital gave up any hope of imposing discipline on these two patients, as if Mount Sinai had become a tale of two hospitals—one dedicated to wellness, the other to decadence. The mountain that gave the world the Ten Commandments was the name-sake of a hospital that couldn't lay down the law for two measly patients.

Any orderly headed upstairs was bound to return disorderly. All doctors who made their rounds on the top of Mount Sinai returned to the lobby flushed and gray-haired, ready to smash two patient charts on top of any golden calf sold in the gift shop. The revelation they received from these two patients could make anyone doubt the existence of God. Around them the Burning Bush dimmed. Miracles of modern medicine were useless against such self-annihilation. These were patients with a death wish, and it wasn't even their terminal illnesses that were bringing them closer to their mortal end.

Inside the red Cadillac, Gleason instructed his driver, Dick Paul, who doubled as a band leader, "To the jai alai fronton, Dick." Oddly, Gleason had never before been to the Miami Fronton, a signature Miami attraction. Sophie intended to teach him all about this Basque game where a pelota takes blistering bounces at Formula One speeds. Players with their loose-fitting white genie pants and hard-shell helmets climb walls with balletic grace, catch the pelota and fire it back, only to watch it return like a looping comet. Jackie and Sophie bet on Joey, her favorite player, and he never failed to either win, place, or show, which was more than could be said for her bets later that evening at the Miami Beach Dog Track at the southern tip of the peninsula, where Government Cut opens wide into the Atlantic Ocean. Here she would taste defeat while Jackie watched with amusement, downing hot dogs slathered in mustard and topped off with sauerkraut. He was Miami's own answer to the Sultan of Swat, yet another Irish giant of immense appetite who appreciated a good hot dog and possessed an unhealthy self-destructive impulse.

Sophie bet many combinations of numbers in selecting her greyhounds, all with colorful names. The dogs' names, however, didn't interest her much. She took her guidance from her left forearm, which gave her a nice option of digits from which to choose. These numbers had been imprinted on her flesh for a decidedly unlucky purpose. Perhaps now, all these years later, those very same numbers could be put to some luckier use. Yet these concentration camp combinations failed her again. She then resorted to the numbers on her hospital wristband; and then borrowed from the band on Jackie's wrist—all to no avail. These bands signaled to the pari-mutuel betters that they were jailbirds due back at the end of the night but easy pickings for now. Like a safecracker who had lost her touch, Sophie was stone cold at the dog track on her night out with Jackie Gleason.

By midnight she and Jackie emerged from the dog track, a trail of losing tickets following them like an omen of bad tidings on Miami Beach.

"Where's the car?" Jackie wondered, squinting into the headlights of revved-up Chevies and Oldsmobiles in the parking lot.

"Fuck the car," Sophie said. "Let's walk along the beach. Have your driver pick us up at the Delano Hotel."

"That's a long walk," Jackie observed, staring north into the twinkling art deco hotels along Ocean Drive. To his right he listened to the steady incoming rush of ocean waves crashing against the First Street Pier, where fishermen were angling for red snapper, suspended above the water and lost in the darkness of the night.

Jackie Gleason was not a man who took walks—even on the golf course. When he played with President Nixon at the Doral Park Country Club shortly before he checked himself into Mount Sinai, whatever sweat he broke was solely from the humidity. Nixon was a born sweater, even in cooler climates. But Gleason was naturally cool because he barely ever moved. His feet touched the fairway only because it was impossible to swing a golf club from his cart. Sophie Posner, however, was used to a man who was unafraid of putting one foot in front of the other—slow though he may have walked, distracted though his mind may have been.

"You sure we're up to it?" Jackie asked. "We're sick patients from Mount Sinai, remember? They've pumped us full of drugs that's supposed to make us sleep. We shouldn't even be out here."

"You're as strong as a horse, and you still weigh as much," Sophie said. "Let's go, Fat Man."

They removed their shoes and held them in one hand. Jackie rolled up his tuxedo pant legs, giving him the unfortunate appearance of a schoolboy wearing knickers—Baby Huey on the Beach. Heading for the shoreline, they then walked north, the surging ocean tickling their feet, footprints vanishing from lapping waves. The full Miami moon hung so low in the black sky, it appeared to nearly kiss the Atlantic. And its brightness was so bright and beckoning, it seemed to Jackie and Sophie to be all but a few short swim strokes out into the surf.

Sophie darted into the water, nearly losing her balance as her bare feet stumbled over rocks, and a fast-moving wave slammed against her body. She splashed water back at Jackie with an underhanded heave and yelled, "Come with me, Jackie, to the moon, to the moon! Like you used to say on *The Honeymooners*. To the moon! We're very close! It's right there! You see? It's full and it's gorgeous!" She pointed at the sphere as if the creator and star of *The Honeymooners* didn't quite know where the moon was.

"Okay, Sophie, very funny. Now come in a little closer, okay? You are drifting too far and you're scaring me."

"We'll swim out and never come back," she said, ignoring her friend. "The moon is where we live. Just us—you and me. Look, see how close it is? If those astronauts could do it, so can we!"

Sophie thrust her hips forward once more; the water was now at her neck. Soon she would have to swim to stay above the waves.

"Are you crazy, Sophie?" Jackie chortled. "It's a million miles away. It's just an illusion. The moon's not right there. And we're not astronauts; we're a couple of drunks. What's gotten into you? Come on, let's go back to Ocean Drive and find the car."

"No, first to the moon!" she insisted. "Come, Jackie, take my hand. Swim out there with me. I will show you. Such a beautiful moon, all there by itself, just waiting for us. We'll be castaways."

"No, we won't," Jackie shouted, this time sounding more serious. "We'll be drowned cancer patients. I'll end up right back here, washed up on the shore. The headlines of tomorrow's *Miami Herald* and *Miami Beach Sun Reporter* will read: 'Beached Whale on South Beach Resembles the Great One.'"

"I don't want to go back there," Sophie pointed at the seawall of Miami Beach as if she were making an accusation. "The car will take us to the hospital. And then we'll be back in our penthouse suites. We'll start again with the chemo medicines and the radiation and the machines and the doctors with their false science. There is no cure for cancer. We'd be better off on top of the real Mount Sinai. We need a Moses, not doctors named Leonard and Norman.

"And I'm finished with the card games and the drinking and the parties with the friends who are paid to laugh with us. These games we play so we can forget the world we come from and the world that we know. I don't want to play anymore. And I don't want my family—not the crime family, and not my own family. They will be better off without me anyway. Enough, already! I want a new life," Sophie pleaded. "I need another escape route. I've done it before—the ghetto, the camp. One more time. I can do it again. But it can't be here on Miami Beach. It's out there," she pointed back at the moon. In those dizzy moments of her lost lament, the ball of light appeared to draw even closer. "I can feel it. Can't you, Jackie?"

The moon dangled in the sky so incandescently, and the Atlantic Ocean appeared to have been sprinkled with powdered sugar as its waves glistened in the vastness of its expanse. She pedaled backward and a freakishly large wave materialized from behind her like an open-armed ghost and crashed against her, thrusting her forward. Her head disappeared under the water.

"Sophie!" Jackie screamed, and then began to wade in himself, moving slowly like an obese lifeguard not wishing to get wet.

Her head popped up like a submerged buoy and she wiped the salty water from her eyes. Sophie was laughing like some demented sea creature, seaweed now attached to her shoulder like a sash. Had some plankton told her a joke just before she reached for oxygen? "You see: we have nothing to worry about. We just pop right back up, you and me. We're survivors. Come on, let's go already! There is nothing back there for us on land but death."

She took another plunge into the water. Jackie paddled in nearly as far as she had drifted, his arms raised high as though being taken prisoner. This time it took even longer for Sophie to surface from the depths of the Atlantic. Jackie was truly fearful, as if he were now alone in the water with no one watching either of them. Could this be his last Miami hurrah? So appropriate, here in the ocean, meters from the seawall and the art deco hotels that he had touted for all those years on his Saturday evening variety show. His death would be of a different variety—not from booze, nicotine, or even his stratospheric cholesterol, but from the black Miami night, bathed in the Atlantic's caress, his head below water and without air. The Fat Man, despite his many talents, simply could not float.

"Sophie, come up!" Jackie screamed to no one. "You're scaring me. Enough with this!"

He knew that his friend was emotionally unstable, and that her sanity was in an even more questionable state. Sophie could have been admitted to Mount Sinai for psychiatric care. But there were so many things wrong with her, so many maladies to address, pick your poison was the grand theme of her medical chart.

Jackie wanted to scream for help, but to whom? They had drifted too far from the shore, and the large stretch of beach that separated the seawall from the shore was at its widest on this portion of the peninsula. He spun around and looked back at the neon-crested hotels with their spunky shapes and deco adornments. From that distance the sand and surf seemed of a different world. No sign of life came into view except for a small boy running beside the seawall and curving with its bend, blond hair bouncing in the night, his gaze straight ahead, his will unshakable, his home unknown.

Sophie and Jackie had much in common: they lived hard, played the odds, took risks, always refusing to do what they were told. But this suicidal side of Sophie was not something Jackie was prepared for; nor did he share in either its excitement or its delusion.

Suddenly he felt the rush of water ascending like a gusher, racing up his back. Sophie surfaced—breathless, elated, rejuvenated like a Miami Beach mermaid rerouted from Poland's Baltic Sea.

"Sophie!" Jackie said, startled. He was now joyful, too. He thought he had lost her; he feared returning to Mount Sinai without her. How in the world would he be able to explain where he was and where she went? It wasn't the cancer that killed her, after all. The woman who once was nearly gassed ended up choking anyway. Fortunately she reappeared, as if washed back ashore after a shipwreck.

Her first order of business: she dunked herself back in, gulped a mouthful of water, and then as she returned eye to eye, proceeded to spit it all into Jackie's face.

"Oh, lovely," the Great One said. "You almost gave me a heart attack with your disappearing act. And now you spit in my face? You want to know who is the crazy one in this friendship, Sophie? You want to know who is the crazy one?"

Gleason's eyes bulged with the same nakedness and electrifying intensity as he often displayed on *The Honeymooners* in one of the many spats he had with his TV wife, Alice. He even balled up his fist, the signature pose before threatening to send her to the moon. In this episode, however, the moon, invitingly perched in the Miami sky, was exactly where Sophie wanted to go.

The two friends walked back from the shore to the seawall separating Ocean Drive from the sand. Their feet and calves were caked in muddy granules, and their hair was damp and matted from the salty Atlantic. Gleason's driver was smoking a cigarette while standing beside the red Cadillac. A peppy breeze nearly converted his chauffeur's cap into a Frisbee.

The Cadillac was filled with a stony silence the entire twenty minutes back to the hospital. Jackie and Sophie walked right through the sliding doors of the front entrance like two bank robbers surrendering to the nearest police precinct. The late-night hospital staff glanced at them, and then instantly returned to their work, registering no surprise. These two patients were off the charts in every way—and their conditions were worsening, too.

Upon reaching the penthouse, Sophie seemed somber. She never wanted this night to end. She wondered whether it was possible not to return. The Atlantic Ocean was only one of several imagined scenarios. Somehow, as her lungs were giving out in the inky ocean, some renewed fire returned to her. Perhaps it was just the obligation to all the Jewish dead not to waste the chance she was given. Swimming back to the ocean's surface, grasping for air, was a play straight from the survivor's manual. The many lessons that had gotten her this far were suddenly called upon again. A less likely reason, perhaps, was the thought of leaving a husband and young son behind on Miami Beach. The father and young boy were already directionless. Could they endure yet another reason to be lost?

"Stop," Sophie said as they passed the nurses' station. "Do you hear that?"

"What?" Jackie wondered, his ears so well attuned to the mechanical white noises that hum in hospitals—the bleeping machines, flashing lights, and screechy floors, along with the occasional cough.

"The music," she said, looking up as if it were being delivered from a floor even higher than the penthouse. "Gershwin."

She was right. It was George Gershwin—"Embraceable You," in fact. "Come on, Fat Man. Take me for another spin, this time with your feet. The penthouse is all ours. The floor is all ours. We can dance until the sun comes out."

Gleason, who was, in fact, a remarkably graceful dancer for a man of his size, took Sophie in his arms, their hospital bracelets nearly interlocking, and he glided her from a spirited waltz into a most tangy tango, and then seamlessly into a dirty dance of some Spanish origin that didn't really have a formal name, a cross between the mambo and a porno.

The nurses on the floor working the late shift were well aware that the penthouse patients had been absent since late that afternoon. Now that they had finally returned in the wee hours of the Miami Beach morning, rather than having their vitals checked and going straight to bed, they were dancing the rest of the night away. Two nurses chased after them as Sophie and Jackie kicked into a few nifty samba steps as they made their way down yet another hallway. The nurses were carrying trays of medication that they, with great difficulty, force-fed their patients in between twirls. Overheard hallway lights flickered to their own fluorescent beat.

By the time Jackie and Sophie had made their way all around the floor and past the nurses' station—the completion of the first of many laps as the entire Gershwin catalog serenaded the couple in the background—the nurses were preparing themselves for an even more complicated maneuver. They corralled the two patients and nimbly connected them to IV stands with rollers on the bottom. So expertly handled was this pit stop that Jackie and Sophie didn't seem to miss even a single step in their fancy-free fox trot that carried them past the nurses' station and down the hall once again. The two dancers now embraced each other with their right arms and with the left hands they held fast to the IV poles; the moving parts to this party had suddenly doubled and they were now officially a foursome.

"You're the greatest," Jackie said to Sophie as he stared tenderly into her eyes, unable to dab the few loving tears that were falling out of his own.

"Gleason, you are such a softie," Sophie replied curtly, not wishing to summon messy emotions that she couldn't reciprocate, or even muster for her own family.

Amid the blinking machines and the dimmed lights, the stillness of the hospital and the hospitality of these always-accommodating penthouse nurses, the dancing continued until daybreak when Miami Beach's awakening but fiery sun put an end to these torch songs and dirty dances. But not before Gleason, his toes still twinkling to a salsa beat and his heart breaking, held Sophie Posner tightly and then dipped her slowly with the grace of a far heftier Astaire. And when his back gave out from a night of such extreme exertion, Sophie nimbly reversed her position and dipped the Fat Man, holding him steady. Two cancer-ridden hoofers maintained their pose—eyes locked and lips nearly touching—while a triage team of nurses raced down the hallway primed to stem these bleeding hearts in a hospital romance both tragic and forbidden.

Seven

The Day Fidel Called Balls and Strikes

"S trike *tres!*" the umpire barked, turning sideways with knees bent
and gesturing with a piston-like arm pump, like an excitable traffic
cop signaling the right of way.

"What are you blind?" a psychotic father bellowed from the
bleachers.

"*Conyo!*" raged a baseball obsessed Cuban. "*Tu madre!*"

"Shake it off, Stuey," came the grating voice of a supportive mother
whose son had just whiffed badly. "You'll get him next time."

"Inning *terminado, vámonos,*" the umpire grumbled, ignoring the in-
sults. It's part of the job, an occupational hazard of calling balls and strikes.
Thick skin was essential; the ump's uniform even came with a chest protector, another layer for cushioning. The chest was protected from foul tips,
but the verbal abuse from parents sitting in the bleachers was not so easily
shrugged off.

This was Little League, after all. Fly balls were lost in the drenching sunshine of Miami Beach, seams rotating in the blinding light and leather cutting through the humid air. Bats felt as heavy as flagpoles. These games

could take an eternity without a disciplined ump. Umpires had to be above the protests from the cheap seats, steeling themselves to the cruelty of parents watching a child's game. It was all in good fun, after all. It's not like the fans would ever erupt in revolution.

"Butterflake is up at bat," he continued. "Score still *dos* to *uno*, two to one, Butterflake in front. *Darse prisa*—hurry up!"

The umpire unwrapped a cigar and bit off one of its ends, spitting it out like a savage. After lighting it he slipped the cigar through the spider web openings of the mask and into his mouth. A black beard spiked out of the mask like seaweed. The cigar wasn't one of those generic Dutch Masters or even the faux Cuban variety from Tampa, but instead authentic, contraband Cohibas, slow burning with even curls of levitating smoke and a bright circle of light on its tip.

"Play ball!" he bellowed.

His accent betrayed no desire to forfeit its authentic Cubano resonance in favor of a more seamless American slang. A large man with a thick beard, a long face, and the loping angular features of a thoroughbred, he flipped off his mask, dropped his small futon of a chest protector onto the clay infield, and removed from his back pocket what was already a drenched wash cloth, which he laid across his face *bandito* style. In this scalding late summer heat and in his khaki green, he was collecting sweat like a kiddie pool. He was surely not unfamiliar with the climate. He loved tropical summers. Summer would always have special meaning—in his soul and body politic. Summer was a time for revolution. Summers, in fact, can give birth to a nation. July 26th was his July 4th, and all the other American holidays combined. But at this moment he was not in his own country but on foreign soil—the dry, dirt infield behind home plate at North Shore Park. Miami was, for him, hostile terrain, and not only on account of the weather.

Summers in Miami Beach do not have a natural cooling-off period. The nights allow for nothing that resembles brisk desert breezes or cool mountain valley frosts. High humidity is a way of life in the tropics. Sticky is the climate du jour. Severe sweat is to Miamians what frostbite is for Alaskans. And the fact that the first pitch was tossed at 6 p.m., and the last out would be called when it got dark, didn't offer any respites, either.

For most cities in America, Labor Day weekend signaled the end of summer and the beginning of a preppy fall with foliage of spectacular and vivid variety and leaves that crackle underfoot like milkless cereal. South Florida offers no such autumnal theater, and no noticeable break from the heat until the darker days of December when heavy dry winds kick sand in the faces of beachgoers and cause coconuts to drop from palm trees like hairy bingo balls. In Miami the coming of Labor Day only means that the bell has rung for a new school year and another telethon is underway for Jerry's kids. Labor Day announced back-to-school shopping sprees. The workingman wasn't being celebrated, but his purchasing power certainly was. Labor Day did not spell any letup of heat, or a solar slumber or, an invitation for milder weather. The sun over Miami Beach was relentless, a fiery workaholic in an otherwise languorous town.

What the end of summer did signify, however, was the conclusion of the city's Little League baseball season. The two city parks that hosted league play and vied for the Miami Beach World Series were North Shore Park, which was located near the northern tip of the city several blocks off the ocean, and Flamingo Park, the larger of the two, which was in South Beach and had just been the mass camp site of smelly hippies from across the country. This festival of seditious teens, hotheaded graduate students, and bitter Vietnam vets had traveled down to Miami Beach to protest at the Democratic and Republican Presidential Conventions. For a brief moment in time Miami Beach was the center of the universe, where the leader of the free world would receive his party's nomination for the presidency of the United States. And the social upheavals of the 1960s would coalesce into one sweaty mob of youthful rebellion. All eyes were on this island peninsula as if it were the Fountain of Youth, which wouldn't have surprised anyone, since this was where America's youth had decided to land like an Apollo mission, so very close to where those rockets blasted off at Cape Kennedy.

But it came to an end almost as soon as it began. All those smug delegates and stoned radicals departed by the end of August, off to ramp up for the general election that would result in a Nixon landslide. And not before long Nixon would slide away from public view, waving good-bye in disgrace from his presidential helicopter. Miami Beach returned to its sleepy small-town rhythms, where nothing of importance ever happened except for the occasional Frank Sinatra, Jackie Gleason, or Muhammad Ali sighting, or an arrest of a local Jewish mobster by the city's top cop, Rocky Pomerance.

Thank God for Little League. A guileless game that pays no mind to the politics of teamwork is the perfect way to close out the summer, and in such an unabashedly patriotic and American way. Baseball was still the national pastime of the United States in 1972, before football gave the country a concussion and caused everyone to forget about its once-most-favored summer game. The Big Red Machine was ascendant that season, although it lost to the upstart Oakland Athletics in the World Series. Miami Beach settled into its own matchup of titans, much tinier in scale, however, with Flamingo Park's Butterflake Bakery taking on the North Shore champion Fun Fair.

Butterflake Bakery was led by its ace pitcher and base-stealing artist, Adam Posner. There was so much to say about this boy, and even more that could be said about his parents. They were not a typical Miami Beach family, for sure, but their oddities surfaced in many ways on this barrier island, like stubborn buoys, and their presence was felt even though most people knew it was better to cast them adrift, to treat them as aliens, which wasn't that far from the truth anyway. Three very strange Miami Beach characters: a walking man, dressed in all white, going nowhere, and very slowly; a woman advisor to the Jewish Mafia of Miami Beach whose mind was untethered to anything wholesome and tangible; and a young boy, on the eve of his bar mitzvah, with legs that enabled him to run very fast, but despite his age and cardio capacity, he didn't have the heart to flee his parents, even though it was doubtful they would have noticed him missing.

Until the boy could fashion an escape that could survive his guilt, he found other ways to put this particular motor skill to work. He never needed much of an excuse to sprint off in any direction—the more aimless the better. Baseball, at least, with its four evenly distanced bases—sixty feet apart in a diamond track—gave his running a purposeful route.

The problem was one mainly of terminology: if only a home run meant running away from home, never making it back home, or racing toward a new home.

"I still don't understand why he is so fast," his father, the walker, would often wonder. "We Posners were not such great athletes back in Europe. We were good with books."

"Over there we did not need to be sportsmen," the boy's mother would intone, pointing in some vague direction that could have benefited from a compass, "but right here, in Miami Beach, after Auschwitz, we are Olympians."

Adam would have gladly volunteered to serve as the designated runner for all of his teammates. It would have allowed them to lounge in the dugout while he used their hits to extend his distance—all except for the fact that he was merely running on a course, making sharp turns, base after base with intermittent slides, racing toward that misnomer of a plate serving as home. In baseball, putting bat to ball and sending it screaming toward the outfield is the starting gun, but the running of the bases is what matters most, and the illusion that there is safety in standing atop one.

There were other misnomers on Miami Beach that summer. For instance, the opposing team, Fun Fair, didn't live up to its sponsor's cheerful corporate name. Those Little Leaguers were not having much fun dismantling the other teams from North Shore and Normandy Parks. Fun Fair played baseball as if someone forgot to remind them that it was, after all, a kid's game—sportsmanship in the spirit of good fun. Instead, they took the field like gladiators, baseball brutes turning an elegant game into a steel-cage match. This attitude did not suit the lazy rhythms of the Florida tropics. Miami Beach was too indolent a town to care about championships, or rivalries for that matter. The city was largely cut off from the mainland, a Florida afterthought. It wasn't the sort of place where grudges festered—at least not with respect to sports.

Also, Fun Fair's Little Leaguers were far from little. They were vastly larger and stronger than the Flamingo Park kids, with stocky builds and thick forearms. A few of the kids had already outgrown their peach fuzz, graduating to facial shadows that blackened by the end of the day. From a distance, deep in center field, they resembled short but fully grown men— Shetland ponies all ready for Pony League—without all that adolescent awkwardness and pimply faces that best described the appearance of their opponents from Butterflake Bakery.

Some of the boys from Butterflake Bakery looked as if they were poaching cookies from their sponsor's ovens, their minds fixated on Danishes and crullers and not on the hit and run. A stick of butter could have been their team mascot. Butterflake consisted mostly of Jewish kids whose parents had come looking for a better life, away from the declining urban areas of the

Northeast, with their race riots, blackouts, and failing schools. This was the very migration to the Sun Belt. These Yankee refugees soon discovered that their children burned all too easily in the sun.

And then there were the other refugees. Fun Fair's more robust Little Leaguers bore little resemblance to their cousins from the other side of the island. They were their own separate community on Miami Beach, having started out from the very opposite direction, transplants themselves, but from an island less than a hundred miles south of Key West. Cuba was the land of sugarcane and late summer hurricanes. And baseball was its national pastime, too.

The team from Fun Fair, while American in origin, was stacked with Cubans. Having so many Cubans on a Little League team in Miami Beach pretty much assured a trip to the city's World Series. These Little Leaguers always looked like they had lived longer, like they had graduated from adolescence without having to take an exam. Puberty was an insult to them. The age on their birth certificates drew attention away from the wives and kids they had stashed away somewhere. They were in a league of their own, and there was nothing little about it.

And, curiously, despite their considerable physical advantage, each summer the team from North Shore Park, looking so unbeatable on paper and ferocious in their uniforms, could not defeat the underdeveloped Jews from Flamingo Park. Their home run swings failed them; their pitchers couldn't find home plate even with klieg lights. Everyone began calling it the Cuban curse, or the Jewish joke—but each summer the doughy and diminutive team from Flamingo Park hoisted the city trophy as Little League champions, while the brawny Cuban kids from North Shore wondered why, given their Marxist origins, Labor Day should be so unlucky for them.

Was this yet another Miami Beach mystery? Perhaps the enduring hope of the underdog is precisely why they call it the Magic City.

The Cuban community had arrived in South Florida with their own exotic immigration tale, not quite as wretched and murderous as the Jewish diaspora, but possessing many of the same elements of survival that will forever mark the twentieth century as the defining era of displaced personhood. Cubans had only recently made their way from Havana and resettled in Miami, and owing to the special circumstances of the Cold War, they instantly became full-fledged Floridians and honorary Americans, welcomed aboard with all the entitlements of natives. Mexicans never had it as good. Haitians, forget it.

The Bay of Pigs calamity and the Cuban Missile Crisis left America with a craziness about Fidel Castro. With Senator McCarthy's witch trials finally over, demonization moved offshore. Now a godless communist became the anti-Christ. Communism was considered too close for comfort; the fear of the bomb raised the temperature on the Cold War and made every day seem like doomsday. At times, ground zero of the Red Scare found itself not in Berlin but in Miami Beach, where from behind the seawall of an Iron Curtain a whole new wave of Americans were getting used to a life of capitalism on crack. There were no Checkpoint Charlies, just the open vastness of the Caribbean Sea and the Atlantic Ocean, crossable by inner tubes and makeshift rafts, and survivable so long as the sharks and jellyfish didn't have an appetite for freedom fighters from Castro's prisons.

With its sun-splashed exterior, no wonder Miami accidentally ended up as a regional pawn in the strategic alliances of the Cold War. It was already a breeding ground for spooks, and home to shady characters. Our man in Havana was easily dispatched to Miami. Yet, Miami Beach was such a curious place to find oneself in the middle of a global conflict. Just north, a hundred miles away in Cape Kennedy, rockets were repeatedly being launched into orbit in search of other planets, galaxies, and life forms, all because of a space race with an ever-shifting finish line. The moon, hanging low and glinting over Miami like a glow-in-the-dark bingo ball, no longer seemed so far away. Just a hundred miles south was Cuba, with Fidel Castro, the Soviet Union's man in Havana—easily the most hated man in Miami. He once had his own missiles pointed directly at Miami and other American cities. Yet the city that was in the center of nuclear Armageddon was bizarrely oblivious to its danger, far more concerned with jai alai and dog racing than with the end of days.

Despite all those *nyets*, UN vetoes, long-winded denunciations, shoes being smacked against tables for diplomatic emphasis, toothless arms control, peppery SALT talks, saber rattlings, and missile silos with their phallic fixations, Miami regarded itself as above it all—even though it was right below. The world played out its chilly Cold War alignments; all the while sultry South Florida served as the only true regional hotspot. In the ongoing clash between capitalism and communism, where else were the beaches this inviting and the sun so strong?

And to make matters more complicated, not all of these Cuban refugees were of the same stock. On Miami Beach there was a special category of Cubans: curious cousins of the northeastern transplants and Holocaust survivors that had settled earlier and presently occupied the middle class of Miami Beach. In 1972, Jews, having escaped tyranny from the right and the left, ended up in Miami's indiscriminate middle. Castro's rejects and Hitler's survivors united in Miami Beach like a parade of the persecuted, sharing notes on tribal anxieties, and trading recipes for kreplach and empanadas. Survival, however, was the special sauce.

They called themselves Jewbans—Jewish Cubans—but in every meaningful way that a people can be pegged as dead ringers for themselves, judged by the manner of their dress, the cadences of their speech, the siesta-inspired way in which they broke up the day, they were creatures of the Caribbean. The Jewbans had little in common with the "huddled masses" and "wretched refuse" of the Lower East Side, even though they, too, had once been rooted to the shtetl and the Pale. Salsa was now in their feet. *Yucca* smothered in garlic sauce was baking in their ovens, but the savory smells emanating from their kitchens equally recalled the borsht soup and stuffed cabbage of yesteryear.

"Play ball!" the umpire called out like a town crier.

Butterflake Bakery was up by a run in a low-scoring game, which was a miracle, given that the team from North Shore was loaded with Cuban hitters who swung at the ball as if it were a candy-stuffed piñata at a third grader's birthday party. The only breeze anyone could feel on that sultry September day was the wind generated by North Shore's stymied hitters, their bats slicing the air like wind turbines. Adam Posner, Butterflake's pitcher, was not only fleet of foot, but his arm was equally adept at generating speed. The ball he hurled toward home plate arrived like an Olympic sprinter with its leathery chest puffed out before landing in the catcher's mitt with a thud. He was a lefty with a hard fastball and the cunning to survive in a city where lefties were always in danger of pissing off anticommunist Cubans.

"Way to throw smoke, Adam," came the encouraging words of Butterflake's shortstop, Brad Isaacson, a graceful infielder who didn't mind getting his yellow uniform dirty. "These guys got nothing on us. They don't even speak good English."

"Just keep tossing strikes, Adam," said Lee Kleinberg, a pudge ball of a catcher whose body type was naturally squat, like a paperweight right behind home plate. With a uniform caked in both infield dirt from the game and chocolate milk from lunch, Lee's long stringy blond hair dropped from his catcher's mask like tassled corn.

Since the game was being played in North Shore Park, Fun Fair was the home team. Miami Beach was a small town, and the distance between the two parks was only six miles, so home was relative no matter the coordinates. Everyone was *home*—well, nearly everyone. Cuban exiles weren't yet sold on Florida. Holocaust survivors weren't buying any of the warranties about residential living and tropical belonging. And the Posner family . . . well, they didn't even understand the question. Nonetheless, the home team had the benefit of a partisan crowd of friendly Cubans.

The bleachers at North Shore were ringing with a decidedly Latin beat. Spanish was spoken almost exclusively behind the backstop. On the day of this Little League World Series, North Shore Park could have existed in any Latin American country—the boys from Panama taking on Little Leaguers from Puerto Rico. And it wasn't only the Spanish language that dominated the conversation: the expended emotion seemed pretty one-sided, too. Butterflake Bakery's game was being derided as the white bread to Fun Fair's more flamboyant brand of Latin American flash. Such nifty glove work and graceful strides in shagging down fly balls. The boys from Butterflake were being cursed out in Spanish, but didn't even know it.

"*Maricón*!" screamed the second baseman who happened to be fielding with a limp wrist.

"*Pendejo*!" the catcher muttered and then farted.

"*Cabeza de pinga*! growled a mini-macho Cubano who was pacing inside the dugout and never got in the game.

The sounds of Afro-Cuban percussion blared from someone's Cutlass Supreme parked at the curb. At a picnic table four men wearing matching guayaberas clacked their dominos like maracas.

It was not as if the parents of Butterflake Bakery's Little Leaguers weren't around to root for their kids, because they were. It's just that they were crowded out, cowed by the Cubans, rendered mute in Miami, reduced to cheerless spectators. Spoken Spanish always pushes the decibels, makes itself heard more prominently than other languages. It usually soars above the other Romance languages and the lingua franca of English—perhaps out of cultural necessity. By comparison, the parents of Butterflake Bakery were cheering in Pidgin English.

Adam and Brad, the two best players on the team, shared not only a love for the Mets and an identical geographic destiny as transplanted New Yorkers, but also a common experience when it came to their fathers. The heads of the Isaacson and Posner households were sickly men, unable to play sports with their athletic boys. In Adam's case his father didn't even show up to watch the games. At least Mr. Isaacson could be seen in the front row, tucked away at the side corner of one the bleachers, frail and leaning against the railing for support. The closest Adam's father ever came to one of his games was when he inadvertently circled around Flamingo Park, walking laps simultaneously with his son as he rounded the bases. A Little Leaguer without parents in the bleachers was unusual in Miami Beach, where fathers were all either semiretired or lazily employed, and seemed to have plenty of time to watch their sons participate in outdoor sports. Mothers were present, too, but Adam's mother was involved in other gaming matters on Miami Beach. The stakes in Little League baseball were too small for her. And the games were played during the day, when she slept, resting up for the action at night.

Another side retired. Butterflake was up at bat again.

"*Seis* inning," the umpire grunted, still smoking a cigar, still indifferent to the casual Spanish being exchanged behind him. He, too, had other business in this city, action more consequential than baseball: revolutionary action, the kind that creates dynasties and preserves dictatorships. Calling balls and strikes were not the most important decisions of his day. For him baseball, even in his own country and without an assist from Butterflake's ovens, was nothing but bread and circuses. But his main calling would have to wait. Everything would have to wait, for now.

Although summer was coming to an end, tropical storm and hurricane season was indifferent to the demarcations of Labor Day. Even as late as September, hard rains and violent winds roared through Miami Beach like carnivals, leaving muddy tracks and pools of rippling puddles. Mother Nature was harsh, even in paradise. And, like the sudden change from night to day, this World Series would not be safe from the schizophrenic changes of Miami's weather. The skies overhead blackened and the clouds seemed to dip like tea bags into the hot water of a Miami Beach sun shower.

"Inside the dugouts, *andale!*" the umpire ordered.

The teams folded themselves inside their respective dugouts like color-coded ants. Meanwhile, the spectators huddled underneath wide-canopied tropical trees. The umpire remained neutral, standing apart from everyone, holding his ground at home plate as if he required no shelter, as if the rain wouldn't dare get him wet. He stared at the huddled adults and the quarrelsome kids with an alien's contempt, like a disapproving father. Within minutes the rains subsided and the clouds brightened. That's how it's done in the tropics—even the rains are all show without substance, a hint of catastrophe but no bust. Smiles returned to everyone's faces even though the bleacher seats were now all waterlogged, the wooden planks sagging like diving boards.

By 1972 the exiled Cubans of Miami came to accept, albeit begrudgingly, that Fidel Castro wasn't going to be deposed anytime soon. Their beloved Cuba, and their relatives, would remain close but untouchable, in a pariah state headed by a third-world rock star who lambasted the United States on every occasion in which he commandeered a podium. Protected by the Soviet Union and endlessly provoking his northern neighbor, Fidel Castro confidently awaited the day when the rising proletariat would add the United States to the list of Soviet satellites. It was inevitable, after all, a dialectical necessity, historical forces making real the teachings of Marx and Engels—even in the tropics.

Meanwhile, the Cubans of Miami seethed, and cursed the day when John Kennedy refused to send in the Air Force to support the Cuban insurgents during the Bay of Pigs. Retaking the island now, after so many years of Castro's oppressive rule, seemed impossible. Fidel had established his authority and gotten used to the job. There were still Cubans, of course, who vowed to unseat Castro and reclaim Cuba. But they were mostly crackpots, their heads filled with arroz con pollo and not common sense. They fantasized about sugar plantations and Havana as a haven for sweet Cuban dreams. But they were fanatics who refused to accept the facts on the ground, unwilling to assimilate and learn the language. Miami, now, and perhaps forever, was home. These exiles would give birth to a generation of Cuban Americans.

There was great sympathy among the general Cuban population for these patriots, however. Somebody had to be the guardians of their ransacked island. Anti-Castro energies throughout Miami were amped up among the locals to crazy-making dimensions. The mere mention of Fidel in any favorable light could result in a car bombing. Once, in retaliation for a news story in the *Miami Herald* about Cuba's enviable healthcare system, newspaper dispensers all over Miami were set on fire. Free speech, when it came to Cuba, was not costless; democracy in Miami required a kind of my-way-or-take-a-hike-on-the-Havana highway mentality. The Cubans in Miami were as implacable and imperious in their hatred of Castro as Fidel was dictatorial about everything on his island. Not a favorable word could be spoken of Cuba's prime minister. All dialogue was nonnegotiable. Family members were singled out for punishment if they broke with the party line.

Tolerance, high culture, and big Pacific coast waves were in short supply in those more placid Miami days. The one thing that everyone seemed to agree on was that Fidel Castro was Miami's very own boogeyman, their personal Hitler—an evil devil dressed in revolutionary green, a cigar in his mouth and tall enough to make for a splendid target and an even better kill. What the community would not have given to get Fidel within their sight lines. But despite all the wishful thinking and backroom deal-making on *Calle Ocho*, they would never got close enough to the man who, by exiling all those talented Cubans, singlehandedly built Miami into a raging bourgeois metropolis. And the Miami Cubans, paradoxically, never forgave him for it.

By the top of the seventh inning and with Butterflake Bakery still ahead two to one, the remaining seats of the bleachers at North Shore Park, which were drying out from the earlier downpour, began to fill up with a few more Anglos—and famous ones. They all arrived fashionably late, in time for the final innings, and they didn't seem to be arriving together. Each entered the park from different entrances, like morning commuters boarding a train. There was Jackie Gleason and his friend Frank Sinatra, who both climbed the bleacher seats to the very top, cheered on by the locals. Gleason scaled the steps like a vaudevillian, hamming it up and high stepping like one of his June Taylor Dancers. Sinatra tipped his swinger houndstooth fedora hat as if he were about to break into a rendition of *My Way*. I. B. Singer, stylishly wearing a three-piece brown suit, read a Yiddish newspaper on a bench underneath a weeping willow while simultaneously making a pass at a blonde divorcee dressed in a tube top walking her dog. Meyer Lansky, the Jewish Godfather, sporting oversized sunglasses on his face that resembled blinders for a greyhound, sat up front with a few of his heavyset henchmen, proudly cheering on Butterflake's pitcher, whom they all regarded as their godson. The local police chief, Rocky Pomerance, always the largest man on any field on Miami Beach, chewed on his pipe and suspiciously eyed the ump, who was puffing on yet another contraband Cohiba. Muhammad Ali, wearing sweats and fresh from a training run, took a center seat while slapping fives to the fans who swarmed like bees around him. The umpire glowered at the self-proclaimed "Greatest," knowing that Teófilo Stevenson could pummel Ali and turn him back into Clay if the dictator had wished to unleash the heavyweight onto the prize-fighting arena.

The bases were loaded and Adam Posner was facing his first really tight jam of the game. Yes, there were two outs, but Adam had just walked the last two batters. He was starting to lose his control, a rare occurrence for a boy otherwise so unusually in control—on the mound and elsewhere. He had to be. Wild was not in his delivery or makeup. He carried himself with the lofty air of self-sufficiency; he was never in need of pointers—one of the side effects of absentee parenting. Even his coach, Stanley Bertman, left him alone in the center of the diamond. Lee, his catcher, threw down no signs. Adam tossed only fastballs all the time. Everything was his call. He seemed to always know what to do, like his namesake, the first man, who, out of desperation and sheer loneliness, was forced to find his way. Adam neither asked nor was given relief—even when he was losing his stuff on the mound.

Exposed to the oppressive Miami heat, Adam was feeling it—feeling everything. These summer months had taken their measure of the boy, what with his impending bar mitzvah in Munich and his radicalized flirtations at the Democratic and Republican Conventions in Miami Beach. And now a big finish, a spellbinding final inning with the ball in his hand, in front of a capacity crowd, with celebrities in the audience, no less. All eyes on Miami Beach were framing him like a picture postcard for the Chamber of Commerce. His unraveling was unthinkable to anyone who knew him. And yet he seemed unnerved by the taunts emanating from Fun Fair's dugout. The opposing team knew the pitcher's vulnerabilities:

"*Tu madre* Mafia!" was followed by, "*Tu padre* loco!"

Over and over again.

"*Tu madre* Mafia!"

"*Tu padre* loco!"

The chain link fence sounded like it was being ripped from its cement bearings. Fun Fair's Cubans were rocking the chains back and forth as if attempting a prison break. Worried about Adam's concentration, Meyer Lansky briefly considered ordering a hit on the entire Fun Fair team.

"Want me to shoot a few of these Cuban kids, Meyer?" Morty the Mohel asked. "They are being very disrespectful to our crew, taking a potshot at Sophie like that."

The rattling of the fence had rattled the nerves of the pitcher whose fastball had until now quelled the Cubans from North Shore Park all game long. He was losing his command, his control, and perhaps even his mind.

"Time out!" the umpire called out. He removed his mask, dropped his chest protector to the chalky dirt, and bounded off toward the boy standing in the center of the diamond. Brad Isaacson, Butterflake's shortstop, began to gather the infielders for a conference at the pitcher's mound, but the ump waved him off like a fastball down and away.

"Hey, what gives?" Coach Bertman wanted to know as he emerged from the dugout with outstretched palms. The ump shot the coach the kind of icy stare that could freeze a body in motion—even in Florida. Bertman meandered back to the dugout, kicking dirt like a sulking scrub trying to get into the game. He knew that this ump was no mere ump, no chump but a tyrant in camouflage khaki.

The umpire stood like a Goliath beside Adam. A green giant and a puny pitcher wearing yellow, they were one communist color away from being a traffic light. The umpire tossed his Cohiba on the rubber of the mound and stamped out the blinking embers of its flame. In a halting but soaring English he said, "Listen, *niño*, I was a pitcher, too. Many years ago . . . before I . . ."

"Before you became an umpire?" Adam asked.

"*Si*, before that."

"Were you any good?"

"*Si*, of course, I was very good, could have pitched in your Major Leagues. The New York Giants gave me a $5,000 contract."

"To play football?" Adam wondered, oblivious to the configuration of baseball boroughs that existed in the days before the Mets.

"No, baseball," the umpire clarified, not exactly sure why the boy so easily confused baseball with *el futbol Americano*. "I had a good arm, a fast-ball like a missile. I can still throw, but as a professional pitcher, I stopped."

"What happened?" Adam asked, looking up at the umpire, whose face and bushy beard were obscured in the backlit sun.

"I went to school to become a lawyer," the umpire replied, "then I fought revolutions in the Dominican Republic, Mexico, and Colombia. I went to prison, and then started a revolution in my own country."

"That's weird," Adam surmised. "After all that, here you are, an umpire in North Shore Park." Adam didn't want to sound rude, but how else could the umpire have heard it? After such a career marked by so many adventures, why was he now slumming in Miami, not presiding over a nation but officiating a Little League game?

"But this is the World Series of baseball," the ump noted.

"World Series of Miami Beach and the Little League—not the Major League."

"Still an important game," the umpire insisted, perhaps trying to justify his Miami ex officio gig. "Every year I come to umpire this game in Miami Beach, and then I go home, back to my own country."

"You're like Santa Claus, except you show up only in the summer," Adam observed and chuckled. This private audience with the ump was definitely settling him down. "You even have the long beard."

This encounter was soon becoming an unbearably long conference. The Miami natives were getting restless in the bleachers. The heckling of the fidgety partisan fans intensified.

The umpire momentarily laughed, then glanced at the bleachers, eyeing the crowd, gladdened by their confusion. There was a jocular warmth in his expression, and a nostalgia for what his country might have become had the forces of history not changed the face of the Caribbean. He stood atop the mound and cut a figure as imposing as the Sierra Maestra. Despite all the distance he had traveled—incognito, smuggled in like Cuban contraband—he realized that here was his home team, too. These were his people, even though they cursed his name each day. They were blinded by all that American bling-bling, the pursuit of happiness, the getting ahead and the leaving behind. They were mesmerized by all that American money. Which Cuban community was brainwashed more—the ones on mainland Miami, or on the island of Cuba itself?

"Your parents, are they here?" the umpire wanted to know, looking out over the grandstand. "They must be proud of you. *Orgulloso.*" He puffed his chest out with ballast as if he was still wearing his protector.

"No, they are not here," Adam said in a thin voice, shyly pubescent. He never knew whether he wanted to see his parents in the bleachers. They would have seemed so out of place, strangely more foreign than they already were. It was enough that his godfather—an actual Godfather—was subbing like a utility infielder.

"But you have parents, *si?*"

Adam hesitated. He didn't know how to answer truthfully. A part of him wanted to hug this mercurial umpire from the sugar canes and tobacco farms of the Pearl of the Antilles, and ask to be taken with him to his home country—wherever that happened to be.

"Yes, *si*, I have parents," Adam finally said. "I guess I do."

The umpire who called balls and strikes didn't know what to make of this kid with his lively arm, forlorn eyes, and lost stare. He looked out over the demanding crowd again. This was the longest time out in the history of North Shore Park.

"Cubans fighting with Jews over baseball?" he questioned. "Mafia on the street? McDonald's? Fat Jackie Gleason and skinny Sinatra—neither knows how to fight in the jungle or mountains, neither knows anything other than a good time—heroes? This is your freedom? A Cold War fought in such hot cities. *Loco.* We should just play a baseball game—pitchers and batters and not with nuclear warheads. In the meantime, I will show them what freedom brings."

The Cubans who had forsaken their homeland would be denied a victory—yet for another year. This was a Cuban park, but it was most assuredly not in Cuba. The umpire returned each year to yank the American dream away from these exiles. For them, rounding the bases was an act of cultural memory, as close as they possibly could get to the motherland without crossing the picket line of the Cold War.

It appeared as if all of Miami Beach was sitting in those bleachers that day, snugly making room for one another, awaiting the crowning of the summer's World Series Little League champion. It had been an eventful summer after all, what with two presidential conventions and an Olympics in Munich. Dramatic geopolitics blended in with the art deco scuttlebutt, Miami Beach wasn't refined enough to absorb it all—or to appreciate its significance. What could the umpire possibly be telling Adam Posner, so many in the stands wondered? Do the rules even allow for such private pow-wows between umpires and little lefties?

"Play ball already, ump!" an anxious Fun Fair father cupped his hands and shouted out onto the infield.

"Yes, we would like to get out of here before the early bird specials end at Pumperniks," said someone's grandmother, a woman who had already called ahead and placed her order of beef flanken. All of her outings ended with a nosh.

"Can you believe this guy? *Maricón!*" an angry Cuban said and shook his fist at the ump. "Who does he think he is?"

Standing on the last row of the bleachers like an obese Moses returning from Mount Sinai—the mountain, and not the medical center—was Jackie Gleason, trying to appease the rebellion below. "Will you's all just relax, for God's sake? It's just a game. Let the man do his job. He's settling down the kid." And then the Great One let it be known which team he was rooting for. "Attaboy, Adam!" he bellowed. "We're all behind you!"

"Knock it to the moon, Ernesto!" a Fun Fair parent beseeched his son to the crowd's laugher.

Gleason's bulging eyes beamed and then twinkled. "How sweet it is!" he roared to everyone's applause.

Sinatra pulled on Gleason's short sleeve, reeling his friend back to his seat. They glanced at one another. It was a joyous time to be them—with their friendships, nightly rituals, nonstop laughter, and command of this otherwise sleepy beachside resort. But the "sun and fun capital of the world" came with responsibilities. The pitcher's parents were nowhere to be seen. The Rat Pack, and the Jewish Mafia, had unofficially adopted this boy as their own—a mascot for the jet set and the jailbirds.

"Okay," the umpire returned the ball to the pitcher. "You have two outs and a one run lead. Throw some strikes and we go home—*voy a mi casa.*"

Adam accepted the ball but not the outcome. The World Series of Miami Beach might win him a trophy, but it would not assure him a home to return to. The umpire was likely to make it back home to the Presidential Palace in Havana. Adam Posner's sense of place was less certain.

The umpire took long strides as he ambled back to home plate while lighting a new cigar. On his face was planted the smile of an expectant father—or was it simply that he regarded so many in the bleachers as his wayward children? He bent down to reclaim his mask, strapped it over his head, and turned to look at the crowd one final time before signaling for Adam to begin his windup.

Meyer Lansky, sitting in the front row, removed his boxcar sunglasses just as the umpire spun around. He stared deeply at the umpire's face—even through the mask. Lansky jolted in his seat as if a bolt of summer lightning had radiated his row.

"Wait a minute," he said, standing as he walked toward the chain link backstop. "That can't be. Huh . . .? The guy who stole my casinos in Havana is now calling balls and strikes in North Shore Park. What the fuck!"

"Sit down, Meyer Lansky, you old fool!" Muhammad Ali joked from the stands, fearlessly. Not even Charlie Nunchucks, Meyer's toughest goon, would dare pick a fight with the world's "greatest" prizefighter. "You're blocking our view! And take off those silly sunglasses. It's getting dark out, and we already know it's you! You can't hide from the IRS, or us."

Lansky turned hastily, not because he was insulted, but because he was searching for Rocky Pomerance—the first time he ever looked to a police officer to make an arrest.

"Play ball!" the umpire shouted.

Adam threw two pitches that were both outside, but the umpire called them as strikes. The Cubans of North Shore Park sensed that this year, too, the fix was in. Each summer no different from the last. The Posner kid was good, but he had help—courtesy of the Cold War. The superpowers fought their battles through surrogates around the world. And now a Little League game was its own theater of war. Perhaps Lansky had a hand in this, as well, a bit of bookmaking aided by a Cuban dictator slumming as an umpire. The Jewish don was always looking for action; he had a talent for picking winners, but this time he was receiving an assist from a most unlikely source. The line at the annual Little League World Series was reliably crooked, for all sorts of nefarious reasons.

Yet, every summer Lansky denied having anything to do with Flamingo Park's winning streak. Obviously he had never before taken a good look at the ump. The odds were rigged, indeed, but all due to the officiating, not racketeering.

"Are you blind?" a stout Cuban jumped to his feet and saluted a profane gesture to the umpire. Two days later, on another island, such an obscenity would have landed the Cuban inside a prison never to be seen or heard from again.

"Go back to where you came from!" echoed the voice of another Cubano.

When it comes to Florida, people expect to see the strange. A fixed Little League game. So what. It's not the worst sin that would befall this sun-kissed city. There would be much more of the inexplicable as Florida grew in demographic importance. Indeed, for many, Florida would become a reliable after-dinner joke, a kooky state where presidential elections get recalled because elderly Jews from Delray couldn't tell the difference between voter ballots and bingo cards, and where Elian Gonzales, another son of Cuba, would be kidnapped and taken directly to Disney World—the seat of capitalist excess, the ultimate insult to the presidente. As a state, as a place of mind, Florida would always be the weird uncle in the attic, under suspicion, a family embarrassment jutting out from the rest of the country like a pesky piece of chewing gum on an overworn heel.

This Little League World Series ended with an asterisk, yet another bit of unfinished Miami Beach business, something else without finality and resolution.

With two strikes and all the base runners taking off on the pitch, Adam Posner tapped his right foot on the rubber of the mound, kicked his left foot back and uncorked a blistering strike that caused the batter to miss wildly and whiz past Lee's catcher's mitt into the bare hand of the umpire, who never flinched.

"Strike *tres*! Game over!"

While it may have seemed that all of Miami Beach had descended on this park at twilight, there were at least two people watching from the cheapest seats of all. Across the street and unobserved stood the Posner parents—eyes squinting, arms wrapped around each other, hearts pounding with emotions they could neither account for nor control. Nor would they show it to their son.

Adam was being mobbed by his teammates, who patted him on the head and brim of his yellow baseball cap, and hoisted him into the air. The Cubans stormed out of North Shore Park as if the justice denied to them in Havana was equally unavailing in Miami Beach. The reviled umpire was nowhere to be found. They looked desperately for the bearish man with the beard, the ump who evoked all sorts of unfathomable feelings, he of questionable calls and a mysterious air. The umpire was gone, as ephemeral as a tropical sun shower, as shifty as a Miami mirage. The disputes that would remain in Miami Beach were beyond his capacity or calling to resolve.

Meanwhile, with the sun rising upon a different hemisphere and twilight leaving everyone on Miami Beach in the dark, the Posners clung to each other without reaching out to their son. He was better off this way. They were useless to him but essential to each other. In the end, who else did they have? Besides, he had already demonstrated an affinity with his own self-preservation and flight.

All forsaken refugees surrender to this magical city and await the arrival of the Miami Messiah, who, of course, never comes.

About the Author

Thane Rosenbaum is a novelist, essayist, and law professor. He authored the critically acclaimed novels *The Stranger Within Sarah Stein*, *The Golems of Gotham*, *Second Hand Smoke*, and the novel-in-stories *Elijah Visible*, which received the Edward Lewis Wallant Award for the best book of Jewish American fiction. His articles, reviews, and essays appear frequently in the *New York Times*, the *Wall Street Journal*, the *Los Angeles Times*, the *Washington Post*, the *Huffington Post*, and the *Daily Beast*, among other publications. He moderates an annual series of discussions on culture and politics at the 92nd Street Y called The Talk Show. He is a Senior Fellow at New York University School of Law, where he directs the Forum on Law, Culture & Society. His nonfiction books include *Payback: The Case for Revenge* and *The Myth of Moral Justice: Why Our Legal System Fails to Do What's Right*. He edited the anthology *Law Lit, from Atticus Finch to* The Practice: *A Collection of Great Writing about the Law*. His forthcoming book is entitled *The High Cost of Free Speech: Rethinking the First Amendment*. www.thanerosenbaum.com